Test the Ice

BLUE DEVILS HOCKEY #4

S.J. SYLVIS

to my hockey romance girlies <3

USA TODAY BESTSELLING AUTHOR

S.J. SYLVIS

One

REESE

MY EYES SPRING open as I jerk awake. My fingers tingle from the sudden alertness.

Is she crying?

I push my hair out of my face and try to figure out where I am. My heart pounds as I search the darkness, but I quickly realize that I'm inside my car and not at the apartment. My phone pings, and I sigh with exhaustion. Pins and needles race to my fingertips as I scroll past numerous Uber requests.

"Goddamnit," I whisper with defeat.

The amount of money I just missed out on because of an impromptu nap makes me nauseated. I'm not making millions or anything, but the tips I get from driving around drunk college students or rowdy Blue Devils fans is a lot for someone like me.

I blow another strand of hair out of my face, as my shoulders slump. I might as well have been throwing dollar bills out the window with each snore.

Ugh.

The clock reads just a few minutes after midnight, which makes total sense as to why I jerked awake.

Charleigh, though eight months old, still wakes up occasionally throughout the night, and it's usually around this time that she starts to cry, demanding my warm arms.

I pull open my texts and click on Zoe's name.

ME

Are you still awake?

Of course my sister is awake. She's a freshman in college.

Not to mention, she's my babysitter on the nights that I'm working.

ZOE

If I wasn't already, I would be now from Char.

I smile.

ME

Like clockwork. Give her a kiss for me. I'm going to try to make a few extra bucks, then I'll be home.

Few extra bucks...make up for my nap. Unnecessary information.

ZOE

Be careful. There's an extra baseball bat in the trunk if you need to knock someone's knees in. Xx

I spin and stare at the backseat of my car.

I'm half tempted to check if she's being serious, but I know she is.

Zoe may be my younger sister, but she's as tough as nails. We both are, thanks to the way we grew up, but she's much more the type to *act now, ask questions later,* and I am the complete opposite of that.

A ride request pops on my screen, and I greedily accept it. I pray it's some drunk girl who's always eager to become best friends. They always tip me well, even if it's the last few dollars in their bank account.

I zero in on the address of the pick-up spot. My foot taps on the brake like it weighs three hundred pounds. If it were any other night, I probably wouldn't take the bait. However, I have to make up for lost time and money, so I can't be picky.

The farther away I get from downtown Chicago, the closer I get to the wealthier part of the city. The streets are clean, free from potholes that could swallow my entire car in one gulp. There are no homeless loiterers wandering about, and I swear if I were to roll the window down, the air would smell cleaner too.

My hands tighten on the steering wheel, and my hackles rise.

Relax, Reese. Benedict has no idea that you have this job.

He's observant, but unless he's stalking me or somehow tracking me like I'm a fugitive on the run, how would he know?

When I pull up to the curb, I glance out the passenger side window and wait for someone to approach. I tap my fingers on the center console and stare at the open bag of Skittles in the cup holder. I pop a red one into my mouth and suck on the sweet candy until the door opens.

A familiar manly drawl hits my ears. "Interesting to see you here, darling."

I nearly suffocate on Benedict's expensive cologne.

How the hell–

There is no way this is a coincidence. I may have some bad luck, but it's not like I broke a mirror and became cursed for years to come.

"Benedict." His name on my tongue may taste like poison, but I've thankfully perfected my *bored* tone when it comes to him.

There is no way I'm letting him know that I'm all riled up. He likes to pretend that he knows me well enough to see right through me, but he doesn't. He didn't two years ago, and he surely doesn't now.

He turns toward me in the passenger seat and stretches his long legs out in front of him. With his 6'3" frame, his knees practically touch the dash. I stare at his fingers tapping up and down on his pant leg.

"So this is your new job?" His tone drips with disgust.

My foot is glued to the brake. I'm not taking him anywhere.

"I've gotta pay the bills somehow," I say.

I learned at a very young age what happens when you don't pay the bills.

Spoiler alert: the electric company doesn't care if it's twenty degrees outside. If you don't pay the bill, you'll nearly freeze to death in your own home.

He rolls his eyes. "You act like there is no other option."

I scoff. "There isn't."

His jaw flexes. There's a tiny bit of stubble dotting the sharp edge of his chin, and I'm pretty sure that's lipstick on the collar of his shirt. He's in expensive slacks, with a white button-up shirt, sans his suit jacket. He either left it at home or gave it to some woman at the club we're idling in front of.

"There is," he argues. "If you were to get over that nasty streak of independence you have and move in with me, I'd take care of you. I could give you anything you want."

A laugh flies from my mouth at the absurdity. Move in with him? Give me anything I want? Why? Just so he can use it against me and guilt me into a relationship with him? No, thank you.

Benedict's smooth expression flickers like a light switch. His eyebrows crowd together, and his lips flatten with irritation.

"I'm getting tired of this cat-and-mouse game, Reese." The charming Benedict is long gone, and in his place is the man he hides well.

"I'm not playing games." I remain calm, but on the inside, I'm sweating with dread because I know what's coming next.

A threat.

I grip onto the steering wheel for stability and focus on the worn leather beneath my palms, digging my nails into its soft skin.

"I think you like the chase." Benedict's voice cuts through the ringing in my ears.

When I say nothing, he adjusts in the seat next to me, his hands clenching to make fists again. His longing stare shifts into a glare, and I start to sweat.

"You fucking love knowing that I can't stop thinking about you, don't you?"

I could smack him.

"What about your daughter?" I snap. "Do you ever think about her?"

I can't help it. No matter how many times I tell myself not to feed into it, I do every time.

Those once-dreamy eyes narrow even more. "Leave the baby out of this."

The baby.

The. Baby.

I grit my teeth together. "She has a name, and she's hardly a baby anymore."

He scoffs.

The very moment I told Benedict I was pregnant and he asked me to get rid of *it*, was when I knew I made a grave mistake. I'll never admit that I regret meeting him, because I got Charleigh out of it, but I wish he'd just leave us be.

"How did you find out about me Ubering?" I ask.

The lone Skittle in my stomach threatens to come back up when he doesn't answer me. Instead, he looks out the window, unfazed by my questioning. Even worse, he seems unbothered from my dig at his nonexistent parenting.

Heavy silence fills the car, and the longer we're stuck in here, the more my hackles rise. The betrayal from his absence in Charleigh's life cuts like a knife to my skin, and each time he pops back up, the knife pushes in a little farther.

"The only reason you ever come around is because you can't stand knowing that I don't want you."

Benedict stiffens.

The air grows tight.

I shouldn't have said that.

Something else I learned about Benedict very early on is that he isn't someone you want to cross. A man like Benedict has too many connections, and his intellect goes much further than my podunk high school diploma and half a year in college.

"Is that how you want this to go?" he asks in a calm voice.

I think I prefer his angry voice instead, honestly.

I dig my nails into the steering wheel again. "This is nothing you haven't heard before. If you want to be in Charleigh's life for honest reasons, then fine. But if you only want to see her to get to me, I won't allow it."

My—*our*—daughter is not a toy.

She will not get stuck between a man who can't take no for an answer and a woman who refuses to settle.

Staying away from Benedict isn't just for my sake; it's for hers too.

Benedict's smooth chuckle brushes against the side of my

face as he shifts in the passenger seat. "I didn't want to pull this card but..."

My heart stalls from his dramatic pause. He's toying with me, and I bet if I were to look at him, he'd be smiling like a fool.

I clear my throat. "Pull what card?"

"The one where I take you to court."

I freeze. My scalp tingles with apprehension. "To court? For what?"

Benedict opens the passenger door. The cool night air rushes inside my car, but it doesn't even touch the heat on my skin.

He swings his long legs around until his feet hit the pavement. With the sudden space between us, I get the nerve to look at him. His eyes pierce right through me, and the truth is as clear as day—he isn't bluffing.

Once he's fully out of my car, I'm half tempted to drive away with the door still open, which is something Zoe would do, not me, so I keep my foot pressed against the brake.

He leans down with his arms laying on the roof of the car. The smile on his face is that of a snake. "It's a shame you keep my daughter from me, sweetheart."

What?!

My jaw slacks. The puff of air that leaves me sounds like a gasp, and it does nothing but feed Benedict even more ammunition to scare me.

"Do I have your attention now?" he asks lazily.

I say nothing. Too stunned to speak.

"If you don't want to be mine, so be it." Benedict taps his fingers along the top of my car, matching the rhythm of my racing heart. "But that means you don't get to keep what's mine either."

Fury blinds me. The words crash right through the warnings in my head not to smack him directly in the face. If he would just lean down a little farther...

"Ah, I've struck a nerve?" he asks through a smirk.

"How can you claim she's yours when you've held her a handful of times since she was born?" And every time, he acts like I should put out for him just because he gave her an ounce of attention.

He shrugs. "I don't think the judge will see it that way when I tell the court about your past...where you live...your many jobs...how you can hardly pay the bills and keep a roof over Charleigh's head."

Just the sound of her name coming from his mouth sends me into a frenzy.

Before I can argue with him further, he slams the door in my face and slaps the top of my car, as if he's giving me permission to leave.

Permission or not, I do exactly that.

I speed off down the street and head home. I dump the rest of the Skittles into my mouth, as if the sweet taste of candy is going to calm me down somehow.

Two

MALAKI

WELL, this night has taken a wicked turn.

I sit at one of the penny slots but make no move to wager any money.

How I ended up at a casino watching one of my teammates drink copious amounts of booze while he sweeps all the other gamblers off their feet at the blackjack table is beyond me.

I'm not here for fun.

I'm here as his babysitter, even if he is wholly unaware of that.

I can hear my teammates now: *Of course Malaki will keep an eye on Kane...he has nothing better to do.*

Just because I'm one of the guys on the team who hasn't settled down with a wife yet, doesn't mean I don't have better things to do. Actually, ninety percent of the team has deemed me the last to settle down, if ever.

Still doesn't mean I don't have better things to do, you know?

"If you're not going to play, can you move?"

I turn and make eye contact with an older woman who has the voice of someone that smokes a pack of cigarettes per hour. She has so many deep wrinkles on her face I'm afraid she may be a witch and cast a spell on me if I don't move, so I spring up from the seat and usher her to sit.

"Go get 'em, tiger," I mutter.

She doesn't hear me. The bright lights and annoying bells on the slot machine have sucked her in–she's preoccupied at the moment.

I sigh and swing my attention back to Kane.

He raises his hand to signal for the cocktail waitress.

Great.

With my long legs, I beat her to the punch and arrive at the table before she does.

"Don't get another drink," I say in a casual tone.

Kane stiffens before turning to glance at me over his shoulder. "What are you doing here?"

I furrow my brow. "Bro, you invited me."

At first, I thought he may be joking. But with the confused glaze in his eye, it's clear that he's not.

"Shit. You're worse than I thought," I mumble.

Where is Daisy?

I texted her at least thirty minutes ago to make his sorry ass leave. One thing I've learned about Kane since moving in with him is that he is as hardheaded off the ice as he is on it. He won't leave just because I ask him to. But he might if she does.

"You're going to feel like shit tomorrow," I warn.

Kane puts his back to me again and focuses on the cards laying out in front of him. "At least I don't look like shit," he mumbles.

I chuckle. *What are we? In grade school?*

I'm tempted to start some *'your mama'* jokes, just to stay

with the theme of dishing out childish insults, but sometimes people take it the wrong way since I'm motherless.

Everyone still expects me to weep at the thought of my mother dying, but that's not how I deal with my emotions.

In fact, I don't really deal with them at all.

Just as the cocktail waitress makes her way over, I spot Daisy walking through the doors of the casino.

"Thank God," I mutter.

With Kane left gambling, I make my way over to her.

I'm not sure what's going on between the two of them, but there's something brewing. If Daisy can get Kane all out of sorts, she's the only one able to get him to leave.

She stands in the doorway and scans the casino, our eyes snagging as I get closer to her.

I place a hand over my heart when we close the gap between us. "My hero."

Daisy laughs quietly but turns serious a second later. "Where is he?"

I inch my chin over to the table that I left Kane at. A groove of worry appears beneath the brim of her hat. She sighs and brushes past me, only to reveal someone standing behind her.

Whoa.

Who is this?

Whoever Daisy was hiding behind her back deserves to be beneath a spotlight at all times.

She is striking, the type of woman that makes you do a double-take. She's the kind of beautiful that stays with you long after she's disappeared, which is exactly what she's trying to do right now.

"Hey," I jog after her. "Wait up."

The woman stops and brushes her long, dark hair over her shoulder. Her thick eyelashes flutter, revealing bright specks of gold within her eyes. *Damn.*

"Are you here with Daisy?" I ask.

It's an innocent question, one that shouldn't give her any clue that I have bad intentions.

Bad intentions, as in...how can I get her beneath me for the night?

"Yes." Even her voice has me sucked in. "I'm her...ride." She rises to her tiptoes, likely looking over my shoulder to spot Daisy across the large area filled with all sorts of noises that I suddenly can't hear.

"Are you two friends?" Another innocent question, right? There is no way she knows I'm only asking so I can figure out if there's a way I can swindle Daisy into bringing this girl around more often.

She glances at me briefly, and I find myself wanting to jump in front of her so she only sees me instead of watching the drama between Kane and Daisy unfold.

"We're–" She pauses. "Yes, I guess you can consider Daisy and me friends."

"What does that mean?" I ask.

An annoyed sigh leaves her, and I sort of like that she's slightly irritated. "I'm her Uber. That's how we met."

She's an Uber driver?

I have never had an Uber driver look like this before. If I had, I'd Uber everywhere despite the fact that I have my own car.

"An Uber driver?" I push my hands into my pockets to appear nonchalant. "I've never had an Uber driver like you before."

She eyes me with suspicion. "What is that supposed to mean?"

Her offended tone makes my mouth twitch.

I shrug. "I either get some guy who uses grunts as a form of speaking or one that is so stunned I'm in his backseat that I have to pretend like I'm not who he thinks I am."

When someone recognizes me, I hurriedly make up a different name and act like I'm not *that* Malaki Young. Half the time, it's for my own protection because I'm afraid they'll kill us both in a wreck before I make it to my destination. Once, I convinced a poor college student my name was pronounced Ma-lock-y, and he believed me.

She looks at me like I'm the biggest loser in the world. "And who exactly are you?"

It's a hit right to my ego.

I place my hand over my heart and act wounded, but my theatrics only last a few seconds. "Shit. Stay here. I'll be right back."

Goddamnit, Kane. I was about to make my new favorite obsession smile, but now I'm headed over to my rather aggravating roommate to stop an altercation before he ends up getting arrested.

"What are you even doing here?" he hisses to Daisy, unaware that I'm walking up to smooth things over.

"I called her."

Kane glares at me. "You have her number?"

Easy, killer.

Doesn't he know I don't want his girl? I mean, there's a perfectly fine one at my back, watching this entire thing unfold. I glance back, just to make sure Daisy's Uber driver is still waiting, and she is.

I quickly reach inside my pocket and pull out Kane's phone. I press it into his chest. "I grabbed her number from your phone. You've got that crazy look in your eye that you get on the ice, which is exactly why I called her to come get you to leave."

Idiot.

"You called *her* to get me to leave?" He laughs, and I know it's sarcastic, because Kane rarely laughs at anything. "Yeah, nice try, but I'm not leaving." He turns to Daisy. "Especially with her."

These two give me a headache.

Unwilling to deal with Kane's temper tantrum and their soap opera romance in the making, I dig into my pocket for my keys and toss them to Daisy.

"You get him home. I'll catch a ride with your Uber…" I turn back to make sure Ms. Uber is still there waiting for me.

She is.

Sure, she may be waiting for Daisy, but I can totally pretend she's waiting for me.

"Her name is Reese." Daisy gives me a look. "And you better tip her well, Malaki."

On the inside, I'm smiling like a fool.

I'll tip her well, alright…if she'll let me.

Three

REESE

I DON'T GET SWEPT off my feet by men.

After Benedict blinded me with his chivalry and tricked me into thinking he was a decent man, I stopped falling for sexy smirks and flirty eyes.

That doesn't stop Malaki Young from trying, though.

I acted like I didn't know who he was, but I knew right away. Each time I drive to the hockey arena to pick up boisterous Blue Devils fans in need of a ride, I spot his face on the little flags lining the street. Most of the players in their jerseys are listed, though his photo always catches my eye first—not that I'm admitting that to anyone.

He nudges me with his shoulder on the way to my car. "Alone at last."

A surprised laugh leaves me. "Alone at last? You just met me two minutes ago."

He smiles, and I'm choosing to pretend that it isn't heart-stopping.

Malaki towers over me, his height casting shadows against my face as we walk toward my car.

His smile digs even further into his chiseled face. "And I already find myself wanting to get you alone," he admits.

My steps falter.

I know all about Malaki from the overly chatty and often tipsy hockey fans I've picked up from the arena over the last several months. He's known as one of the best defensive players in the league with speed that outshines all the rest. He's even up for MVP of the year. But I don't let those facts deter me from steering clear of that tempting twinkle in his eye.

"Hey..." he starts quietly. "I'm only kidding."

I peer up at his tall frame, and he wears a face of worry.

Suddenly, I'm offended by the thought that he doesn't want me alone.

Wait, what? *Why do I care?*

"I'm over here." I point at my car.

Malaki follows behind, silence settling in between us.

I reach for the door handle, but he steps in front of me, leaving my hand outstretched in between us. I pull back out of shock, half irritated that he's blocking me from my car. "What are you–"

I drop the question when I'm met with an opened car door. Malaki's large hand remains on the door handle while the other rests on top of my car. He motions for me to get inside, his eyebrows rising to his forehead like he's confused that I haven't moved from the spot on the pavement.

"Oh." I slowly sit down in the driver's seat and allow my lips to form a forced smile. "Thanks."

Malaki dips his chin, a playful smirk twitching on his lips. "You're welcome, Dimples."

My nose scrunches at the nickname. It's been a long time since someone has pointed out my dimples. "Very original."

He chuckles before shutting my door.

I'm tempted to just drive away, because I've been alone with this guy for two minutes, and he's already managed to make me laugh.

Sure, he's a little arrogant, and I'm certain his gentlemanly tactics pull girls into his bed like some sort of siren call, yet I find myself staring into his eyes for a second too long, which is never good.

Not to mention, I need the money.

I start to set up the Uber ride on my app when the passenger side door opens.

Malaki sits nonchalantly in the front seat, and I can't help but snort.

He glances over at me. "What?"

"Nothing." I busy myself with the phone, but I can still feel his gaze lingering on the side of my face. "It's just–" I peek at him and roll my lips together. "Most people sit in the back."

Malaki, with his wide shoulders, turns and glances at the backseat.

Thank God I took Charleigh's car seat out.

"Looks small back there," he notes.

It is. If I could afford an SUV, I'd get one. The bigger the car, the more money I'd make.

I run my gaze over his large frame and shrug. "You'd fit," I say.

He would be super cramped back there, and I'm pretty sure there's a wafer stuck to the seat from attempting to appease Charleigh earlier when she was getting antsy from our trip to the store, but it's fun to act unimpressed by Malaki and his sturdy body.

His ego could surely afford a few hits.

"I'm over six feet," he argues.

I purse my lips and openly gawk at him. "Oh, you looked much shorter than that."

He huffs, and I turn away to hide my amusement.

After getting the Uber drive set up, I have him tell me his address. It doesn't take long for me to realize that he lives in the same complex as Daisy, and I'm no rocket scientist, but I'm pretty certain he's Kane's roommate.

"I think you just don't want me next to you," Malaki says. "Because you and I both know that I tower over your tiny frame."

"I am not tiny," I argue, putting the car in drive.

He grunts, and I glance over at him. He's staring out the passenger side window, but even from the glimpse of his profile, I can see his lips twitching with humor.

If only he knew that I had a baby nine months ago, and my body isn't quite the same as it used to be. I'm still thin, mostly because I don't have time to eat, and even when I do, healthy food is much more expensive than junk food, but my belly isn't as tight, and it's hard to fit my hips into those skinny jeans I wore a year ago.

"You are tiny," he says. "But you're also mighty."

I can't help but laugh. "Mighty? What makes you say that?"

Our eyes catch when I stop at a red light. I ignore the way my stomach flips, because *absolutely not.* There is no time or place in my life for a smooth talker like Malaki, even if he has made me laugh more times in the last twenty minutes than I usually do in an entire day.

"I don't know..." he drags his words out while simultaneously running those blue eyes over my body.

The light turns green, and I silently thank it for giving me a reason to look away. Being under Malaki Young's scrutiny gives me hives.

"You just seem...independent?"

Okay, so he can read people. *Big deal.*

I remain quiet as I turn onto his street, the tall apartment building standing like a beacon of light.

"I can tell you don't put up with anyone's bullshit."

I used to, but I'm much less likely to do so since leaving that run-down trailer on the south side of town. I took my sister, gave my dad the middle finger, and removed us from *trash*, as Benedict likes to refer to it.

I park in front of Malaki's apartment building and end the ride. His phone pings, but he doesn't touch it. Instead, he stares at me from the side. The longer I look at him, the faster my heart beats. It isn't until he grins that I turn away.

"It's sort of hot," he admits.

I roll my eyes, pretending like I don't care that he just referred to me as hot.

Get a grip, Reese. Just because it's been nearly two years since I've been with a man, or had an interaction with one that didn't make my skin crawl, doesn't make me desperate.

I do *not* crave a man's attention or his compliments. *Nope.*

"Let me take you out."

I freeze in the driver's seat. The butterflies in my stomach, unfortunately, do not. Apparently, I *do* crave a man's attention.

My refusal comes swift as I turn toward him. "No."

His lip lifts, and I hate that it makes him so much more enticing. I could totally see myself getting lost in his blue eyes, and paired with that smirk? *Jes-us.*

"How'd I know you'd say that?" His half-grin turns into a full-blown smile. His teeth are bright white and perfectly straight. Some hockey players have missing teeth, but not Malaki. That'd be such a shame, considering his smile makes my head spin.

I turn away and stare out the windshield to get out from underneath his spell.

"I don't date," I say.

"So you're taken." He says it like a statement instead of a question.

A laugh erupts from my mouth, as if I have the time to date.

He hums quietly. "So you're not taken..."

I think he's talking to himself more than he's talking to me.

He shifts in the passenger seat, his knees nearly hitting the dash. "Why don't you date?"

The excuses are endless: I don't have time to date. I have an overbearing ex who is threatening to take custody of my daughter if I don't force myself to love him. Oh, and then there's the little tidbit that *I have a baby!*

What Malaki won't understand is that he and I aren't compatible even in the slightest. Maybe we could've been if I didn't drop out of college to wash bottles and change dirty diapers several times a night. I have responsibilities that leave zero room for a fling with a guy like him.

A few seconds of silence pass before he blurts, "Are you a lesbian?"

I'm shocked, but only for a second. I slowly turn toward him and raise an eyebrow. "You think that's the only logical reason as to why I won't let you take me out?" I cross my arms and scoff. "Talk about arrogant."

His jaw drops slightly, but I still see the hint of mirth lingering on his face. "I didn't say that. I was just throwing out suggestions."

Instead of getting out of my car that's still idling in front of his complex, he seemingly grows more comfort-able. He leans back in the passenger seat and pushes his legs apart a little, this time his knees actually brushing against the dash. I stare at his fingers as they tap against his jeans, and I have no idea why, but it's sort of attractive.

"Dinner and a movie?"

My gaze slides from his hand, all the way up to the grin on

his face. When our eyes catch, he shakes his head. "Okay, not your thing. What about..."

I hate that I want to laugh.

"Bowling?" His eyebrow hitches, and I have to bite the inside of my cheek to keep him from knowing I'm amused.

He rolls his eyes when I stay quiet. "Bowling isn't my thing either. I suck."

I feign surprise. "Admitting you aren't good at something? Wow."

His flirty gaze slices to me. "There are plenty of things I'm not good at...but there are also things I'm *very* good at."

A rush of heat whips at my cheeks, and he winks, as if he knows exactly where my mind went. My thoughts have taken a sudden detour, and somehow, I've ended up in a porno with Malaki Young. A coil of lust pulls at my belly, and my pulse quickens. It's been too long since I've done anything with anyone. The last time I was kissed was by Benedict, and it ended with a slap to his face.

Malaki's growing list of date ideas pulls me from my dirty aspirations. I hear the tail end of his next idea. "Water park?"

"Water park?" I give him a wary look. "There's a water park here?"

He chuckles. "No, but I'm running out of options."

"I'm not dating you," I repeat.

There's a challenge in his eyes. He squints and then smiles. My lips beg to smile, the dimples I've had since I was a baby threatening to appear.

"Then let's hang out as friends," he suggests.

I laugh sarcastically. "Said no guy ever."

"You haven't been around the right guys, then," he says matter-of-factly.

I sigh and reach for my Skittles. The bag crinkles, the Skittles tacky in my hand. I pop a few into my mouth and suck on the ends of my fingers.

I catch Malaki's eye, and he's staring at me. He blinks once, twice, then slowly turns away and stares out the windshield. "Fine," he sighs. "You pick the activity, and text me when you figure it out."

I snort. "You're not getting my number."

He turns toward me with one eyebrow raised. "Who says I don't already have it?"

I pause. *Does he?*

I mentally shake my head. There's no way he has my number.

My phone pings, and his attention snaps to it. Before he has a chance to grab it and text himself my number, I snatch it from the dashboard mount and press it against my chest. His cheek twitches, like he wants to smile.

I glance at the screen and read Zoe's text asking when I'm coming home.

She probably wants to go out with her friends, because that's what college girls do. Instead, she's at home, babysitting her niece.

"Oops, looks like I have another ride request," I say.

Malaki's mouth turns down into a disappointed frown, and I hate to admit that I'm kind of bummed to see him go too. But it's better this way, and I know it.

"Alright," he says.

The door opens, letting in the Chicago city air, and just when I think he's accepted that I won't go on a date with him, he leans toward me with his elbow on the center console. His low voice slips into my ear. "Thanks for the first date. It was fun, Dimples."

A surprised gasp leaves me when he backs away.

"This was not a date," I argue.

"Felt like one to me," he says, sticking his hand into my bag of Skittles.

"Hey!" I blurt.

He pops a few Skittles into his mouth, winks at me, and then shuts the door.

I speed away before he makes it to the door of his apartment complex, as if leaving him sooner is going to wipe away the blush covering my cheeks.

My phone pings just as I turn the corner, and I see the five-star rating and astronomically high-dollar tip he's left me. Since I'm all alone, I let myself smile, but if he was here to see me, I'd make sure to roll my eyes.

Four

MALAKI

I KICK my feet up onto the coffee table and rest my hands behind my head. The apartment is quiet without Kane here, and although I've spent a lot of time alone, even when I was a kid, it's sort of nice having a roommate.

With Kane in full denial about his little obsession with our neighbor beneath us, he's preoccupied. In other words...he's hook, line, and sinker. *Taken.* Gone. He is no longer single nor the leader of the party clan. The majority of my teammates are either in a serious relationship or married. Good for them.

That's not for me, though.

Not now, and maybe never.

To allow yourself to get that close to someone requires careful consideration. It has to be deliberate, and in my opinion, loving them has to be worth the fear of losing them.

I mean, I read that somewhere once, but it makes sense, especially after losing my mother and being left with essentially no one but *me, myself, and I.*

Most of the men I surround myself with are getting

engaged, having babies, or stalking their best friend's sister—that's directed toward Kane, of course—but that doesn't mean I have to do that. I'm the guy who's just happy to have a good time.

I *am* bored, though.

My phone rests face down on the couch beside me. I grab it to scroll through social media again. After a few swipes of my feed, mostly filled with hockey highlights and more of my friends posing with their girls, I get a message.

KANE

I need backup.

Say less.

ME

Backup how? Are you about to fight someone?

Kane has always been the troublesome type. That man has skeletons in his closet. It's part of the reason I moved into his apartment with him. I have my own house, on the other side of town, but when there's a friend in need, I'm your guy. Can't cover the rent? I've got you. Need a ride from the bar? Get in, loser.

KANE

Maybe.

I'd bet my lucky hockey stick that this has something to do with Daisy.

Which just so happens to give me the best idea I've had all night.

I eagerly exit out of my messages and pull open another app. I grin and click on *request a ride*.

Do I have my own car? Yes.

Can I drive it to the club? Also yes.

But how would I see that pretty, brown-eyed angel of an Uber driver that I can't stop thinking about if I did that?

I climb from the couch and head to the bathroom to get ready. It takes me less than three minutes, and by then, I've already canceled two trips due to them not being Reese.

I request again and again, even narrowing my search to *female drivers only.*

Ten minutes have passed, another text from Kane, and then it happens.

Her information pops up, showing me the make of her vehicle, and when she'll be arriving.

I smirk, dab on some cologne, and head out the door.

I watch her on the map as I make my way to the elevator. With each descending floor, my hope dissipates more. Her car remains idle, unmoving in the direction it needs to go.

Reese clearly knows it's me. I mean, how could she not? I tipped her more than I've ever tipped anyone when she brought me home the other night. You'd think she'd be eager to be my Uber driver again. Unless she isn't a girl who's motivated by money. I'm not trying to buy her, though. I'm just trying to make our time together worthwhile.

I rest against the side of the apartment complex and allow a few more minutes to pass before I pull up the messages.

ME

Are you broken down? Need a hero to come rescue you?

Despite being fatherless from a very early age, I was still taught basic survival skills every man should know: how to fix a flat, how to change the oil—you know, those sorts of things. My mother made sure I was well versed in basically anything life could throw at me before she died. I'm well-versed in laundry and baking too.

REESE

Did you request me on purpose?

My mouth flattens. *Psh. What? No.*

ME

You can't request certain drivers on the app. Must've just been a coincidence.

I exit the message and pull up her map again. She still isn't moving.

REESE

Don't you have your own car?

ME

I may have a few drinks. Can't risk driving back, and I would rather not leave my car downtown.

Instead of waiting for her to come to me, I'll just go to her. There. Problem solved.

Once I'm a block away, I click on the tip I had originally given her for the last ride and edit the amount while smiling to myself.

3...2...1...

REESE

Are you bribing me to give you a ride?

How dare she assume that.

ME

What do you make on a typical night of Ubering?

I only spent a half hour with her—tops. Yet, I can picture her eyeroll as she reads my message.

REESE

Just depends. Why? Thinking of getting a side job?

I chuckle.

ME

As if I have the time for that.

Turning the corner for the street she's on, I scan each parked car. Blue, red, black...*there.* Her white Honda snags my attention. I stop on the sidewalk with my phone in hand and wait for her to respond, my fingertips tingling with excitement.

REESE

You have time to pester me, so surely you have time to Uber.

Pester. Flirting. I see how she can get the two mixed up.

Just to push her buttons a little more, I go back and re-edit my tip again. This time, I triple it.

She messages me within seconds.

REESE

I'm not a prostitute! Stop sending me hefty amounts of money!

ME

Fine.

I put my phone away and head directly for her with a teasing smirk locked away until I'm on the passenger side of her car.

Five

REESE

HE'S INSANE.

Not in the way that Benedict is, but insane, nonetheless.

I stare at my earnings from his last ride. I wasn't even aware a rider could get back into the app and adjust their past tips, but apparently you can.

Did he google that? Does he adjust his Uber tips often?

I switch back to his message with my heart beating too fast. I'm not a woman who gets impressed by a hefty bank account. I've been there, done that.

However...if Malaki is going to tip me this well for a ride, I'm not sure I can say no. I may be independent, but I'm not stupid. The more money I have in my bank account, the more prepared I'll be for Benedict's lingering ultimatum in the back of my mind.

If he is serious about taking me to court for custody, I'll need a lawyer—a good one.

Part of me wants to believe it's an empty threat, but the

second I think Benedict has moved on and is going to leave me be, he materializes out of thin air.

Another message comes through.

MALAKI

Are you ready to go?

My cheeks fill with air, and I squeeze my eyes shut.

I don't know how long I argue with myself over whether or not to take the bait, but suddenly, there's a tapping on my window, and I spring my eyes open. A bloodcurdling scream erupts from my mouth at the same time my phone flies out of my hand, landing in the backseat.

Through the passenger window, I see Malaki's flirty grin staring back at me. My fear switches to annoyance in an instant.

I roll the window down with my heart flying through my chest. "Don't do that!"

His grin widens. "Jumpy much?"

"You try being a female Uber driver on the streets of Chicago," I mumble.

Despite wanting to refuse him a ride, I unlock the door. I angle my back toward him when he opens it, but the rich scent of his cologne fills my senses anyway.

He smells so incredibly good.

"Maybe you shouldn't be Ubering," he says, drawing out his words like he's a father disappointed in his daughter's choice of employment.

I snap my attention to him. "I don't really have a choice."

The hours are flexible, and all you really need is a driver's license. It's not like I'm able to get hired somewhere that is flexible and pays decent with a half-finished college degree.

Silence settles between us, his gaze roaming all over my face, like he's trying to read me or something. I have every urge to turn away, and I should. Except, he leans in close, and all I can focus on is his cologne.

What is he doing?!

Why is he so close to me?

And why am I not moving away?

I stop breathing in an attempt to snap myself out of the hypnosis his cologne is putting me in, but it doesn't work.

He leans in even closer, and I feel my lips part. Malaki gulps, the deep dip of his Adam's apple moving slowly against his neck. Warmth sprinkles against my skin, and I realize right away that my desperation runs deep. Malaki is practically a stranger, and yet, I'm longing for him.

He isn't even touching me, and somehow, I feel him everywhere.

"Here," he says, voice husky.

"Huh?" I mutter.

Malaki's eyes shoot down to the small space left between us. His hand is there, palm up, with my phone in it. Heat rushes to my cheeks as reality settles back in.

He's just trying to give me my phone!

He must've grabbed it while I was stuck in a fantasy land with a knot in between my legs from just looking into his eyes.

I jerk backward.

"Oh. Thanks." I quickly reach for the traitorous device, and our fingers accidentally brush. A line of fire shoots up my arm, and I freak out. I fumble my phone, and it goes flying— *again.*

"Are you okay?" he asks, a line of worry digging in between his eyebrows.

"I'm fine," I rush out. "Let's just go and get this over with."

Malaki chuckles and settles back into his seat. He adjusts it, sliding it backward, just like he did the other night. It wasn't until I was hauling Charleigh's car seat into the backseat that I had noticed, which then led to me googling how tall he was. Two hours later and I had a full background on Malaki Young.

He's from Manhattan. Only child. No father was listed, just a mother who died several years ago from breast cancer. He signed a hefty contract with the Chicago Blue Devils and is currently in the running for MVP of the year. He finished college with a degree in political science before being drafted into the pros on a third-round pick.

Impressive? Sort of.

It sure puts my unfinished fashion and marketing degree, single mom who is Ubering to make ends meet self to shame, that's for sure.

I'm driving for a total of five seconds before Malaki's smooth voice fills the car.

"Two hundred?"

I briefly glance at him to see if he's talking to me or if he's on the phone. He's looking directly at me.

"Two hundred what?" I ask, bouncing my attention back and forth between him and the road.

"Is that how much you make in a night?"

This again?

I focus back on the road to hide how uncomfortable I am talking about money.

I hate that I'm ashamed.

I've been poor all my life—a bottom feeder, a few dollars away from the electric being turned off and freezing to death, hand-me-down clothes with holes and stains until I finally learned how to sew in the third grade. It's even worse because I know Malaki is well-off, just like Benedict, and he never held back from making me feel like shit for my financial burdens.

"Two hundred fifty?"

I remain quiet.

Malaki hums. "Two seventy-five. Final answer."

I trap a laugh behind my lips. He sounds like he's on some type of game show.

"Going once... going twice..."

The laugh slips out, and I give in. "It just depends," I admit. "When you guys have a home game?" I shrug. "Around that, yeah."

Silence fills the car again, my shame filling the air with a heavy stench. I glance out of the corner of my eye and see Malaki fiddling with his phone.

Is he texting someone?

Is he meeting some girl at the club?

Ugh, why do I care? I hardly know him!

I have more important things to worry about, like how I'm going to balance everything while raising an eight-month-old on my own, support my sister, avoid Benedict and his bribes, find a better job...

My spiraling thoughts pause when my phone goes off. I quickly scan the screen and gasp. My foot slips to the brake, and we stop suddenly, my car jerking.

Malaki's hand shoots out to the dash to steady himself while the other comes across my chest to do the same to me. "Whoa, girl. Need me to drive?"

"Why did you just tip me five hundred dollars?!" I exclaim, ignoring his forearm pressed against my breasts.

Once Malaki removes his arm and places it on the center console, I start driving regularly again.

"Now you have a reason to get off work early." He shrugs, almost sounding bored. "You can come hang out with me at the club. Daisy is there too."

My thoughts are all over the place, and I try to find something reasonable to say. As much as I want—and need—the five hundred dollars, I cannot accept it. I'm not a charity case, even if I hear Benedict's voice inside my head, telling me those exact words more often than not.

"I'm not hanging out with you at the club," I argue. "And I can't accept that much money."

"Why can't you?" he asks. "And yes, you can."

I scoff. "Because!"

"You can't hang out with me because why? Because you have to work? I just paid you more than what you'd typically make in a night, right?" He pauses, and I'm pretty sure he's waiting for me to agree with him.

I make a left turn, my heart beating faster and faster the closer we get to the club he's going to.

"Should I tip you even more?" he asks.

"No!" I exclaim.

I glance at him as I park my car beside the curb, my eyes dropping to his lap. He's messing with his phone again, and I panic.

"Fine!" I blurt, reaching for his phone. I put my hand on top of it, our fingers brushing again. "I'll go"—*for a second*—"just stop paying me."

His chuckle is irritating and addictive at the same time. He's so proud of himself for winning.

How this night started off as a regular night of work and ended at a club with the most persistent man I've ever met is beyond me.

I angle toward him after shifting my car into park, the light of my dash illuminating the side of his face. Malaki's triumph nearly suffocates me.

"This is not a date," I remind him.

It doesn't take long for his cheek to curve on one side. I drop my attention to his mouth, and fuck my stomach for flipping.

"Okay, Dimples..." His voice is as smooth as butter. "Friends?"

I narrow my gaze before eventually giving in. "Fine."

He outstretches his hand in between us for me to shake. I

stare at it like I'll be trapped for life if I place my palm in his, but I have a feeling I won't be getting out of this car until I surrender. So, I gingerly peel my fingers off the steering wheel and give in.

The moment our palms touch, sparks fly to my hand. I manage to keep the shock off my face, but my nerves are fried. The small space we're tucked in crackles, and I pray it's all in my head.

"Not a date number two... here we come." He winks at me before removing his hand from mine.

We both open our doors with an eagerness that is hard to deny. Though Malaki is probably just excited because I finally gave in to his persistent attempt to hang out with me, I'm rushing to put space between us because his smirk does wild things to my body, even if my head is refusing to admit it.

MALAKI

REESE and I walk into the club, and we couldn't be more contradictory if we tried. Not only is she the most gorgeous woman in here, turning heads from the bouncer all the way to the bartender across the dance floor, but she's clearly unimpressed to be here with me. Whereas I'm feeling pretty fucking elated to have her by my side, smirking at every guy who's jealous of the hottie next to me.

Well, she *was* next to me.

I find her within seconds, my attention clinging to her like a magnet. She's casual, wearing jeans and a loose-fitting sweater that just so happened to slip off her shoulder on the drive here. She's chatting away with Daisy, who looks confused to see her friend here. My roommate is staring at them, his quick glimpse in my direction only lasting half a second.

I walk closer and overhear Daisy asking Reese what she's doing here.

It's a natural reaction for me to slip my arm around

Reese's shoulders, but I don't miss the way she tenses. "I convinced her to come out with me."

She raises an eyebrow, seemingly hesitant to believe me. I don't think they've been friends for long, but with how difficult it was to get Reese to agree to come out with me, I'm betting she doesn't do much of anything other than work.

Reese makes a sarcastic noise, her warm breath coating my hand. "If requesting several Uber drivers until you get me as your driver is your way of convincing, then okay."

Daisy tries to hide her smile, but I make no effort to hide mine.

Reese sends me a scathing glare, and it's awfully tempting.

I've never had a woman so uninterested in me before. She's different, and I'm fully entertained by it.

"I have to get back to work," she announces, shrugging my arm off her shoulder. "Malaki said you were here, so I just wanted to say hi real quick."

She's leaving already? I think not.

After she gives Daisy a hug, she heads for the door without so much as looking in my direction. I watch her weave in between couples and men whose gazes linger a little too long. Before she makes it to the door, I rush over and wrap my arm around her waist. I spin her toward me, and a hot little gasp slips from her mouth.

Ah, fuck.

"Stay a little longer," I beg.

A girly growl rumbles out of her chest, and I have to bite my cheek to keep my chuckle at bay. Reese is headstrong—that much was evident from the very moment I met her, and it's surprisingly attractive.

"I can't just...skip out on work and go clubbing." She shoves my arm away, and I drop it willingly.

I tilt my head. "Why not? It's not like you are missing out on the money."

Reese glances away, the wheels turning inside her head for another excuse.

I dig into my pocket for my phone and open up the Uber app. When she finally glances back at me, her eyes immediately fling to my phone screen.

"Don't," she hisses.

I feign innocence. "Don't what?"

She leans in close, her sugary breath messing with my head. "Stop paying me to hang out with you!"

"How else will I get you to stay?" I ask.

The song from the DJ picks up volume, so I stare at her mouth to read her lips. "Why do you even want me to stay?"

"Because..." I lean in closer, my mouth hovering over her ear so she can hear me better. "Friends don't leave friends at the club alone."

She pulls away and shoots me a look that makes me grin.

"Friends?" The word coming from her mouth is as sarcastic as it gets.

"We're friends." I shrug. "Right?"

I can tell she's thinking about staying. Her eyes bounce back and forth between mine as she tries to decipher how persistent I really am.

Spoiler alert: I'm the most persistent person in the room.

Since she's tossing the idea around inside that pretty head of hers, I push her a little further into the right direction. "When was the last time you had some fun, Dimples?"

She glances away, her rosy plump lip trapped between her teeth.

"Exactly," I say.

Our eyes catch, her brows crowding with frustration.

"Ugh." She scowls. "Fine! Just stop calling me Dimples."

"Show them off more often, and I will."

She's still scowling at me before she stalks off toward Daisy. Those curvy hips sway as she stomps across the floor, and I don't even have to look to know that every man has stopped to stare.

Daisy's arms wrap around Reese's neck for a hug, and then they're off to the dance floor. She says something in Reese's ear that makes her smile, and the sight of those dimples sort of makes my dick hard.

I'm not even sure why I'm trying so hard when it comes to Reese. It's clear that she isn't interested in me, and she's definitely not the type of girl to climb in my bed for a one-night stand.

There's something about her, though. Something that pulls me in.

A challenge?

The breath of fresh air she gives me because she's not willingly throwing herself at me?

Boredom?

Am I really that bored with life that I'm putting this much effort into a woman who refuses to even smile at me?

I think she's rolled her eyes at me more than she's smiled at this point.

I shake my head and head to the bar. I ignore the loud group of college girls staring at me as the bartender hands me a beer. I rest my hip against the edge and stare out onto the dance floor.

A few nights off from hockey and I don't even know what to do with myself other than force some woman I barely know to the club with me to babysit Kane so he doesn't get into a fight over his best friend's little sister, who is currently pulling every one of his strings.

Daisy and Reese break apart as Daisy starts to dance with a random guy.

Kane's ears are bright red, his anger not so subtle. They're both glaring at each other, playing their own type of game.

I casually slip my attention back to Reese while taking a

swig of my beer. The malty flavor coats my tongue, not even coming close to distracting me enough that I'll stop staring at her perfect ass in those tight jeans.

She catches my eye, the strobe lights from the dance floor coating the side of her high cheek bone. Her eyes quickly shift elsewhere, like she doesn't want to admit she was looking for me.

I smirk because she totally was.

I place my beer on the bar and stand up a little taller. She's on the complete other end of the club, avoiding me, until a man comes up beside her.

She immediately searches for me, and when our eyes meet, a hint of worry shows within the shadows across her face. My chest tightens, and the beer on my tongue dries out.

Before my brain can catch up to my body, I'm halfway across the dance floor to reach her. I've lost Kane and Daisy, but I can't really seem to care. He's on his own for now. If he wants to keep his spot on the Blue Devils, he'll think twice about getting into some fight.

Same goes for me, which is something I remind myself as I come up behind Reese and the guy whose name is about to go on my shit list.

"No, I'm good," Reese squeaks. "I'm here with someone."

Me? She's referring to me, right?

"Who?" the man asks. "A boyfriend? Because I don't see him."

Reese stalls.

She reaches up on her tiptoes to look past the man in the direction of the bar, where I just was.

"That's because I'm behind you," I say, slipping out from behind the man. "She's here with me."

My arm finds Reese's waist right away, and I pull her in close. She's a perfect fit against my body.

"Fucking figures," the guy mutters. He runs a hand

through his hair and disappears to look for the next willing female to lure.

Reese's shoulders fall, a soft sigh escaping her mouth.

"You good?" I ask.

"Yeah." She nods. "Thanks."

Before she puts any space between us, I grab onto her hand. Her chin jerks upward, the warm color of brown in her eyes sparkling with surprise.

"Now you owe me a dance."

She gives me a look that's nothing less than a warning, but I pull her onto the floor anyway.

Seven

REESE

MALAKI'S HAND slips into mine, and he pulls me further onto the dance floor.

One thing is for certain: Malaki does not give up.

I hate to admit it, but I sort of admire his tenacity. His persistence isn't unusual. Most men refuse to give up, but he pairs it with patience, and that's seemingly unconventional.

Still, I refuse to dance with him.

"Malaki." I dig my heels into my shoes and try to stop him from taking the center of the dance floor with me in tow. "I'm not much of a dancer."

His eyebrows fold together. "I just watched you dance with Daisy, so nice try."

My lips flatten. "That's different."

Malaki comes in close, our chests almost touching. "How so?"

"Because," I stress, "she's my friend."

His huff, hinted with the scent of beer, hits me in the face.

He places his free hand against his heart. "I thought we were friends."

I hate that he makes me want to laugh. I suck in my cheeks and look past his shoulder. "We hardly know each other," I remind him.

Malaki's hands land on my hips, and I pause. There's chaos around us, couples touching intimately and girls dancing with their friends as their drinks slosh around, but with Malaki touching me, it fades.

"That's not true," he argues. "We know plenty about each other." He guides my hips back and forth, and I let him because I'm too interested to see what he'll say next.

"Like what?" I ask.

His lips turn up on the side, and *God,* he could be a model for some high-end clothing line. Handsome with perfect, kissable lips and a double-edged sword for a jawline.

"Well, let's see..." Malaki spins me around and puts my back against his chest. The pads of his fingers dip underneath my shirt, and goosebumps fly to my skin.

Shit.

"We know where the other works," he notes.

"Kind of hard not to know when you're on various posters in the city." I angle my head, tipping my chin to look up at him to see his reaction.

He smirks. "I can't help that the city is obsessed with me."

I roll my eyes and go back to looking at the dance floor.

"What else...I know who your best friend is."

Okay, so he knows two things about me. That's nothing compared to everything else going on in my life. It doesn't even come close to the surface.

"Is that all?" I ask.

Malaki spins me again. This time, he takes my hands in his and places them around his neck. I clasp my fingers together because apparently my body didn't hear the warning inside my head.

"I know your favorite candy." Our eyes catch. "Skittles."

I narrow my gaze. "But you don't know my favorite flavor."

There. Take that, Mr. Know It All.

Malaki flashes me a half-smile. "Strawberry."

My mouth parts, a slight gasp slipping in between us.

How does he–

"Want to know mine?" he asks.

Our dancing has become less stiff and a lot more relaxed. My hips sway to the beat, and for the first time in at least two years, I find myself getting lost in the moment instead of looking over my shoulder or worrying about what tomorrow brings.

"Let me guess." I bite my lip and pretend to think. "Yellow?"

"Wrong."

The music shifts, the song still upbeat but much more intimate. At some point, Malaki and I end up pressed against each other. My body is suddenly aware of every little thing, like how hard his chest is against my breasts.

I guess again. "Orange?"

Malaki shakes his head. "Wrong."

I pout and spin around, putting my back to him. "Purple?"

Malaki's mouth hovers over my ear, and goosebumps crawl against my neck. "Nope."

I go over the colors of the rainbow in my head. "Green!" I exclaim.

His chuckle rumbles along my back. I turn my head to give him a dirty look, but before I can look away, he takes his hand, snakes it up my body, and grabs a hold of my chin.

"You're forgetting the most important one." Malaki stares at my mouth, and my heart stutters in my chest.

Oh god, this is bad.

When he leans in close, I tell myself to move away, but I can't. I'm too captivated by how close his mouth is to mine and how nice it feels to have his hands on me.

"Strawberry," he whispers.

"But that's my favorite," I say, as if he isn't allowed to like something that I like.

"Then it looks like we have another thing in common, Dimples."

My tongue slips out to lick my bottom lip. Malaki snaps his eyes back to mine, something highly enticing swimming in the blue color, before dropping back to my mouth.

I want him to kiss me *badly,* and I think he can tell.

"Hold that thought," he says quietly.

"Huh?" I breathe out.

Someone comes into my peripheral, breaking my trance. I step away quickly, and reality comes crashing back in.

What in the hell am I doing?

I have a baby at home and an ex who is trying to scare me back into his bed. I can't be out at the club on a random Thursday with a guy like Malaki.

"I can't find Daisy or Kane anywhere. Do you know where they went?" A guy, who I'm assuming is Daisy's brother, River, steps in between us.

"Uh..." Malaki glances around the dance floor, looking just as out of it as I feel. "Let's go outside and look."

I lead the way, eager to get out of the club.

Malaki's low voice sweeps into my ear. "You're distracting."

I glance at him. "Me?"

He thinks I'm distracting? What about him?

"I came here to keep an eye on Kane because he and your

best friend are playing a very dangerous cat-and-mouse game, but when I'm with you, I can't focus on anything else."

At this point, I think we're the ones playing the dangerous cat-and-mouse game.

I'm officially forfeiting.

"Maybe Daisy doesn't want to play the game," I say. "Not every girl wants to be chased."

Malaki pauses before tugging me through the door. "And what about you? Do you want to be chased?"

I pause.

Say no, Reese.

I'd be a liar if I said I didn't want to be chased by a guy like Malaki. I'm desperate to know what it's like to be kissed with passion instead of bowing down to someone who yields too much power. I want to let go and indulge in something, instead of giving away parts of myself to people who don't deserve them.

But I can't.

Maybe in the future, when things aren't so messy, but right now, I just *can't.*

I open my mouth to answer Malaki, who's waiting patiently, like he knows I'm teetering with the idea of allowing him to chase me, but our attention moves to Daisy's brother.

"Found them," he says.

Malaki tugs me through the door after him, our fingers still intertwined. Once we make it outside and the cool Chicago air brushes against my flushed cheeks, reality sets in, and I pull away.

He notices, but he doesn't say anything.

"Where did you go?" River asks Daisy.

Daisy and Kane are obviously guilty, but she's quick to feed her brother a lie. "I got overheated. Kane came with me to cool down out here."

River sighs. "It was probably the drink. I knew you shouldn't have had one. Your cheeks are red."

I walk toward Daisy as she argues with her brother. Unable to stop myself, I find myself looking at Malaki. He catches me staring, and my cheeks warm. If this were before Benedict, I'd probably end up going home with him. But it isn't, and I'm a lot more conscientious than I was before.

Malaki steps forward. "We leave for the road tomorrow afternoon, so we should probably go."

The rest of the group nods, and I leap to take the bait. I pull my keys out from my back pocket and wiggle them. "Let's go. Your chauffeur awaits."

I sort of want to decline him a ride so I can put some much-needed space between us, but he did pay me after all. The least I could do is drop him off at home, right?

I should be able to keep myself in check for a twenty-minute ride back to his apartment complex before turning in for the night.

I'm not a wild sorority girl any longer. I can do this.

Malaki saunters up beside me, his arm landing on my shoulder. He pulls me to his side and whispers into my ear, "Ready when you are."

My stomach dips.

I'm not sure I'm ever going to be ready when it comes to him.

MALAKI

REESE'S CAR idles in front of my apartment complex, and the longer I sit in the passenger seat, the hotter I get. She reaches for the air conditioner knob and turns it up before she angles the vents toward her face.

Is she all hot and bothered like I am from our impromptu dancing?

Those hips.

The sweet scent of her perfume.

Her slender neck sparkling with a slight sheen of sweat.

She's the whole package, and I want her, which is exactly why I can't get out of the car.

"Well?" She glances at me with her eyebrows raised high.

"Well, what?" I ask, purposefully acting oblivious.

Those pink lips move with a half-smile, the slight divot in her cheeks showing off her dimples. "This is your apartment, right?"

She knows it is. I know it is. Yet, I lean forward and squint through the windshield. "I don't know. Maybe we should go inside and check?"

A cute laugh leaves her. "Nice try."

I chuckle and lean farther back into the seat, seemingly becoming more comfortable. "It was worth a shot."

She angles herself toward me, one leg coming up to prop against the steering wheel. "Don't you have a game tomorrow?"

I nod.

"Well, shouldn't you be sleeping?" she asks.

Part of me wants to turn on the dash light, just so I can get a good look at her to figure out what's going through her head. She refuses me at every turn, but there are times when she slips up. I can read between the lines. She was enjoying dancing, and for a second, I thought she was going to push up on her tiptoes to kiss me.

"Did you have fun tonight?" I ask.

Her eyes flick past me, and although we haven't spent too much time together, I know she's about to tell a fib. "Not really."

A chuckle flies from my mouth. "Liar."

Reese's lips flatten, but she can't fool me—she wants to smile in the worst way.

"You did," I argue. "Just admit it."

"Never," she counters.

Without putting any thought into it, I poke her side like I'm back in high school, flirting for the first time. Her laugh fills the car as she tips her head back, and *damn, she's pretty*.

She slaps my hand away as another laugh leaves her, and I poke her again.

"Malaki!" she shouts, amusement backing her scold.

"Admit it, and I'll stop." This time, I don't just poke her side. Instead, I wrap my hand around her waist and squeeze. My fingers softly dig into her skin as I tickle her, causing that quiet laugh from before to get louder. Her dimples are deeper than ever, and I'm fully mesmerized.

"Stop–" She laughs when I give her a squeeze again. "Fine!" The word comes out choppy, her fingers landing on my wrist to stop me. My heart stutters from the touch, my skin sparking with heat beneath hers. I haven't been this sensitive to a female's touch since I was a thirteen-year-old going through puberty.

The effect she has on me is fascinating.

She glances at her hand on my wrist, and I do the same. Her laughter fades, and the fun energy in the car takes a nose-dive to something much hotter. I bet if I were to light a match, the entire car would burst into flames.

I attempt to break the hot tension, but I make no attempt to remove my hand from her body. "So you had fun?"

My throaty voice is very telling.

Reese slowly brings her attention to mine, her eyelashes fluttering.

It's hard to know what she's thinking. I act like I can read her well, but I can't.

When she zeroes in on my mouth, my pulse picks up its pace.

I want to grab her around the waist and pull her into my lap, just to know what it feels like to have her there. My head is spinning, and I can't figure out why I'm so out of control when it comes to her.

Reese shifts, and I hear the sound of her seatbelt unclicking. The strap slowly slides off her body to reveal the easy access to the button of her jeans. It would be so fucking easy to slide my fingers from her waist and end up right *there*–

Her fingers dig into my skin, and I release her from my grip. My dick takes the hit, the sparks dying before they even make it to the tip, but suddenly, they come to life again as Reese takes me by total surprise.

Instead of leaving me high and dry, she quickly climbs over the center console and lands right in my lap. Her hands grip my shoulders, her legs falling to my sides to straddle me.

Fucking yes.

Her mouth seals against mine, and I'm lost. She's sweet like that candy she was just sucking on, but her tongue moves against mine like a sin.

I waste no time.

I skim my hand up her body and cup the side of her face. My fingers disappear into her dark locks to tug her in even closer. At the same time, I flex my hips, and a sweet noise escapes her.

She's needy, and I'm willing to give her whatever she asks for. Money? It's hers. My bed? As long as she doesn't mind sharing. My last name? Let's make it official.

With one hand keeping her face pressed to mine so I can explore every single inch of her mouth, my other moves against her body so I can memorize every part of her. She's soft and warm with curves that make my head spin.

I pull away from her rushed kisses for a second. "Let's go up to my apartment."

She shakes her head, never taking her eyes off my mouth. "No."

No?

As if she can taste the confusion on my tongue, she pulls back after kissing me again. Our eyes catch, the dazed look in her eyes making my dick even harder than it was before.

"The shame will catch up to me," she admits.

"Shame?" I repeat. "You'll feel shame from this?"

It's not like she dropped her panties for me the second we met or jumped into my bed after one drunken meeting. In fact, she's been pretty persistent with keeping her distance when it comes to me.

"Shh." Reese places a finger against my lips. "Stop talking

and kiss me." Her eyes bounce back and forth between mine, the dazed look switching to a plea. "*Please.*"

My muscles tense. Fire flies to my fingertips.

Having her like this and hearing her beg just does something to me. If she wants me to kiss her outside of my apartment complex instead of going upstairs, who am I to deny her?

Nine

REESE

I'M SIMPLY out of control.

This was not how the evening was supposed to go. When I left Charleigh at home with Zoe to go work, I never once dreamed that I'd end the night in my car with Malaki, especially after spending the night dancing against him at the club.

The word "please" involuntarily slips from my mouth, and my entire body heats with embarrassment. Could I sound any more desperate? Why don't I just stamp the word on my forehead for all to see?

I expect Malaki to hesitate. At the very least, I suspect him to question my desperation, but he does the exact opposite. He grips the back of my head and pushes my face close to his. The hint of Skittles lingers in between us, my tongue likely red from the way I sucked on the candy just a few minutes ago. I close my eyes, and he kisses me again, this time deeper. My back arches with his hands roaming, his tongue moving with finesse, like kissing is an art.

I'm in a daze as his rough calluses rub over my skin and

send chills to the surface. My eyes flutter with pleasure as my head tilts to the side. His lips move to my throat where he peppers the delicate area with kisses and nips from his teeth.

"Gorgeous," he whispers.

His fingers move with a deft speed as he pushes the button of my jeans through its hole before unzipping them. I place my hands on his chest and shift up to give him more access.

I make every effort to push away the quiet thoughts in the back of my head that this is wrong, because is it? How could something this good feel wrong?

There is nothing *wrong* about Malaki Young.

A fire brews in between my legs as Malaki sweeps his fingers against the top of my panties. It's been so long that I'd forgotten how good it feels to be touched by a man.

"Lift up for me, babe."

I waste no time. I push myself up by anchoring my palms to his shoulders. Malaki shimmies his hand farther into my unzipped jeans, and pleasure sweeps over me.

He curses under his breath, and I get a quick glimpse of his face. His pupils dilate, his jaw clenching. The moment his finger swipes against my clit, I cry out.

"When was the last time you were touched, Reese?"

God, even his voice is hot.

I can't answer him.

My body is too riled up; my mouth refuses to form words.

I move against him, craving more. His fingers move faster, one pushing inside of me while he rubs against my clit with another. Each touch unravels a tightly woven bow that's been tied for far too long.

His hands are just as talented with a hockey stick as they are with my body. One grips my waist as the other works its magic in between my thighs. *It feels so good.* My fingernails dig into his shoulders as my body tenses, the orgasm swiftly peaking and taking me under.

It's earth shattering.

I shake in his grip.

I'm still reeling when he grips the back of my neck and brings my face to his again. He presses his lips to mine, and I open up as if his mouth is a key to a lock. Hot strokes of his tongue lap against mine, and I match every single one.

A groan leaves him, echoing into my mouth.

I regret not taking him up on his offer—we should've gone upstairs to his apartment.

Being here with him like this puts a pause on all my responsibilities, and it's the best escape I've ever had.

"Fuck." He curses against my mouth and crushes me against his chest. "Don't move."

"Huh?" I blink several times and try to find my way back to planet Earth.

Malaki's warm breath lingers against my ear, which *does not* help. "There is someone walking a little too slow past the window."

I tense, my spine snapping into place. *Oh my god, we're in public.*

"Relax," he says. "I've got you."

Panic races down my spine. What was I thinking? What if Benedict walked past? This would give him plenty of ammunition to take Charleigh from me. Instead of being at home with her, I'm in a car, getting fingered by some guy! This is considered public indecency! A judge would do to me exactly what they did to my mother. They shamed her, called her a bad mother, and listed every one of her mistakes for all to see, and in the end, they took us.

It wasn't like she cared much, but I would.

As if fate can hear me, my phone starts to ring from the dash. I jerk away from Malaki and practically flip into the driver's seat with my pants still unbuttoned. My long hair is a tangled mess from his fingers gripping the strands. I quickly brush it away and leap for my phone.

I answer quickly. "Zoe?"

Her voice comes over the car's speakers instead of the phone. I snap my attention to Malaki.

Shit! I fumble with the device, attempting to take it off my car's speakers.

"You need to come home." Zoe's tone is clipped.

"What's wrong?" I ask, losing my battle with the Bluetooth button. "Is it Charleigh?"

Malaki stiffens, his hand forming a tight fist against his leg.

Zoe's panicky voice pulls me right back to the phone call, and I ignore Malaki's reaction.

"No." She sounds concerned, which is never good.

I turn it off Bluetooth just in time.

"It's that fuck face, Benedict."

Shit.

"I'm on my way." I hang up the phone, and silence fills the car.

I don't even have to say the words for Malaki to catch the hint. The door opens, the unlock button causing me to jerk in the driver's seat. Before he slips out to disappear into his apartment, he peers at me with one leg out of the car.

"I thought you said you were single."

I open my mouth and close it again. *What?*

Malaki mumbles quietly to himself about me being a cheater. It does nothing but offend me.

"I *am* single," I stress, defending myself.

He chuckles, but I'm pretty sure it's sarcastic. "Then who is Charleigh?"

I blink a few times, my thoughts a tangled mess.

But then it hits me.

Charleigh is a gender-neutral name, and his brain automatically went in the direction that I should have expected.

I could take the time to explain myself, but what's the point? This was a mistake.

I break our stare-off and gaze out the windshield. "I have to go."

I don't like the way my stomach aches from the loss of something that was never mine and never would be.

He makes a noise of sarcasm, huffing under his breath. "See you around, Reese."

As soon as he shuts the door, I take off in the direction of my shitty apartment.

Ten

REESE

I MAKE it home in less than seven minutes. The drive from Malaki's apartment in the uppity part of the city is far enough away from downtown that being back at my place seems like a whole different world. The homeless wander about, and you never want to look at someone for too long in the eye.

I rush out of my car and lock it on the way to the stairs. I skip every other step with my heart in my throat. The long hallway comes into view, and I stop dead in my tracks at the sight of Benedict.

Why is he here?

"Nice place you have," he muses without looking up from his phone. One shoulder is leaning against the wall with one foot crossed over the other.

I slow my steps. "Why are you here, Benedict?"

He shuts his phone off. The quick flick of his gaze causes my breath to falter.

Can he tell?

"The question is, why aren't *you* here, Reese?"

I cross my arms defensively. "I was working."

"Oh, really?" He raises an eyebrow. "Interesting."

I was working–until Malaki convinced me to stay out with him. Convinced, *paid*, whatever.

The air in the stuffy hallway is so tense I'm afraid to move.

Benedict opens up his phone again, his movements slow and lazy.

"I wasn't aware that Ubering had a double meaning, sweetheart."

I cringe. I hate when he calls me that.

"The court is going to love seeing the footage of you dancing and having a good time while our baby is at home alone with a teenager."

My nostrils flare. "Zoe is in college. She is perfectly capable of babysitting Charleigh while I work."

Benedict smirks. "While you work?"

This is a disaster. An utter fucking disaster.

Before I can think, Benedict moves like a lion after its prey. One second, I'm standing with my arms crossed, and the next, my back is against the wall with his presence trapping me.

His hand digs into my hair, and I turn my head away to stare at my apartment door. Fear prickles my skin. He pulls on the strands hard enough to make me wince.

"Your hair is messy," he hisses.

I push myself into the wall in an attempt to get away from him. He leans in close to rub his nose against my jaw. He sniffs twice and growls. "You smell like him."

Blinding anger zips to my fingertips. I lift my hands and push against his chest to slip out from under him. Surprisingly, he lets me go with a gruff chuckle following close behind.

"I'm allowed to see other people," I argue.

It doesn't matter that I'm not dating Malaki or even considering seeing him again. Benedict needs a reality check.

"You think a court is going to side with you after they learn that you're out whoring around with some random guy while our daughter is at home?"

The nerve.

Our daughter?

"And you think the court is going to side with you after they learn that you wanted me to *end my pregnancy* and have only held Charleigh a handful of times?" I scoff. "What happens if the court sides with you, Benedict?"

I've struck a chord. His eye twitches, and his jaw clenches.

His plan is to force me back into a relationship with him so we can act like one big happy family, but doesn't he know that a broken home, filled with fear and hate, is much more damaging to a child than the one Charleigh currently has with me? She deserves to be surrounded by love and warmth, and that comes in all shapes, forms, and sizes.

Do I struggle to make ends meet? Sure.

But I'd rather work odd hours to pay the electric bill than live in a mansion where I'd have to turn my head every time Benedict came home late from the bar with the scent of perfume on his collar.

Benedict glares at me. "Who is he?"

I inch toward my apartment door. "Have you been having someone follow me around?"

My legs are heavy as I take another step away from him. The knot in my stomach tightens when he clicks his tongue and smirks.

There is no fear as powerful as the thought of someone taking your child from you.

"I asked you who he is. Is he a one-night stand? I sure hope you don't get pregnant again."

I swallow past the lump in my throat and open my mouth. "What if I tell you he's my boyfriend? Would that make you leave me alone?"

Anger brews in his eyes, the blue becoming as dark as a midnight storm. "You think just because you call him your boyfriend that means anything?" He laughs sarcastically. "How long have you known him? An hour? That's how long you knew me before you were opening up those legs."

This bastard.

"I've known him for years," I lie right through my teeth. "You'd know that if you actually knew me."

Benedict's upper lip rises with obvious irritation. He takes a step toward me, and I panic, but at the last second, the apartment door swings open, revealing Zoe holding Charleigh. She's in her pink footy pjs with her wild dark hair hanging in her eyes. I smile when our eyes lock, her expression matching mine.

She babbles while bucking against my sister's hip. "Ma-ma–mama."

"Hi, sweet pea," I coo.

"You need to leave." Zoe pops her hip out with an edge of anger to her tone, and I take Charleigh from her.

I glance over my shoulder at Benedict. He's glaring at Zoe, and surprise, surprise, he completely ignores Charleigh.

"You going to make me?" he asks.

A challenge flashes over my sister's face. *Oh no.*

Benedict knows that Zoe and I come from a different background. When he was opening presents on Christmas morning from Santa, Zoe and I were cleaning up our father's vomit on our living room floor from his drunken rage the night prior. When someone knocked on our front door, it wasn't a delivery man with a package of goodies; it was someone demanding money—or worse, CPS.

It shouldn't have come as a surprise to him or me when Zoe disappears for a moment and pops back up with a baseball bat in her hands.

"I can definitely make you leave." She twirls the baseball

bat in her hands, and all I can think is, *where the hell did she get a baseball bat?*

"You're fucking crazy," he mumbles.

Zoe hauls the bat up higher with Charleigh eagerly reaching for it.

Benedict slowly backs away, shifting his gaze in between us. "A baseball bat when I'm just trying to see my daughter..." He acts appalled, his head shaking back and forth.

"You are not here to see your daughter," Zoe argues. "You know it, I know it, Reese knows it, and it won't take Char long to figure it out too."

"Zoe." My heart pounds with the realization that Benedict is cataloging every last interaction between us so he can compile it all into a nice and tidy folder if he ever decides to follow through on his threat. "Stop."

My sister's steps falter, the bun on top of her head bouncing from the sudden movement. "Please tell me you're not siding with him."

Of course I'm not.

She knows me better than that.

I give her a look, stressing my quiet thoughts. She eventually rolls her eyes before putting the bat back where she found it and disappearing into our small living room.

I move Charleigh to my other hip and glance at Benedict once more before quickly shutting the door and fumbling with the lock.

Zoe flops onto the couch and puts her long legs on the Goodwill coffee table we snagged weeks prior. An empty baby bottle, binky, and three toys are scattered on top. "Is it bad to wish death on someone?"

I sigh. "Yes."

Zoe unravels her bun, and the dark strands of her hair fling off the back of the couch as she slumps down farther. "Why did you tell me to stop?" she asks. "I remember you taking a baseball bat to Scary Larry, and in my opinion, Benedict is worse."

Scary Larry—a name Zoe and I came up with one night when we were tucked away in the same bed because we were afraid that our dad's creepy friend would try to sneak into our room at night like the boogie man—*was* worse than Benedict. She was just too young to remember. That's why I took a bat to his knees.

"There's more at risk with Benedict," I explain.

"Like?"

I begin cleaning up the living room, gathering everything in my free hand. Charleigh reaches for her pink binky and plops it into her mouth. Her eyes droop, and she lays her head on my shoulder.

"Like the fact that he keeps threatening to take me to court for custody."

Zoe is on her feet in seconds. "What?!"

I put my back to her to hide how terrified I am. I'm the strong one of our sister duo. I can't show her that I'm worried.

"Yeah," I say over my shoulder from the kitchen. "So it's time to be on our best behavior."

Silence fills our small apartment for so long I'm able to wash Charleigh's bottle with one hand and put it on the drying rack without any interruptions.

When I walk back into the living room to snag her pink blanket, Zoe is nibbling on her lip. With Charleigh's head resting against my shoulder, well past asleep, she lowers her voice. "Is that why you told him whoever you were with was your boyfriend and that you've known him for years?"

My lips flatten. "You never did grow out of eavesdropping, did you?"

Her classic cheeky grin appears, and she shrugs. She's almost to her room before she turns around with an even bigger smile on her face. "I sure hope that boyfriend of yours gave you an orgasm tonight. Might as well make it worthwhile, right?"

I snatch one of Charleigh's toys and chuck it at her head. Knowing me almost as well as she knows herself, she quickly shuts her bedroom door to avoid being hit. The toy hits the wood before falling to the floor with a quiet thud.

"He did give me an orgasm, thank you very much!" I whisper.

Little does he know, I just told my overbearing ex that Malaki and I are much more than what we really are, especially after tonight.

Eleven

MALAKI

I WALK inside the locker room for our annual charity event, and it's buzzing. The sounds of shuttering cameras ride a wave in between all the quiet murmurs, and young kids step forward while staying close to their parents who look at us with admiration and gratitude. I scan the crowd and–*ah, shit.*

I pause in the doorway and stare. Reese is hard to overlook, even standing beside Daisy all dolled up in her Blue Devil mascot costume. I have no idea what she's doing here, but I'm not necessarily unhappy about it.

Days have passed since I've last seen her, our night ending on less-than-ideal terms. Yet I still can't seem to get her out of my head. It isn't often that a woman lingers for this long. Is it because we were interrupted? Or is it because my attraction to her is unmatched? Maybe it's because I was metaphorically left on unread when I asked her who Charlie was.

Her sassy response to my unintentional jab is on repeat: "*I am single!*"

Even during practice, it circled around my head like it has

any business being there while I'm working gap control or battling behind the net.

I pull my eyes away from Reese when there's a tug on my pant leg. Two wide eyes stare up at me, suddenly reminding me why I'm here.

I get down on the little tyke's level. "Hey, bud. What's your name?"

He looks down with the slip of his name. "Jackson."

"Jackson," I repeat. "Give me some knuckles." I throw my fist out, and he eagerly pounds it with his own. "Should we get a picture?" I ask.

He shakes his head.

No?

I try again. "Do you want an autograph?"

He pauses and seemingly looks around for something to sign. He disappears for a moment and runs over to his parents to tug on their pant legs like he did to me. I watch him for a second before shifting my attention to the prettiest girl in the room.

Reese is staring directly at me.

Pride fills my chest. I grin, my lip hitching on one side.

Knowing she was caught, she turns away quickly, but not quite quick enough, because I spotted the blush rush to her cheeks.

I get back on Jackson's level and sign the puck he brought me, but before I hand it to him, another grand idea comes to mind.

"Hey, want to be my partner in crime?" I ask him.

This time, there is no hesitation. He nods his head eagerly, more than willing to partner up with me.

There's a nearby bin of pucks for signing. I sneakily grab one and write, *Who is Charlie?* on it with a permanent marker and hand it to Jackson. "Okay, partner. Can you deliver this puck to that girl right there?" I point over at Reese, who is doing everything in her power to avoid me.

She stands alone, looking at Daisy and Kane arguing while simultaneously posing for pictures with kids.

She's leaning against my locker. Coincidence? I think not.

Jackson disappears to deliver the puck to Reese while I busy myself with signing more autographs and posing with other kids and their families. I catch quick glimpses of my little partner in crime when he hands Reese the puck, and I suddenly can't look away.

She bends down to get on his level and pushes her soft wavy hair over her shoulder. Her warm smile sucks me in, and the fluttering of her eyes? I'm a goner.

Reese quickly stands up straight after taking the puck from Jackson and raises an eyebrow in my direction.

I shrug innocently.

Her lips flatten.

Humor fills me, and I find myself wanting to smirk as I'm pulled away to socialize some more. I photobomb several of my teammates while they pose for their own photos with tiny fans and win the laughs of everyone in the room, even Reese.

Kane saunters up beside me, huffing and puffing.

"Lady trouble?" I ask.

"Fuck off," Kane growls.

We both look out into the sea of kids who somehow seem more interested in Daisy and Reese than us. Jackson continues to stand near Reese, making no move to come back over to me.

Little traitor. Not that I can blame him.

I glance down when someone taps on the side of my leg.

This time, it's a little girl with pink glasses and two pigtails. She's holding up a puck for me to take with wide eyes. She's cute and reminds me of Rhodes' daughter.

Though, Ellie is as sassy as they get.

After signing the puck, I swoop the little girl up into my arms. She doesn't talk, and her parents explain that she's mostly deaf yet refuses to wear her hearing aids.

"Do you have them with you?" I ask them after posing with her for a photo.

The dad nods and pulls out two purple devices.

I place the little girl back on her feet but stay on her level. I pop both hearing aids into my ears, and she giggles. Not knowing sign language, I turn to her parents. "Can you ask her if she likes them? If she thinks they look good on me?"

The mom laughs while signing to her daughter.

She shakes her head and giggles again. Before I know it, she's reaching forward and snatching them out of my ear. It only takes her a few seconds to put them into her own.

"I agree." I nod. "They look much better on you."

I wink at her and stand, her laugh still lingering below.

Her father shakes my hand and expresses his gratitude.

I brush them off. "Don't worry about it. I'm happy to help."

I eagerly scan the room after they move on to another one of my teammates.

Back to the target, I tell myself.

Reese stands in the same spot next to my locker, with her lip tucked in between her teeth. There's a softness lingering around her, those brown eyes warm as she flutters her eyelashes in my direction. We keep catching each other's eye until the room begins to clear out, taking her best friend and Kane too, as they both rush through the door.

I move toward Reese while giving each of my teammates a look that says, *She's mine.* A few of them smirk; some roll their eyes. She sticks out like a rose in a bunch of thorns. So pretty and soft, surrounded by gruff hockey players who are hoping I blow my chances so they can try to win her affection too.

I lean against Kane's locker, which just happens to be next to mine. "Did you get my note?" I ask her.

Reese plays with a delicate gold necklace around her neck, refusing to look at me. "Hm?" she says. "What did you say? Something about a note?"

I chuckle. "Maybe I should go get those purple hearing aids for you."

She sucks her cheeks in, and I know it's because she's trying not to laugh at my joke.

I nudge her with my elbow. "Did you like that?"

She finally glances at me. I immediately drop my gaze to her mouth. Kissing her the other night really messed with my head because here I am, thinking of doing it again, while I just so happen to forget about the whole *Charlie* thing.

"Did I like what?" she asks.

I flick my chin to where I was standing previously. "My little stunt with the hearing aids?"

She rolls her eyes playfully while her fingers continue to fiddle with the necklace.

Silence begins to settle in the locker room, my teammates ready to end the evening but not before stopping to talk with the manager and trainers. Reese's lips open out of the corner of my eye, like she's going to say something, but then they close again. She does this a few times before finally giving in.

"You're good with kids."

Rhodes walks past with his gear in tow. He doesn't even make eye contact but still manages to say, "That's because he's a kid too."

"Fuck off," I mumble.

Reese quietly laughs, and yeah, okay, fine. He's not necessarily wrong.

I like to have fun, and if that makes me a kid, then so be it.

I shift to rest my shoulder against the locker so I can see her better. She doesn't so much as twitch. Her back stays straight as a board as she stares out into the emptying locker room, almost like she's afraid to move.

Afraid I'm going to kiss her again?

"What exactly are you doing here?" I ask, crossing my arms. "Did you come to answer my question?"

A huff of air leaves her. "No."

"You came to see me, though, didn't you?" I can't help but rile her up.

"What?" She crosses her arms like me. "No!"

I hum. "Whatever you say, Dimples."

Her hip pops with attitude, and excitement creeps into my blood. I love her saucy manner. It's entertaining and enticing all in one. She turns to face me, little lines of anger on her forehead. "I'm here because I help with some PR stuff occasionally. I was the one who designed Daisy's costume, and I had to fix a few sequins."

Oh?

"And," she presses on, "I'm also Daisy's ride."

"So you're an Uber driver, you make costumes, and you help out with the team's PR?" I pretend to count. "What is that? Three jobs?"

She scoffs, like she'd rather be anywhere else than in this locker room, talking to me. "I wouldn't consider making one costume a job, and I only helped Cindy a few times. It's nothing permanent."

"Damn," I sigh. "I thought I might get to see you while on the ice."

She pushes her hair over her shoulder and turns away. "Sorry to disappoint."

It is a disappointment. I like seeing her. I like being around her too.

I move without thought and end up right in front of her with my hands on her hips. Her eyes widen, and she jerks backward, bumping into my locker. A soft gasp slips from behind her lips, and I somehow forget all about the whole Charlie thing and how dismissive she is with me most of the time.

"Excuse me," I say under my breath. With my hands around her waist, I scoot her over some so I can get into my locker. Reese's chest is unmoving, air trapped inside as she holds her breath. A smirk works itself onto my face as I remove my hands from her waist. "Breathe, Reese. Or you might pass out and force me to give you mouth to mouth in front of my coach."

She responds with an exhale, her sweet breath fanning in between us. Satisfaction fills me up to the brim, to the point that I almost miss her fleeing.

"Um, excuse me," her sweet voice carries throughout the room while she dodges a few people.

She waves at Cindy, the woman in charge of our PR, before she slips through the door.

I chuckle as she scurries away.

Doesn't she know that I'm annoyingly persistent? As if I'm not going to chase after her? The flare of attraction between us burned so bright with my hands around her waist that I'd be a fool not to. My pretty Uber driver with secrets that she's unwilling to spill is doing nothing but tempting me by running off like that.

She's about to find out the hard way that I'm relentless.

Twelve

REESE

I TIPTOE out of my bedroom, careful not to wake Charleigh, and pause. Zoe sits on the couch in front of the coffee table with three lit candlesticks as her light.

"What are you doing?" I whisper. "A seance?"

Zoe doesn't even glance up from her book. "A seance? Who the hell would I want to contact from the dead? I already know plenty about our mother. No need to ask her from hell."

"Zoe," I warn.

She glances at me and shrugs. "What? It's true."

It *is* true, but still.

The only thing I learned from both of our parents is what *not* to do. The electric bill is due? Any sane person would pick up some more hours so they can afford it. My parents used to rip the bill up and throw it into the trash.

Out of sight, out of mind.

Until the power shuts off, and somehow, they're both shocked. My dad would take it out on my mom with his fists, and she would disappear for days at a time, leaving my sister and me to fend for ourselves.

What can I say? They were great role models.

I plop down onto the couch beside Zoe and sink into the worn cushions. "God, it feels good to sit."

Zoe remains quiet as she pulls her textbook closer to read. It's so dim in the apartment that I have no idea how she's able to see the text. I stare at the flickering flames on the candles and then slowly move back to staring at her.

It clicks a moment later.

My stomach slowly slides to the floor with the weight of the world on my shoulders again.

"Zoe," I say her name slowly. "You can turn the lights on. Stop working by candlelight like we used to do in high school."

I drag myself off the couch and head over to where my purse hangs.

Was I planning on working tonight? No.

But all it takes is one tiny reminder of how bad off we really are to kick me into gear.

Zoe peeks above her textbook. "What are you doing?"

I try to act energetic and walk with a pep in my step toward the door. "I'm going to Uber for a few hours."

Her textbook slams shut behind my back. "Reese, no. Take the night off."

"You're literally working by candlelight," I joke from over my shoulder. "That means you opened the electric bill before I did, and that means it's probably a lot higher than expected."

Her shoulders drop. The wavy strands of her dark hair sway with a heavy sigh. "You deserve a night off."

I ignore her. "You're in for the night, right? In case Charleigh wakes?"

"I've got our girl," she says, opening her textbook again.

"Love you, mean it," I say in the doorway.

We started saying it years ago, when things at home became messy. Zoe is as strong as they come and independent too. But when she was younger, she would scream if she was forced to leave me. One day, I tried to reassure her that I'd see her after school and that I loved her. Her face screwed up, her cheeks turned a bright red, and then she said, *"Yeah, but do you mean it?"*

I couldn't blame her for questioning the meaning. Plenty of people told us they loved us, and then their actions told us a different story. That's where the *'mean it'* part came into play.

"Love you, mean it," she says quietly.

I smile to myself and shut the door.

After logging into work, my phone immediately starts blowing up. Three rides later, a total of $20 in tips, and I'm being directed to the hockey arena.

The Blue Devils must've had a game tonight, which explains why the Uber requests are piled high. I do a great job of not thinking about a certain hockey player until I pull up to the curb with hundreds of fans wearing blue and black fleeing from the arena. So many of them wear his number that it's impossible not to let his annoyingly hot smirk creep inside my head.

Damn him.

I grip the steering wheel and wait for my rider to approach the car. I peek through the window to search for someone with that deer-in-the-headlights look, but it's no use. Rowdy fans with their foam tridents–one of my marketing ideas–loiter around, making it difficult to breathe let alone spot my little Honda off to the side.

I open my car door and stand on my tiptoes in search of some guy named Nathan. A gust of wind whips my braid around as I step up onto the curb with my phone in hand.

Where are you? I type, wondering if he's gotten a different ride.

All of a sudden, the crowd parts, and a guy comes barreling toward me. I take a step backward and lean onto my car.

"Reese?" He glances at his phone and then up at me.

I nod. "Yeah, that's me."

"Whew." He wipes sweat off his forehead and flings it off to the side. "Sorry. For a second, I thought I missed my ride."

I shake my head and direct him to my car. "It's no problem. I know how crazy it gets after the game."

It isn't until I'm about to step off the curb when I realize that people are staring in my direction. I pause with my foot hovering above the road. Nathan wipes more sweat off his brow with his other hand on the passenger side handle.

Weird.

I hurry around to my side of the car and slide inside. The sugary smell of Skittles fills the air as I grab the wheel. I turn to make sure Nathan is getting in–and scream.

"What the hell are you doing in here?" My hand flies to my chest to keep my heart from barreling out onto my lap.

The back door slams shut. Nathan sucks in air so quickly, he squeaks.

Malaki, relaxed as ever, shrugs nonchalantly. "Getting a ride."

My mouth opens, but nothing comes out. I'm too shocked to form a sentence.

Malaki angles himself toward the backseat. His large frame takes up so much space I have to move backward so his arm doesn't brush mine. "You don't mind if I tag along, do you?"

Nathan blinks three hundred times in one second. "What? Yes. I mean–" He shakes his head, frustrated with himself. "No! I mean, no! I don't mind. You...you're Malaki Young."

Malaki's jaw drops. He looks at me with surprise and then back to Nathan. "I am?!"

A laugh bursts from my mouth.

I slap my hand over it.

I can't let him know he makes me laugh!

Malaki's mouth curves on the side, but he says nothing. Instead, he reaches into the back with his hand outstretched. "It's nice to meet you, man."

"Um, yeah..." Nathan gingerly shakes Malaki's hand. "You too. That was a g–good game."

Malaki turns back around—as if he's supposed to be in my front seat—and continues the conversation. "Yeah, it was alright. We won, and that's all that matters, I suppose."

Nathan's seatbelt clicks, but I still remain unmoving.

"I can't believe I'm in a car with Malaki Young," he says under his breath.

"Me either!" I hiss in Malaki's direction. "What are you doing here?" I whisper, trying to keep our conversation somewhat private while Nathan gives himself a pep talk in the backseat about keeping it cool.

"I told you..." He leans over the center console, closer to me. His warm breath fans onto my face and–*are those Skittles I smell?* "I'm getting a ride with my favorite Uber driver."

I freeze when he reaches across me to grab my seatbelt. He pulls it across my chest and clicks it into place. The small act shouldn't cause my brain to fizzle, yet I can't breathe.

I almost forget that Nathan is in the backseat until he clears his throat. It snaps me out of my near blackout. I quickly shift my car into drive while Nathan and Malaki ramble on about the hockey game for the entire seven-minute drive to Nathan's drop-off point.

"Can I have a quick autograph?" Nathan asks, door half-opened in front of some club with a line wrapped around the building. "Do you have anything to write with?" Nathan looks around my car. "And, like, maybe something to write on?"

Malaki, who acts like this is his car instead of mine, opens the center console and rummages around for something. He finds a pink permanent marker—from my college days, I assume—and...*oh my god.*

My eyes almost pop out of my skull.

A nursing pad?!

Malaki furrows his brow while he flips over the cotton circle a few times.

I stopped nursing months ago but never disposed of the pads because they could come in handy at some point. Apparently, like right now–for a freaking autograph!

If someone could ram into the back of my car just enough to send the pad flying, that would be great.

Eventually, Malaki shrugs and signs the nursing pad before tossing it to Nathan.

"There you go." He shoves the marker back into the center console, and Nathan thanks him over and over again while climbing out of my car.

He tips me before moving away toward the line.

"Wow," I whisper, staring at the amount.

Malaki adjusts himself in the front seat, spreading those long legs. "You're welcome."

I cross my arms, making no attempt to drive anywhere with him still inside the car. "For?"

"Admit it, Dimples." His blue eyes twinkle with mischief. I hate the way my breath catches. "You make more money when you're with me."

I huff. "That's because you pay me to hang out with you!"

Malaki scoffs and points to the backseat. "How about what just happened? I gave him an autograph too. Imagine if I had told him no, or if I kicked him out of the car and took his Uber completely, leaving him stranded at the arena."

"I should leave *you* stranded at the arena," I exclaim. "What are you even doing in my car? You have your own!"

He turns and stares out the window. "It broke down."

"Liar."

I can see his smirk through the reflection. It makes me want to smile in the worst way–that or hit him. I refuse to do either. "You're insane."

"I'm not insane," he argues. "I'm persistent."

"You mean annoying," I quip.

"Charming."

"*Irritating.*"

"Handsome."

I can't help but laugh.

He shows me his heart-stopping smile. "I'm funny too."

I give up. I drop my head against the back of my seat and sigh. "Well...where am I taking you? Home? Back to your car that is most definitely not broken down?"

Malaki rests his head against the passenger seat just like me. We both turn and stare at each other with nothing but the air conditioner whirring in the background. "You can take me wherever you want...after you tell me who Charlie is."

This again?

I bite the inside of my cheek.

It's not necessarily a secret. I'm not hiding that I'm a mother from Malaki for any reason other than I don't like people privy to my life. I'm protective of not only my daughter, but of Zoe too, and our well-being. I'm cautious. It's as simple as that. Which is why Benedict's threat has my stomach turning every time I have to make a decision that could give him or anyone else ammunition to use against me.

"You've given me no other choice," Malaki announces.

I squint at him. "What–" I gasp when I realize he's staring at my Skittles. "Don't you dare."

He eyes me from the side as he reaches for the bag of candy. I quickly sit taller, my spine locking. He wastes no time. He moves just as quickly as he does on the ice. The wrapper crinkles in his grip, even more so when he tips his head back and opens his mouth.

"Tell me, or I'm eating every last one," he says, his neck bobbing up and down.

I jump into action and undo my seatbelt. I lean over the center console as a single Skittle drops into his mouth, the candy clinking against his teeth. Malaki turns towards me now, our faces inches away. He proudly shows me one lonely Skittle resting on his tongue.

"Give my Skittles back," I stress, half-playful, half-annoyed.

I know it's absurd, but the candy is sort of like a protective blanket to me. I've been indulging in Skittles since I was a kid, and somewhere along the way, they became more than just a sweet treat.

"You're going to have to take them from me."

The candy is beginning to melt on his tongue. I flick my gaze to his, and the teasing glint in his eye sweeps me right off my feet.

Malaki is challenging me, and I know I shouldn't play this game with him, but being this close to him jumbles me up.

I narrow my eyes and smile. He does a double-take, tilting his head to one side.

"Fine," I say.

I brace myself as I press my mouth to his. It surprises him so much that I'm able to brush my tongue against his without trouble. The sweet taste of strawberry fills my mouth, and I'm seconds from stealing it until I'm brutally ripped away by a sharp rap against my window.

I fly back into my seat and turn.

Benedict stands outside my car in his victorious stance. His arms cross at his chest with a cunning smile to greet me.

"Shit," I whisper.

Thirteen

MALAKI

IT DOESN'T TAKE a genius to know that the man standing outside Reese's car isn't a stranger. The energy shifts, a hot sticky feeling of panic filling the gap between us.

"Is that Charlie?" I ask.

Fuck. It definitely is.

He may punch me.

Am I ready to take a hit for this girl?

I run my tongue along my bottom lip, tasting her. *Yeah, no question about it.*

"Fuck, fuck, fuck." The curse words fly from her mouth.

There's another *tap, tap* on the window, and she exhales.

Instead of opening her door and climbing out of it, her shaky finger presses down on the window button. It rolls down slowly, squeaking as it lowers. The man leans into the car, and his sharp gaze skips her to land on me.

"Get out of the car, Reese."

My eye twitches. Where are his manners?

Reese straightens, seemingly sitting taller in her seat. "Do you need something, Benedict?"

Benedict? So this isn't Charlie?

I relax some, but I'm still strung tight. He puts her on edge, and I want to know why.

Reese is a mystery, and I think it's making me crazy. What am I doing in her car right now? After playing the game I just played, I should be a walking dead man from exhaustion alone, but all it took was one glance at her car pulling into the arena parking lot, and I was summoned like a damn vampire.

"Do I need something?" Benedict repeats her question in a condescending tone. He chuckles, shaking his head. Not a hair moves out of place–there's too much fucking gel to do that.

"I don't need anything..." his voice lingers. "But you're going to need something real soon, sweetheart. Especially being out here, late at night, making out with some guy."

I drop my attention to Reese's lap where she moves her fingers to pinch her thigh, like she needs something to keep her in line.

"Get out of the car. Your fuck buddy can stay in there." He rounds the front of her car and sits along the hood without any worry that she'll take off with him on top.

Reese scrambles to roll her window up.

"Who the hell is that–"

She cuts my sentence off with a sharp look. "Just...stay here."

"No fucking wa–"

Her door shuts in my face. I unclick my seatbelt. I'm not leaving her out there to deal with this douchebag on her own. Plus, he's wrong. I'm not her fuck buddy. I wish I were, but I'm not.

Reese's eyes shoot to mine briefly as I climb out of her car.

I remain casual as I walk toward them. Benedict continues to throw insults at her without paying any attention to me. She chews on her bottom lip nervously–the poor thing is going to be raw by the end of this ordeal.

"Out here whoring around–"

I stop dead in my tracks, my feet scuffing along the pavement.

"I know you did not just insinuate that Reese is whoring around." The pitch of my voice is as neutral as always, but my shoulders tense with irritation. I haven't known Reese for long, and according to her, I don't know her at all, but what kind of man would I be if I stood here and let him talk to her like that?

Benedict glares at me briefly before turning back toward Reese. "This doesn't concern you, so if you're going to be our audience, do me a favor and shut the hell up."

I step off the curb and stand beside Reese.

"This absolutely concerns him!" she argues.

It does?

"Oh, does it now?" Benedict rolls his eyes. "How does this concern your fuck buddy, Reese?"

"He isn't my fuck buddy!" she seethes.

I wish.

Benedict raises an eyebrow. "So what? He's your... boyfriend?" He chuckles sarcastically.

Irritation races up my spine like a chill. I put my arm around Reese and tug her to my side. It's *almost* as good as sticking a knife in his chest. "Boyfriend..." I repeat, playing with the words.

I can act like her boyfriend.

No skin off my back.

"No." Reese intertwines her fingers in my hand hanging off her shoulder. "He's my fiancé."

I blink. Did she just say that I'm her fiancé?

Her fingers squeeze mine, and I quickly smooth my face.

Benedict snorts before he throws his head back with a laugh. "Bullshit."

I don't have to look at Reese to know she's worked up. Her entire body trembles with nerves.

Or is it fear?

Either way, I'm in.

Fuck this asshole.

I chuckle, and it pulls Benedict's sharp gaze to me. A crowd is beginning to form, and I have no doubt that the guy I shared an Uber with showed everyone my autograph inside that club, and they're all out here to get their own.

"What? You can't believe that she'd find someone better than you or...?" I let my words linger, and I hope they leave a sting behind.

Benedict abruptly stands from sitting on the hood of Reese's car. She attempts to take a step back as he heads for us, but I refuse to let her do so.

He isn't going to intimidate her with me standing here.

The moment his fingers wrap around her delicate wrist, a touch of anger skims my skin.

"I don't see a ring," he snarls.

She doesn't bat an eye. "It's being sized."

Damn, she's good.

I eye the crowd. Their cell phones are already being pointed in our direction. I lean toward Benedict and lower my voice. "Take your hand of my fiancée before these cameras catch something you'd be embarrassed about later."

Out of the corner of my eye, Reese glances at me, but I hold Benedict's stare until he releases her wrist. She quickly grabs my hand again, her palm sweaty with nerves. Benedict smooths his pressed shirt and sits back down on the hood of her car, apparently with more to say.

Get a clue, bro. She isn't that into you.

"Has Charleigh met him?"

Reese's fingers clamp onto mine.

Fuck, I really need to find out who this Charlie person is.

She scoffs. "Of course she has!"

She?

Charleigh is a she?

"Hey! Are you Malaki Young?" I turn toward a group of guys standing outside the club with none other than my Uber partner lingering behind them with his glasses perched on the end of his nose.

Benedict pops up from Reese's hood. "Well, then... I guess you'll be hearing from my lawyer." Before he makes it to the curb, he turns and winks at Reese. "Don't say I didn't warn you, sweetheart."

A lawyer?

What the hell did I just get myself into?

The subtlest gasp from Reese hits my ears, pulling my attention to her face. Her eyes are glassy, that lip of hers white with the force that her teeth are putting into it.

I'm not one to waste time when I'm a spectacle, so I pull her over to the passenger side of her car and open the door. She looks up at me, a million and one emotions flickering across her face. My hands find her hips, and I slowly guide her to sit. Her hands are shaking, so I pull on the seatbelt and strap her in before jogging over to the driver's side.

I may not know everything about my mystery Uber driver, but now that we're engaged, I suppose we have plenty of time to get to know one another.

Fourteen

REESE

"FUCK, FUCK, FUCK," I mutter quietly. "What am I going to do?"

I bounce my eyes back and forth, moving them from the windshield, to the dashboard, then back to the windshield.

My lip hurts from the incessant chewing, and all I can hear is Benedict's voice in my head on repeat: *You'll be hearing from my lawyer.*

A tremble wracks my body. "Fuck," I say again.

Malaki is quiet. We've been driving around Chicago for at least thirty minutes, going nowhere. He hasn't asked a single question as I sit here mumbling under my breath like a psych patient.

"Take a left."

Malaki puts the blinker on and does exactly what I say.

Another few minutes pass, with all sorts of scenarios racing through my mind, when I say, "Take a right."

Again, he follows my command quietly.

He is as casual as they come, drumming his fingers on the

steering wheel, seemingly enjoying the silent drive toward downtown.

"Left."

I see my apartment up ahead, along with some of the homeless dragging their belongings in stolen shopping carts with worn blankets trailing behind them.

"Park up there." I point toward the curb and try not to think about the fact that Malaki is probably judging me up and down right now. The apartment complex is falling apart. Bricks are missing on the side of it, a piece of spray-painted plywood covering it in an attempt to keep the critters out.

As soon as the car is in park, I jolt from the passenger seat.

The sooner I lay eyes on Charleigh, the sooner I can process whatever the hell I just did with Malaki as my witness.

Fiancé. I said he was my fiancé.

"I'm so fucked," I say as I run up the stairs.

The elevator hasn't worked in months.

Maybe Malaki will attempt to use it and get stuck in there, then I won't have to face the consequences of my fuckery.

I lift up the dead house plant in front of the neighbor's door and steal my key out from below.

"Clever," I hear from behind.

Damn, he's fast.

My face is hot with embarrassment, so I keep my back to Malaki. The door pops open, and I rush inside, Malaki seemingly right behind me.

Zoe, still on the couch with a pencil in her hand, springs to her feet. "Why are you barreling in here–" Her mouth shuts with surprise. "Oh?"

I ignore my sister and rush toward the one bedroom that we share. I slowly push on the door and search for Charleigh.

Zoe whisper-shouts from the couch, "What's with you? Charleigh is fine."

My heart slows when I see her.

There, sprawled out in her hand-me-down pack-and-play, right next to the bed, is my daughter.

I allow myself to breathe deeply for the first time since seeing Benedict. My chest fills with contentment and comfort, but then I hear Malaki's voice, and I'm right back to the shit-show I was in moments ago.

I tiptoe backward and quietly shut the door to my bedroom.

I turn just in time to see my sister gawking at me from the couch. Her mouth curves, and a laugh fumbles out. "Oh my god." She can hardly contain her laughter as she grabs her phone from the coffee table and speaks to whoever is on the other end. "I gotta go. I think my sister is trying to get laid."

"What?! No, I'm not!" I pinch the bridge of my nose and press against the wall until I'm sliding down to the floor. I bring my knees up to my chest and bury my face. I can't even make eye contact with Malaki without bursting in flames.

I'm humiliated, embarrassed, ashamed, and so many more things.

"What the hell was I thinking?" I say into my knees.

Zoe snorts. "I'm pretty sure you were thinking that he's hot."

Malaki chuckles for the first time since Benedict showed up. "Whoa. That's no way to talk to your future brother-in-law."

Oh my god.

Zoe laughs awkwardly. "What?"

"I am such a fucking idiot," I whisper.

There's a ringing in my ears that doesn't stop until I feel the slight brush of someone's hand against my arms. I slowly peek through my knees and see two deep blue eyes looking back at me. Malaki is crouched below with my sister looming over his shoulder. When he sees that he has my attention, his lip lifts slightly, and he reaches into his pocket. A crinkling noise echoes around my small apartment, and I take the bait. I unwrap my arms from my knees and raise my head.

There, in the center of Malaki's palm, is the torn packet of Skittles from my center console.

He raises an eyebrow. "You need a hit?" he asks, like it's a cigarette or something.

How he can make me crack a smile right now is beyond me.

"Can someone explain what the hell is going on?" Zoe exclaims. Her hands fly to her hips with frustration as she stares at the two of us. "Why is this random guy in our apartment?"

"Random guy?" Malaki mumbles. "I'm one of the best hockey players on the Blue Devils."

Zoe scoffs. "I don't do sports."

I steal a Skittle from the packet in Malaki's palm and suck on it. He eventually stands so I take full advantage of the space between us and head for the kitchen in an attempt to sort my thoughts without him distracting me.

"Well..." Malaki shrugs. "Your sister proposed to me."

I laugh like a maniac because that's exactly what I am.

He's my fiancé. What the hell was I thinking?

Zoe gapes at Malaki, then slowly shifts her attention to me and my crazed laughing. She inches her way across the living room.

"Reese?" She says my name as she carefully eyes Malaki and then dives for the baseball bat propped in the corner by the door. "Should I beat him?"

My eyes widen, and I scramble out from behind the counter. "Zoe!" I screech her name as quietly as I can, careful not to wake Charleigh. "Stop it, or he'll think we're both crazy!"

I place my hands on top of hers while she glares at Malaki from over my shoulder.

To no surprise, he stands there, observing the pair of us, without a care in the world. His face smooth, hands in his pockets.

Maybe he's the crazy one.

"Put the bat down!" I grit between my teeth.

Zoe rolls her eyes but eventually follows suit. The metal bat clanks against the wall when she places it in its rightful spot, followed by her arms crossing as she stares at the pair of us.

"Well, someone better start talking," she retorts.

Malaki and I make eye contact. I have the urge to cry and laugh all at once.

We speak at the exact same time:

"Your sister asked me to marry her–"

"I have a daughter–"

Malaki's eyebrows crowd together with shock.

Zoe laughs hysterically.

And me? I die a slow, painful death.

MALAKI

DID she just say what I think she did?

Reese's sister's laughter fills the tiny apartment.

"I'm sorry, what?" she asks, hardly able to form words.

She turns toward Reese, who is staring at me with those glassy eyes again.

Zoe points at me over her shoulder. "Did he just say you asked him to marry you?"

She has a daughter?

I quickly scan her from head to toe. She's a mom?

My eyebrow crooks. If so, she's the hottest mom I've ever laid eyes on.

"I need a drink," Reese mutters.

She struts into the kitchen and flicks the light switch, bathing the small space in fluorescent lights. They flicker a few times before eventually turning right back off. Her shoulders fall, but she brushes it off with a relaxed expression and a quiet *"everything's fine"* under her breath.

Zoe follows after her sister as I stand back and observe.

The apartment complex is the nicest on the block, but it's still a shithole. Pieces of brick crunched beneath my shoe as I followed Reese after she ran through the doors. My first thought was how badly it smelled. A mixture of mildew and cat piss burned my nose, and the elevator had a sign taped to it that had the word "broken" on it, only it was spelled incorrectly.

Reese's place seems nice on the inside, but if you look close enough, you'll notice that it's a trick of the eye. The colorful woven rugs hide how uneven the floor is, and it's so small I could jump from the living room and be in the kitchen. There is an incessant buzzing noise coming from the refrigerator, and when she opens it, there's practically nothing on the inside.

She swings the door shut with her foot while holding a jug of apple juice in her hand.

"What does he mean you asked him to marry you?" Zoe places her hands on her hips. "What the hell happened? I thought you were going to work!"

Reese places the juice on the counter. "Benedict happened."

Her sister growls. "That mother fucker."

I've gotta admit, Zoe is sort of terrifying.

I can tell she's younger than Reese, but I get the vibe that she's protective of her older sister. I mean, she did just try to hit me with a baseball bat.

"Zoe!" Reese furrows her brow. "Language."

"Sorry," she says sarcastically. "I mean...that mother... trucker."

I chuckle.

Reese's eyes flick to mine.

Did she forget I was here?

She mutters something under her breath and unscrews the lid to the apple juice to take a swig.

"You do know that's apple juice, right?" I ask.

Zoe glances over her shoulder at me. "She refuses to drink anything harder than juice."

"That's because I make stupid decisions when I drink!" Reese blurts, slamming the jug onto the counter.

I raise a brow. "Well, that's intriguing."

"She hasn't drunk a sip of alcohol since being impregnated by Benedict," Zoe confesses.

Never mind. That's not intriguing at all.

"One drunken night and now look at me!" Reese exclaims. "A baby, a shitty job, an even shittier apartment..."

"A hot fiancé..." I say, winking at her.

Her cheeks turn red again, and she reaches for the apple juice.

I do my best to keep a straight face, but she's drinking apple juice while pretending it's something stronger. It's amusing.

Zoe and I stand in silence as we watch Reese screw the lid back on. She undoes her long braid and quickly throws her hair into a high ponytail while muttering to herself. Zoe turns to face me and leans back against the counter with her arms still crossed over her chest defensively.

I feel like she's about to interrogate me, especially with the shitty lighting in this apartment.

"Since my sister is clearly spiraling, I need you to fill in the gaps on what happened tonight."

I run a hand through my hair. "Uh, well..."

I don't even know what happened. It's all a blur. Kissing Reese, then the asshole who was belittling her, the whole "he's my fiancé" thing, and now to find out that she's a mom?

Shit, maybe I should ask for the apple juice.

"Benedict showed up." Reese is staring at the counter. Her hands rest against the top, her ponytail hanging low over her shoulder. "And I panicked."

"Yeah, well, maybe you should carry a baseball bat with you," her sister retorts.

Reese shoots her a dirty look. "That'd go over well. I can't even sit inside my car without him banging on the window and threatening me."

I raise an eyebrow. "He was threatening you?"

She averts her gaze.

"He threatened to take you to court again?" Zoe asks, neither of them acknowledging me.

I know when to keep my mouth shut–though most of my team would disagree–but this seems a little more serious than I originally thought.

Reese's entire demeanor changes. Her shoulders sag, and her voice quivers. "He was going on and on about how I'm whoring around, picking up random guys at clubs–"

Zoe interrupts her. "Picking up random guys at clubs? Yeah, because you're an Uber driver! That's your job! It's not like you open your legs for them!" She huffs. "For fuck's sake, you won't even drink alcohol because you're afraid to step a toe out of line! As if you'd be sleeping with random men!"

And just like that, it clicks.

All the excuses, the comment from the other night about feeling shame.

I'm beginning to dislike this Benedict guy more and more.

Once Zoe finishes her rant, Reese continues, "He kept referring to Malaki as my fuck buddy." She glances at me before biting her lip nervously.

Suddenly, I feel the need to defend her. *Us.* "We aren't," I add.

"Still, I was afraid he'd twist things and use it against me..." Our eyes catch again, and I know exactly what she's thinking.

When Benedict tapped on the window, we were mid-kiss.

He saw us.

"So..." Reese exhales deeply. "In a desperate attempt to save my reputation and kill any type of proof he has against me that I'm a terrible mother who leaves her kid at home to sleep around...I...sort of..." her sentence trails.

"Sort of what?" Zoe is impatient. "Spit it out!"

I finish the sentence for her. "She told him that I was her fiancé."

Silence settles in the apartment. Nothing but the annoying buzzing of her fridge cuts through the quiet.

Zoe stares at me with an open mouth before she erupts into belly-clutching laughter again. Her laugh fills the apartment, and as serious as this is, I can't help but laugh alongside her.

Reese glares at us from the kitchen with a reddening face and furrowed brows. "Stop it!" she stresses. "This is serious!"

"Benedict..." Zoe tries to hide her amusement. "Benedict believed you?! That you two are engaged?"

Reese throws her hands out. "I don't know! It's not the first time I've used the excuse that I have a boyfriend! He just doesn't care, so he keeps coming back to torment me."

"Okay, hold up." I place my palms face down on the island like Reese, careful to avoid the chipping edge. "Why is he threatening to take you to court?"

Reese moves her attention to the bedroom door. Her lips tug into a frown. "He's threatening to take Charleigh from me. He wants full custody."

Oh.

"He doesn't *want* full custody," Zoe argues. "He's just a fucking asshole who can't stand that Reese doesn't want to be in a relationship with him, so he's using Charleigh as leverage."

Reese growls. "Zoe! Again with the language."

I shake my head. "Let me guess...he's given you an ultimatum?"

He isn't getting his way, so of course she can't get hers.

Reese pauses before eventually nodding.

"Ah," I hum under my breath. "So if he doesn't win, neither can you. Is that the game he's playing?"

She exhales. "Yeah, I guess so. He didn't want her to begin with. He wanted me to terminate the pregnancy, and I refused. I was fine with doing this on my own. But once I had Charleigh, he popped back up, and..." The words fade, and she drags her gaze elsewhere.

She does that a lot.

Shies away from me when things get real.

"And he wanted you back?" I finish for her.

Zoe snorts. "You could say that."

I stay locked on Reese. Her eyes widen in her sister's direction, and she gives a little shake of her head.

Now, *that's* intriguing. Another secret? What else doesn't Reese want me to know?

I mean, I am her fiancé after all. Doesn't she know that her secrets are safe with me?

To take the pressure off Reese, I break the silence. "Alright, so he knocked you up, wanted nothing to do with you, and then he waited until you had the baby to come back and... what? He wants to be a family now, and you don't? So he's trying to threaten you into a relationship with him?"

Reese shrugs. "Yeah. Pretty much."

I reach across the counter and steal the *not-vodka* from Reese. I unscrew the top and place my mouth right where hers was moments ago and chug.

Her lips curve at the sides a little when I wipe my mouth with the back of my hand.

Zoe pops up onto the counter, her legs dangling below. She takes the juice from me and gulps it too, as if the three of us are passing around a bottle of liquor. "So now what?" she asks. "Should I start planning a wedding?"

Reese scowls at her. "You're not funny."

She laughs. "Yes, I am."

"I'm going to have to make up an excuse," Reese mutters, talking more to herself than us. She's going over a list of excuses, all ranging from calling the wedding off to telling Benedict that I suddenly died.

I press my palms onto the counter and think things through as she aggressively chews on her lip.

"That's ridiculous," Zoe says. "You can't say he died..."

"Do you have a better idea?!" Reese exclaims. "If he knows I lied, he'll use that against me too! Knowing him, he probably has an entire filing cabinet with information about me. Our past. God, what if he has a private investigator following me?"

She's pacing now. Her tone squeakier as the minutes pass.

"I have a better idea."

Reese stops dead center in her tiny kitchen and eyes me.

Zoe stops swinging her legs. "Alright, let's hear it."

I stand up tall and cross my arms. My heart beats a mile a minute, and I can't tell if it's from excitement or dread. "We stay engaged. We fool him and everyone else. Either he'll give up on getting you back, or he'll follow through and take you to court, where we'll prove to the judge that every delusion he's created to tear you down turns out to be just that: a delusion. It'll make him look like a desperate man who can't take no for an answer."

Silence cuts through the apartment.

Reese opens her mouth to argue, but nothing comes out.

Eventually, enough time has passed that Zoe jumps off the counter. She walks over to me and pats me on the chest with a cunning smile on her face. "Welcome to the family."

Sixteen

REESE

I NERVOUSLY TAP my fingernails against my steering wheel outside of the Devils' arena as I wait for Malaki. I pinch my leg again, just in case the first few times I did it were a fluke, but unfortunately, the tiny bite of pain is still there, which means this is *not* a dream.

If we go through with this–*wait*, no. We are *not* going through with this.

I am not engaged to Malaki Young.

Through the windshield, I watch the bus until it comes to a halt in front of the arena. A group of Blue Devils players exit the arena and head for it with their suitcases. They have an away game and soon will be on an airplane out of the state.

Which is good, considering I'm about to tell Malaki that even though he was awfully convincing last night, I still haven't changed my mind. We can't fake an engagement.

My breath catches as soon as I see him.

At least I had enough sense to pick a good-looking fake fiancé, even if it is the shortest engagement in the world. His formal attire isn't overdone by any means–blue dress pants, a white button-down with a few buttons popped, and a matching suit jacket. One single strand of his perfectly messy hair hangs over his forehead, and I'm thankful he's wearing sunglasses. That way, I don't have to look into his dreamy blue eyes.

Suddenly, he's standing in front of the passenger window. He grins and mouths, "Unlock the door."

Oh, right.

I quickly unlock it, and he slides into the passenger seat. His cologne swarms my senses, and I have to pinch my leg again to pull myself together. He adjusts the seat so he's able to fit better before brushing his hand down his dress pants, smoothing them out.

God, he's hot.

It's a contradiction.

He's a contradiction.

No one this sexy in a suit should have an air of unease around him too. My pulse quickens, and I wrap my fingers around the steering wheel.

"I got you something," he finally says.

"I hope it's a divorce," I joke.

His jaw unhinges. "We're not even married yet, and you're asking for a divorce?"

I roll my eyes playfully and somehow keep my mouth from forming a smile. "We're not getting married, and we're not engaged," I remind him.

Malaki lifts a hip and shoves his fingers into his pocket. He keeps his hand clasped and holds it over my center console. "Open your hand, Dimples."

I sigh and do as he says. "If this is a ring, I swear–"

My sentence is cut off by that *exact* thing dropping into my palm.

"You swear what?" Malaki mocks.

"*Malaki.*" I plan for his name to sound like I'm chastising him, but instead, it comes out as an airy whisper.

I stare at the prettiest diamond I've ever seen.

I've never held something so expensive before.

It makes my skin itch.

I clear my throat. "You know the only reason I asked to see you this morning was to tell you that we cannot go through with this."

And fine. Maybe I wanted to see him one more time.

For what?

I don't know. I just...did.

Zoe is all for this engagement.

Malaki too, if that shiny ring has anything to say about it.

Apparently, I'm the only one not.

Malaki steals the ring out of the palm of my hand, his fingers sweeping against the skin quickly. Heat races up my arm, and I jerk my hand away.

This is exactly why we can't go through with this. I'm too affected by him, too blinded by shiny things. If I entertain this idea of a fake engagement with a pro hockey player in an attempt to trick Benedict and the justice system into thinking I have my shit together, it'll blow up in my face. Because newsflash: I do not have my shit together.

Malaki twirls the ring in between two fingers and gazes out the passenger window. Some more of his teammates are walking toward the bus with their bags slung over their shoulders, which means he's going to have to go.

"I thought I was pretty convincing last night," he says, gliding his gaze over to me. "I mean, I already got you a ring."

I push my back into my seat. "I didn't ask you to do that, though."

An airy chuckle leaves him. "And that's exactly why I did it."

There's an argument on the tip of my tongue, ready to come out, but he cuts me off.

"Your sister said you'd do this."

I'm instantly irritated. "Do what?" I ask.

He reaches for my hand again, his fingers wrapping around my wrist to gently pull on my arm. With a determined look in his eye, he uncurls my clenched palm to slip the engagement ring onto my finger. "She said you'd push back because you hate when people help you."

"Well..." *Damn her.* "I don't need help."

Malaki snaps his eyes up to mine, and my heart leaps. His blue eyes, dreamy and soft, deepen.

I think he could convince me to do anything.

"Yes, you do, Reese." His tone is grave.

I glance to the diamond on my finger and then back to him.

"And you're going to take my help," he demands.

If it were anyone else, like Benedict, I'd recoil at the dominance. But with Malaki, it's different. It's sincere, and he's highly persuasive. Whether it's regarding an Uber ride, staying at the club to dance with him, or remaining his fake fiancée, I find myself agreeing.

There is so much ease with Malaki. It makes him dangerously convincing and outwardly trustworthy.

I gingerly pull my hand away from his. "And what if I don't?"

Am I going to go through with this?

Can we pull this off?

"You will," he says matter of fact.

The ring is like a brand, searing itself with guilt and sin around my finger. "You act like you know me," I say.

"I know enough."

I huff. *He does not.*

His phone goes off, but he ignores it. "I know that if

you're willing to work as hard as you do to provide for your daughter and your sister on your own, then you're willing to do almost anything to keep what you've built so far."

His phone goes off again, and this time, he reaches for it.

"I'm coming," he says into it, hanging up a second later.

I should take the ring off and give it back to him. The diamond sparkles beneath the morning sun, but I pull my gaze away and look into the rearview at Charleigh's empty car seat.

Give him the ring.

This is crazy.

You can't.

I barely know him. Sure, he's willing to act like my fiancé just to help me, but...

He smiles at me, and my stomach dips.

"I'll see you tomorrow...future Mrs. Young." He grips the door handle and slips out of my car.

My mouth hangs open with shock as he strides toward the bus with ease, as if he didn't just leave me with an expensive ring on my finger.

He disappears onto the bus, and I get a text.

It's an address.

That's it.

Then another message comes through.

MALAKI

Movers will be at your apartment in an hour
to get your things. See you at home.

I quickly fling my attention out the windshield, but Malaki and the bus are long gone.

———

"Oh my god, stop being so dramatic about this!" Zoe spins

around the foyer of the address Malaki gave me with bewilderment. "Look at our new place!"

I refuse to call it ours, because it's not, but apparently, Zoe didn't get that memo.

Charleigh claps aggressively in my arms, bouncing up and down as she watches her auntie twirl over the marble floor.

"Even Char is excited!" she says.

"That's because you're acting like a maniac!" I hiss.

"Says the girl wearing an engagement ring from a man she hardly knows."

My jaw drops. "You're the one who told me to go through with this!"

Zoe's laugh echoes throughout the empty space. "I'm kidding! Of course I'm all for it. It's like killing two birds with one stone. A better place to live, and we're getting rid of Benedict? I mean, why wouldn't you?"

I turn my back to Zoe and ignore the small stack of boxes from our apartment in the middle of the floor. The moving company showed up with four hefty men, thinking they'd have to move loads of furniture and household goods down three flights of stairs, but in reality, it was four boxes, and most of the things were Charleigh's.

"Because," I stress. "I feel like a charity case."

My head spins the longer I stand unmoving in the foyer of a house that I'd never be able to afford. It's in a historical part of town where the homes are even more expensive, with pretty windows for natural light and bricks that are fully intact and not at all crumbling.

There's even a little yard full of green grass in the back for Charleigh to play on.

I slowly walk throughout the house and remind myself that this is all fake.

I can't get invested.

Zoe follows me, and we both stare into the kitchen. It's

pristine with state-of-the-art appliances and a modern feel. Zoe steals Charleigh out of my arms and helps her stand on top of the kitchen island.

"We've been a charity case our entire lives." Zoe scrunches her nose at Charleigh. She bounces up and down, her little bare feet leaving footprints on the marble. I spy her two little bottom teeth and can't help but smile too. "What's a few more months?" she finishes, raising an eyebrow at me.

Charleigh squeals, and my shoulders drop.

"A few months?" I take Charleigh from Zoe. "You think that's all it'll take? Just a few months of acting happily in love with some hockey player and playing 'family' with him?"

Zoe tightens her ponytail and heads for the stairs. "A few months, a year? I guess we'll see." She jogs up the steps and shouts over her shoulder. "Either way, I get the biggest room."

"Yeah right!" I call after her. "You're going back to the dorms!"

"Never!" she shouts back.

I laugh to myself as Charleigh wiggles in my arms again.

"Ma, ma, ma, ma, ma," she babbles.

"Okay, *fine*." I press my nose to hers. "We can stay. But don't get attached. This isn't permanent."

"Ma, ma, ma, ma, ma." Her little hand lands on mine, and she is immediately distracted by the ring on my finger. Her lower lip pops out as she studies it, concentrating on the shine that continues to catch my eye too.

"Don't get attached to that either," I whisper, more to myself than her. "It isn't permanent."

Seventeen

MALAKI

"WHAT DO you mean you're moving out?" Kane studies me from across the ice.

I toss the puck to him, but he lets it slide right past. I skate a circle around him. "You know you're going to move Daisy in eventually, so why do you care?"

I opted to use my house on the other side of town as an Airbnb and moved in with Kane when he found himself in a sticky financial situation, but I wouldn't really call us roommates. He's sort of a loner. The quiet, broody type.

I decided to drop the news now as we warm up for the last period of the game. We're up 2 to 1, but we all know that doesn't mean anything. I figure it's better to tell him while we're winning, versus after, in case we lose.

Most of the team will be fuming if we leave defeated, especially Kane.

Don't get me wrong, I hate to lose too.

I'm just a little more in control of my emotions than the rest of these hotheads.

"The rent is paid for the rest of the year," I add. "Is that why you're looking at me like I just broke your heart?" I lean in close. "Don't tell me you're heartbroken that I'm moving out. I didn't realize you liked me that much."

"I don't," he snaps.

Rhodes, an even grumpier version of Kane, skates past, and I take the opportunity for what it is. "Hey, Volkova." I tap him with my stick, and he stops immediately, ice flinging up from his abrupt pause. He glares at my stick against the front of his jersey.

"What do you want, Young?"

I fling my chin over to Kane. "Kane is sad that I'm moving out of the apartment. Figured you'd want to see him shed a tear or two—you know, to confirm that he does have feelings."

Rhodes glances at Kane and then to me. "Do you ever shut up?"

Kane is the first to answer. "No. He doesn't."

Rhodes grins and skates off with Kane following close behind. I trail them because I still haven't broken the news to them—or to anyone, really.

"Don't you guys want to know why I'm moving? Or where?"

Rhodes turns, skating backward with his stoic face smooth. "Not unless it's because you're being traded, which I know isn't the case...so, nope."

He skates away, and I let him.

I steal a puck from the floor, the crowd becoming louder as the minutes tick by. I toss the black biscuit back and forth before heading to center ice to fling it at our goalie.

Olson blocks it with his killer reflexes before doing the same to Kane's.

"Damn, he's good," Kane mutters.

He is.

I'll admit, our team had a lot of work to do at the beginning of the season, but adding Emory Olson to the roster as our goalie has completely turned this season around. We're not bad, and the league is beginning to notice.

"Okay, fine," Kane gives in. "I'll take the bait. Where are you moving?"

The buzzer sounds, and we're quickly pulled back to the bench. "Back to my house on Oak."

I tip my head back and squirt water into my mouth.

"Oak?" Rhodes, who must've been listening, repeats the name of the street.

I smirk. "Oh, so Daddy *does* want to know where I'm moving."

He narrows his eyes. "Never call me Daddy again if you want to make it back to your house on Oak."

"Young, go."

I hop up from the bench at the sound of Coach's voice.

Before swinging my leg around to climb onto the ice, I mention to Kane that I'm going to be living with Reese.

"Reese?" he repeats. "Daisy's Reese?"

The blade of my skate touches the ice, and I nod. "Yep."

My chest grows tight, but I still can't figure out if I'm excited at the prospect or scared out of my fucking mind.

Not only are we about to be living together...but she has a kid.

I've been known to seek out a challenge a time or two, but this? This is uncharted territory, and there's a lot more at stake than something like getting MVP of the year.

I shut my car door and stare up at the house.

I bought it when I first moved to Chicago, because the price was right, and it was close to the arena. Since moving in with Kane, it's been listed as an Airbnb just to keep things running smoothly.

It's fully furnished, and the appliances are brand new.

I wonder if Reese likes it.

If she doesn't, I suppose we can just move someplace else.

My hand freezes with the key inside the keyhole. *What?*

It's late, and clearly, my thoughts aren't making sense.

Not only was I in a different time zone earlier today, but I had nearly twenty-eight minutes of ice time, which is more than average. That's the only valid reason as to why I'm falling for this make-believe stunt that Reese is actually my fiancée, and we're going to live happily ever after in a house we choose together.

It's not like I want that or anything.

I'm just helping out a damsel in distress by pretending to be her fiancée.

I chuckle to myself.

Reese is the furthest thing from a damsel.

If anything, this whole experience of living with a single mom will be entertaining, right?

The house is pitch black when I walk inside. I shut the door quietly and use my phone as a flashlight to make sure her sister isn't lurking somewhere in the corner with a baseball bat, ready to attack me.

She scares me.

I slowly place my bag on the floor and scan the foyer.

It smells nice, and I can't decide if it's from the cleaning service I hired last minute or if it's an indication that Reese is somewhere near.

The thought that she isn't here definitely crossed my mind, but I confirmed with the moving company that they did, in fact, deliver her things from her apartment.

After finding the downstairs empty, I make my way up the stairs.

It's quiet, and I suspect that Reese, her daughter who I've still yet to meet, and sister are all sleeping.

Which is fine.

We can work out the rest of the logistics tomorrow over breakfast.

I head for the master bedroom.

Maybe I should get donuts for breakfast—a little *'just engaged'* treat to tease Reese.

I turn the knob to my room.

Wait, do babies eat donuts? Do they have teeth yet? I don't even know how old Reese's daughter is. When I texted Daisy and asked her, she told me to ask Reese and followed it with a **chicks before dicks** text.

Very immature.

Almost as immature as my follow up text: **bros before hoes.**

I pull out my phone and shoot a quick message to Rhodes.

ME:

Do babies eat donuts?

He texts back before I even make it into the room.

RHODES

You're a moron.

The room is dark, and my eyes have yet to adjust. I reach for a light switch, searching the wall, but come up empty-handed.

"Where the hell is the light switch?" I mutter, angling my screen toward the wall for light.

A gasp comes from somewhere in the room, and I quickly turn around in the direction of it. My elbow hits something soft, and suddenly, I'm in a vortex of confusion with a yelp, blinding light, and a looming, headless figure coming right toward my face.

"Fuck." I form a fist and punch whatever is attacking me.

A loud thud comes next, and I lurch backward, bumping into something else. I twist, and my hands fly forward to steady the next thing falling toward me.

My eyes adjust, my palms warm from Reese's skin. She stands there in the skimpiest pair of pajamas that I have ever seen. The tank top ends above her belly button, and my hands remain wrapped around her bare waist.

"Jesus." I glance over my shoulder to see a tattered mannequin laying on the floor, now with lopsided mounds for breasts from my attack. "What the hell is that?"

Reese shakes her head to clear the damp hair from her face. "What are you doing here?" She's breathless, and it takes just about every ounce of respect in my body not to drop my eyes to the cleavage peeking out from her tank top.

I raise a brow. "I live here...with my fiancée."

Her long eyelashes flutter with confusion. "No, I...I know," she stutters. "I mean...I thought you had a game."

"Sometimes we fly back through the night."

"Oh." Her gaze drops to my hands still wrapped around her.

Mm, right. I remove my hands from her warm skin and bend to pick up my victim. The headless mannequin is wobbly when I place it up right.

"Don't worry," Reese brushes me off. "Stella was like that before."

"You named it?"

Her dimples appear, and my chest constricts. She shrugs coyly while pulling on her tiny shorts.

I tear my eyes away and run a hand through my hair while searching the room. It's the same as it was before I left—my boxes still unopened in the corner—but now there's an opened suitcase, a mannequin that nightmares are made of, and a shiny ring on top of the dresser that should be on Reese's left finger.

My fatigue from earlier has long disappeared as Reese and I stare at each other. The warmth from touching her skin has given me energy to toy with her. If anything, maybe she'll show off those dimples again before escaping to a different room.

"So..." I glance at the bed. "Sharing a bed with me tonight?"

Faint wrinkles of worry appear on her forehead. "What? No!"

I walk over to the dresser and lean against it. I unbutton the top two buttons of my dress shirt, eager to get out of my stiff clothing. "You can if you want." I grip the edge of the dresser behind me and watch the prettiest shade of pink spread over Reese's cheeks.

"I don't!" she blurts. "I only came in here to get ready for bed. Zoe was in the other bathroom, so I used this one..." She looks nervous. "I'll make sure to use the other one from now on."

I tilt my head to the side. "You're welcome to use this one whenever you want. This is your home too."

Reese shifts on her feet. "No, it's not."

I narrow my gaze. "Yes, it is."

She sighs and pops her hip out. Her arms move to cross against her chest. *Thank God.*

"This is your house," she says, emphasizing the word *your.*

"Yeah..." I push off from the dresser and grab one of my boxes. I open the dresser drawer and dump the contents in there, gathering some clothes to change into. "But *you're* my fiancée," I remind her. "So, what's mine is yours, babe."

With my back to her, I start to unbutton my shirt. I peek at her through the mirror, but she's staring down at her bare feet instead of at me. "I think you're insane," she mutters. "I can't believe I'm going through with this."

I shrug my shirt off, letting it fall to the floor. "Going through with what? Marrying me?"

"I'm not marrying you!" she shouts.

I turn around, and her jaw drops, right along with her eyes. She scans my chest, all the way down to my waist, and then back up to my face again. Her lips slam together, and she's suddenly looking everywhere but at me.

"Most women would kill to be my fiancée. Fake or not."

Reese darts over to her suitcase, shoving her clothes back inside. "Well, I'm not most women."

That much is obvious.

Doesn't she understand that's the entire reason I've taken such an interest in her?

I have to hold back a laugh as she drags her suitcase and Stella over to the bedroom door. "What are you doing?"

She looks to the bed again, and then her eyes flit in a different direction. "I'll sleep in the other guest room."

I can't help but smirk. "If that's what you want."

"It is."

I hum to myself, and she rolls her eyes.

Before she gets too far, I stride over to the door and call down the hall. "We have breakfast plans tomorrow."

She stops walking, her spine straightening.

"Kitchen. Eight am. See you then, Dimples."

I shut my door and head to the bathroom to get ready for bed.

The steam from her shower lingers, and the smell of her shampoo fills my head. I tell myself not to do it, but the last thing I think about before falling asleep is Reese and those teeny-tiny pajamas.

Eighteen

REESE

"YOU SHOULD HAVE NEVER DROPPED out of college." Zoe tosses the paper back to me where my neat handwriting remains, with a list of boundaries that Malaki and I have to follow in order for this whole thing to work out.

"Well, I wouldn't have, but..." I look at Charleigh, who's crawling all over the kitchen.

Zoe bends and kisses Char on the head before moving toward the door. "I'm heading out to catch the bus. I have class in an hour."

I glance at the clock.

Malaki said we had breakfast plans at eight, and I have no idea what that entails. Are we going somewhere? He remembers that I have a daughter, right? She's pretty much with me all the time unless I'm working, and even then, she sometimes has to tag along.

"If you want to wait, I can probably drop you off," I say.

"You have plans." She walks backward toward the door.

"With your *fiancé*." She says this with a French accent, and I can't help but laugh.

"That's the worst accent I've ever heard."

She gives me the finger and disappears through the back door. It's just me and Charleigh in the kitchen, waiting for Malaki. Nerves lie quietly in the pit of my stomach at the thought of him meeting her. It's silly, but what if he changes his mind and doesn't want to go through with this anymore after learning what it's like to have a baby around?

Charleigh is a good baby. She's happy, and her giggle is infectious, but she's still a baby. She cries sometimes. Is he going to be okay with that? Benedict wasn't. The first time he held her, she screamed bloody murder, and he quickly shoved her back into my arms.

I nibble on my thumbnail and get on the floor with Charleigh. Sweet potato-flavored puffs are scattered around her, so I pick one up and hand it to her. She gnaws on it with her gums before taking it out of her mouth and trying to feed me.

"No, thank you." I laugh. "That's yours."

Charleigh puts it back into her mouth and then looks over my shoulder to stare.

My heart stalls.

I follow her line of sight and peer at Malaki standing in the hallway with a pink box in his hands.

His boy-next-door smile appears. "We've just met, and she's already ratting me out."

I quickly stand up, leaving Charleigh on the floor with her soggy puffs.

Malaki walks farther into the kitchen and places the pink box on the table, his attention remaining on Charleigh the majority of the time. "I was waiting to see if you were going to put that in your mouth," he says to me.

I choke out a laugh, but words fail me when I watch

Charleigh hold out another soggy puff. Malaki and I share a quick look as he squats down in front of her. She cranes her head, the crazy wisps of her dark hair flying backward.

Malaki gasps dramatically. "For *me*?"

Charleigh wiggles against the tiled floor and scoots closer to him, which is her way of saying yes. The soggy snack, falling apart in her tiny fingers, remains outstretched between them.

"Charleigh, I don't think he wants–"

Malaki opens his mouth and allows Charleigh to shove the puff inside. My hand comes up to cover my own mouth.

Charleigh squeals with excitement after Malaki sits back on his heels, pretending to chew the puff that no-doubt fell apart the second it touched his tongue.

"Mmmm," he says as he nods. "That is delicious."

I laugh so loud they both look at me. Charleigh giggles, and Malaki smiles proudly, like he's passed some test.

And okay, fine. Maybe he did.

"I can't believe you just ate that," I say through a laugh.

"When a girl as cute as her offers you something, you take it." He heads over to the pink box on the table. "I learned that the hard way from Volkova's daughter."

I scoop Charleigh up in my arms, along with the container of puffs. She bucks against me, wanting down again. I sigh, place her back on the ground, and stand to see Malaki holding out the pink box for me.

He raises his eyebrows. "Donut?"

I stare into the box and pause when I see that some are missing. "How many did you eat on the way?"

The box is big enough to hold a dozen donuts, yet there are only four inside.

Malaki shrugs. "I only had three. Your sister took the rest."

"What?" *Zoe!*

Malaki places the box on the table but leaves the lid open. "Yeah, and I let her take my car too."

I gape at him. "Did she ask to take it? Oh my god."

He moved us into this nice house, and now he's letting my sister take his expensive car? What's next? A pony for Charleigh?

Malaki gives me a strange look. "No. But I would rather her not take the bus to the university. It's not the safest, plus I have my own personal Uber driver." He winks at me.

"You don't have to go out of your way to take care of us," I stress. "And if you don't want Zoe living here too, that's okay. She can always move back into the dorms. She was only living with me because it was easier with her watching Charleigh."

It was part of the deal: I co-sign for her student loans, she watches Charleigh for me.

Malaki pulls out a chair and gestures to it. "Sit."

I want to argue, but I don't. Instead, I sink down into the seat while keeping an eye on Charleigh crawling around.

The donut box is shoved toward me. "Eat."

"I'm not really hung–"

My stomach growls, and Malaki glares at me.

Fine.

I reach forward and grab a donut with pink icing. He smirks and closes the lid.

"What?" I ask.

"I knew you'd grab that one."

"How?"

"Because red Skittles are your favorite. You clearly like the taste of strawberries." He sniffs the air. "You smell like strawberries too."

"My shampoo is strawberry scented." My teeth sink into the donut, and I almost moan. *God, that's good.*

Malaki leans back in his chair and watches me chew. "And here I thought you just smelled of Skittles because of how many you've eaten since I've met you." He flashes me a teasing smile, so I tear a tiny piece of my donut off and throw it at him.

To my surprise, he catches it with his mouth.

He chews it slowly while keeping his sights set on me. A swallow works against his throat, and my stomach dips, which reminds me...

I clear my throat and eye the paper I spent an hour on this morning while giving Charleigh her bottle.

Boundaries.

I slide it over to him and hastily remove my fingers so he doesn't accidentally graze them with his.

"What is this?" he asks in a low tone.

"Read it," I say, mid-chew.

Charleigh has crawled over to me and tries to pull herself up by using my leg. I beam at her and quietly say, "What are you doing trying to stand, little missy?"

"Boundaries?" Malaki stares at the paper with his eyebrows drawn together.

After a few minutes, he smooths his forehead and smirks. "Does this mean you're going to accept that we're engaged?"

I purse my lips. "We're fake-engaged."

"Same thing," he mutters.

I nod to the paper. "Not according to those boundaries."

They're not really to protect me, but more so for him.

I've been groomed to believe I'm an inconvenience, a nuisance—a leech, if we're talking specifics here. The last thing I want is for Malaki to think I'm using him any more than I already am.

There's the thought of him not being the person I think he is either. What if something happens between us, and he runs off to tell Benedict about our ruse? There's a part of me that trusts him. Otherwise, I wouldn't be in his house, along with bringing Charleigh around him, but trust is fragile.

I clear my throat. "If, for some reason, we have to be in

public, we will obviously have to act like a happily engaged couple so we can keep up with the facade that Benedict believes. But behind closed doors? We remain professional. I'll keep my job so I can help pay rent..." My words trail as I glance around the kitchen. It's bigger than my entire apartment. "And I will obviously cover all the things I need, like baby food for Charleigh and–"

Malaki chuckles deeply, cutting me off mid-sentence. He waits until my mouth is shut to shake his head. "No."

I jerk backward. "No?"

"You're not paying rent."

I sit up straighter. "Yes, I am."

Malaki sighs. "Reese, do you really think Benedict is going to believe that you're engaged to a pro hockey player if you're working as an Uber driver?"

I glance toward Charleigh who has moved on from pulling up on my leg.

"Don't tell me you're one of those guys who thinks women shouldn't have jobs," I mutter, pushing my donut off to the side.

Malaki pushes it back toward me. "Of course I'm not. My mom worked her entire life up until she got sick. If she were alive, she'd kill me if I thought that. But Ubering isn't your dream job, right? According to your sister, you dropped out of college to take care of Charleigh, and you work as an Uber driver because of the flexible hours and fast cash. Oh, and she mentioned something about you selling hand-stitched quotes in college too."

That's it. I'm kicking Zoe out and back into the dorms.

"What were you in college for?"

I turn my nose up. "It doesn't matter."

He taps his fingers on the wood table. "Says who?"

"Says me." I avert my gaze to Charleigh again, who's clapping her hands like she's cheering us on.

"Fashion?"

I pause, and he smiles.

"How did you know that?" I ask.

Malaki doesn't answer. Instead, his smile grows deeper.

"Fashion with a minor in marketing," I finally say. "But I can't do anything with half a degree, and I have to work, Malaki. I have to save money somehow, and my measly embroidery business made next to nothing." My voice shakes with panic.

I get up from my chair to pace.

"Babies are expensive, and I don't want to be any more of a hassle to you than I already am."

And again, what if he suddenly decides to turn on me and tells everyone that I've been using him? If Benedict were to find out, he'd have plenty of proof that I'm an unfit mother with unstable finances.

I turn my back to Malaki and place my palms onto the counter. I hold my breath before exhaling deeply.

It isn't long before there's a tap against my shoulder. I glance backward, and to my surprise, Charleigh is face level with me. Malaki is holding her with one arm while taking her hand in his other to tap me on the shoulder.

My lips twist, and a quiet laugh slips from in between them.

Charleigh smiles, her two lonesome bottom teeth cuter than ever.

I turn all the way around, unable to keep myself from smiling.

Malaki stares at me. "You're not a hassle." He turns toward Charleigh. "But I understand where you are coming from and your need to save money. We will come up with something."

I take Charleigh from Malaki. "Well, surely whatever we come up with can't be any worse than me telling my ex that you're my fiancé."

Malaki scoffs. "That's the best idea you've ever had. What are you talking about?"

I roll my lips together, hiding a smile.

"Come on." He reaches out and pokes my cheek. "Let me see them."

Don't do it.

Charleigh wiggles in my arms and smiles at Malaki.

"Charleigh shows me her dimples," he says, giving her a lopsided smile.

I grimace and try my hardest to ignore how easy this seems. I feel too safe. My guard is already wavering, and it's day one.

Maybe I should've written *no giving me butterflies* on my list of boundaries, because at this point, I am completely screwed.

Nineteen

MALAKI

I CRACK MY KNUCKLES, push my fingers back into my glove, and focus. We have one more drill to go, and then we're done for the day. I've been distracted, and when questioned, I blamed it on being tired from traveling late last night, but it has nothing to do with lack of sleep and everything to do with that piece of paper Reese handed me this morning.

Boundaries.

My first thought was *lame*. But after scanning the list, I sort of became...agitated? It wasn't a list of boundaries that benefited her. Instead, they all benefited me. Like she was trying to protect me from herself.

Her vow to never invade my privacy or cross any lines beyond a business-like relationship is permanently engraved into my brain. Right along with her promise to help contribute to the bills, keep the house as tidy as possible, and she mentioned she'll never ask nor require any help with Charleigh.

I know that our engagement is a ploy, but how does she

expect anyone to believe it if we're practically strangers? It'll be obvious, especially to someone who is paying close attention: like Benedict.

Spit flies from my mouth when my body suddenly tumbles through the air. I slip on my back and land with a thud on the hard floor. "What the hell," I groan and turn over to cradle my stomach.

Ice shavings fling into my face from Kane's sudden stop. "Dude, pay the fuck attention."

"I was," I argue.

"No, you weren't," Emory adds from the bench.

He must be done for the day. Goalies have different drills and spend most of practice off doing something else.

I turn with a wince. "I need your help with something," I grumble through the pain. The wind must've gotten knocked out of me from the fall, because I can't seem to catch my breath.

Emory reaches down and pulls me up by the collar of my practice jersey. "I'm not giving you mouth to mouth."

I try to chuckle, but I come up short.

One of our trainers comes over wearing a grave look. "Tell me you're not injured."

Coach growls, "He better not be."

"He's fine." Emory sits back on the bench. "Just got the wind knocked out of him."

I nod and hold my hand up. My teammates head for the locker room, bypassing me off to the side. I'm back to normal by the time the ice clears, my breathing less strained and my lungs loose. I glance at my surroundings, making sure no one is too close to eavesdrop—though I think I may be the only one on the team that really cares to do that. I lean my elbows on the edge of the wall.

"How did it work with you and Scottie? When you two were fake married?" I ask.

Emory's jaw flickers. "We weren't fake married." It's apparent by his tone that he's annoyed I'm even bringing this up.

Sure, they're still married, and it's nothing less than real. But at first, it was out of total convenience. I think he may have even hated her at first.

I quickly try to rectify his rising irritation. "Let me rephrase. How did it work with you and Scottie when you were still in the early stages of your blossoming love story?"

If looks could kill.

"Why?" Emory's glare remains, but I've definitely garnered his attention.

Slipping further off to the side, I move and sit on the bench beside him to start removing my blades.

"I'm fake engaged."

Emory snickers. "You're fucked."

My leg starts to bounce up and down with sudden jitters. "Thank you for your support."

"Wait, you're being serious?"

"As a heart attack."

Emory's head tips backward, and he sighs loudly. "Why on earth would you enter a fake engagement? You know my reasoning for marrying Scottie and how I paid her because she needed the money, so what's yours? Boredom? Jealous that all your friends are in relationships?"

"Maybe." I shrug.

Emory stands, and my leg suddenly stills.

"Break it off before it blows up in your face," he says.

"It's complicated," I blurt, hoping he'll sit back down and give me some real advice. "I offered to help her in a shitty situation, and now we're kind of stuck."

Stuck isn't the correct word. I don't feel stuck, but I didn't really have a choice after I found out the whole story.

Emory's lip lifts slightly, just enough for me to question if he's smiling or not. "Okay, so what do you want to know?"

I huff. "I don't know. Like, how did you two make it look real?" I bite the inside of my cheek as I think back to Reese's boundaries. "Did you two practice?"

Emory's loud laugh echoes around the empty rink. "Practice what exactly?"

"You know…" He knows what I'm referring to, but nonetheless. "Acting like you two were in love."

Emory looks off in the distance, and his head tilts. "Not intentionally. We were forced to act like we were in love in front of the cameras, and then…it just kind of happened." He looks at me. "Who are you two trying to fool?"

My leg starts shaking again. "Her ex…?" *Charleigh's father?*

"Sounds like there's more to that sentence."

I wiggle my jaw back and forth.

Fuck. Fine.

"She has a daughter, and he's trying to take her to court for custody as a way to punish her for not getting back into a relationship with him."

Emory curses under his breath before standing up. "Like I said…break it off before it blows up in your face."

"Mmm, sort of sounds like you think I can't achieve this."

Emory shakes his head and walks off, leaving me alone with his half-ass advice.

He and Scottie had an agreement. She helped him with his image in exchange for money.

That may work with Reese. I could hire her for a job of some sort and pay her.

It's either that, or the alternative, which I know she'll refuse.

———

I eagerly jog up the porch stairs and listen intently as I walk through the front door. Reese's faint voice lingers from the kitchen, and I follow it like a kid in a candy store. My plan to ease her financial burdens has me walking down the hall with a pep in my step.

"Oh, Dimples..." I sing. "Say goodbye to Ubering and hello to–"

I stop abruptly, my feet coming to a complete halt.

Reese, barefoot, stands in the middle of the kitchen in nothing but a skimpy bra and jeans. She holds her cell phone up to her ear with one hand while the other holds Charleigh in a diaper–who looks to be as content as ever.

Reese on the other hand, seems mortified.

Her cheeks are bright pink, her eyes as wide as saucers.

She adjusts the phone up to her ear and shuts her eyes. "I'm not video-chatting with you, Benedict. If you want to talk about something regarding visitations, then I'm open to talk. But your reasoning for video-chatting has nothing to do with where Charleigh is living and everything to do with where I'm living."

She winces from whatever he said, and I have a hunch that it's something her fiancé wouldn't approve of.

As if we need any more chaos, the back door opens, and Zoe walks in, dangling my keys in her hand. She lands on me first then glances at her sister, coming to a complete stop next. "What the hell did I just walk in on?"

Reese tries her best to keep her composure. Charleigh kicks against her mom when she lays eyes on Zoe. Her squeal is so high-pitched my ears ring, but it's still cute somehow.

Zoe turns toward me. "Who is she on the phone with?"

I answer by raising my brow because Zoe is no dummy. She grimaces, but before she can act, I step forward.

"I've got this," I say.

For a second, I think Zoe is going to ignore me and still

threaten to hit Benedict with that baseball bat she keeps nearby, but she gives me her trust instead. She offers her arms to Charleigh and swoops her onto her hip to take her to the other room.

"Video-chat with him," I say to Reese.

She shakes her head in a panic, so I wind my hand around her waist and whisper into her other ear, "Trust me."

I spin her around so her back rests against my chest. Keeping a hold of her, I reach up and move her hair behind her shoulder and do my best to ignore the fact that she's in nothing but a bra and a tight pair of jeans.

Not caring if Benedict is still talking, I take the phone from her ear and replace his voice with mine. "Did he find out that you don't live in the apartment anymore?"

Reese's gulp is deafening. She nods.

I chuckle quietly. "Then let's show him exactly where you're living and who you're living with."

She glances at me briefly, and I wink. Her warm sigh falls to the arm I have wrapped around her waist, and I make the grave mistake of looking down. Her cleavage catches my eye, the sun-kissed skin begging for my mouth.

Fuck, she's perfect.

"Wait," I quickly say.

I let go of her and tug my shirt up and over my head. I grab a hold of the phone, hit the video button while simultaneously pulling my shirt over her head. Her small arms find the sleeves just as Benedict hits accept.

I tug her to my bare chest, and she relaxes against me.

"He lost his privileges to see you in a bra," I whisper into her ear.

One of her dimples pops out, and pride fills me to the brim.

"It's about time–" Benedict's voice cuts mid-sentence. His jaw flickers with annoyance, and I smile at him like a fool.

There isn't much, other than winning a hockey game, that can make me feel superior, but having Reese pressed against me and her asshole ex scowling through the phone most definitely comes close.

"Hey, bud." I dip my chin at him. "Reese said you wanted to video-chat?"

Benedict leans back in his computer chair with the skyline of Chicago in the background. I knew he was a businessman by the way he carried himself, and this proves it.

Reese's hand finds mine around her waist, and I grip her wrist. Her pulse slams beneath her skin, and I'm not sure if it's because we're on the phone with Benedict or because she's pressed against me.

"Yeah." Benedict snaps his gaze to Reese while talking to me. "I didn't know you were there."

I flick an eyebrow. "Well, we do live together..."

Reese shifts to peer back at me, and my words fade. Our faces are so close that Benedict is likely to have an aneurysm.

"She is my fiancée after all," I remind him, forcing myself to look at him. "We're together most of the time."

Benedict scowls. "Yes, so I've heard. Odd that I haven't seen any photos circling with the two of you. There seems to be plenty of you, Young. But Reese? None."

He's beginning to dig.

Noted.

"Well, we wanted to keep our relationship private. Reese has some issues with people digging into her personal life. You know?"

Benedict's eye twitches, and I smile on the inside.

Silence passes between us, and although he's trying to be discreet, I watch him survey the house. Unfortunately for him, my arms are around Reese, and we take up so much of the frame that he can't see much. I find it strange that he hasn't asked to see his daughter, but I guess that just proves that he really did just want to video-chat to snoop out her new place.

He's trying to catch Reese in a lie, but I'll go to the grave with this secret if that's what it takes. I don't like him, or the way her entire body tenses when he speaks to her.

"Well…" I'm hoping to make him feel like an idiot with our abrupt exit. "We're a little busy, so we're going to go."

"Busy…" The word drags out of his mouth as he lazily scans Reese. "What are you wearing?"

I answer for her. "My shirt. It looks better on her, huh?"

Benedict says nothing.

I grin, and then he does too.

His gaze shifts back to her. "I can't help but notice that you're still not wearing a ring…"

Come on, Reese.

She finally speaks. "It's being sized."

He chuckles darkly. "No, it isn't. I've called every jeweler in the city, and not a single one of them has an active order with your name or your fiancé's."

Tension springs to my shoulders. "That's borderline stalker-like."

Benedict ignores my insult, but I refuse to let him come out on top.

"But if you must know," I start. "the order is closed because her ring has been picked up."

"Then why isn't it on her finger?" His jabs are starting to aggravate me.

Reese's skin is warm to the touch, and it only gets hotter the longer we talk to him.

"Because…" I keep my words as smooth as possible. "We got distracted…if you know what I mean."

A touch of red creeps up his neck, just above that crisp white collar of his. I reach for the phone with a shit-eating grin on my face. "Talk to you later, bud."

As soon as I hit end, Reese exhales so hard I have to hold her hips steady so she doesn't collapse. Her hands cover her face, her words muffled. "He definitely doesn't believe that we're engaged."

Zoe's scoff comes from behind us. "Ya think? You two need to get your story straight, and put that ring on!"

We both turn to look at her holding Charleigh, who, per usual, is smiling. "Ba, ba, ba, baa."

Zoe shrugs sheepishly. "Even she agrees."

Twenty

REESE

"YOU WANT ME TO WHAT?" I'm scrubbing my spit-up covered shirt in Malaki's kitchen sink while Zoe gives Charleigh a snack. I only let her stick around because I know she'll just eavesdrop if I don't.

Malaki repeats what he just told me. "I want you to work for me."

"I don't understand." My bicep burns from how aggressive I'm scrubbing. "Work for you? Doing what?"

Malaki, still bare-chested, leans against the counter beside me. I stare at the no-longer-there stain on my shirt so I don't accidentally stare at his flickering stomach muscles. I still feel the roughness of his five-o-clock shadow against my face when he whispered into my ear no more than ten minutes ago, and it takes everything in me not to graze my hand over my cheek.

Having him close puts me on edge, yet I find myself looking forward to it. My body sends all sorts of mixed signals to the parts of my body that are very much out of service, and I pray he doesn't notice.

Malaki drags a hand up his chest and winds it around his neck to give it a squeeze. "I'll pay you to cook..."

Zoe snorts, and I glare at her. I may not be the best in the kitchen, but it beats mac and cheese from the box.

"And clean," Malaki adds.

I pause my scrubbing, my hands covered in sudsy water. "So what you're saying is that you're going to pay me to be a housewife?"

"House-fiancée," he corrects.

My lips flatten.

He grins. "Oh, come on. It's that, or I just pay you for simply existing."

An argument is on the tip of my tongue, but Zoe interrupts me mid-thought. "Can you pay me for existing too?"

"Zoe!" I snap.

She shrugs. "Worth a shot."

Malaki laughs, and I roll my eyes. He pops up from resting against the counter and nudges me out of the way with his hip. "You start tomorrow. Oh, and lasagna is my favorite food."

He grabs my shirt covered in soap and rinses it under the cool water before grabbing Charleigh's onesie that's in a damp ball off to the side. My lips part. I glance at Zoe, and she looks just as surprised as I do.

For the first time in her life, Zoe is speechless.

I laugh, and it breaks her out of her stupor.

"I'm sorry, what the hell are you doing?" she asks.

Malaki's jaw catches the light just right as he looks over his shoulder at her, the defined curve sharper than ever. "Helping?" he says questionably.

He goes back to the project in front of him.

"My mom grew tired of me coming home with grass stains on every pair of jeans that I wore when I was younger, so she taught me how to get the stains out myself."

I try to picture Malaki as a young boy.

What was he like? What was his mom like before she passed?

I suddenly want to know everything there is to know about Malaki Young. Maybe if I did, I wouldn't be so surprised that he does things like this.

"Oh." Zoe huffs with sarcasm. "That explains it, then…" She glances at me with a roll of her eyes. "We didn't have a mom growing up, so no stain lessons for us. She didn't teach us how to make lasagna either."

Malaki's hands freeze mid-rinse, but only for a second.

Zoe's sarcasm keeps coming, her grudge over how we grew up flying out of her mouth without boundaries.

"So your mom taught you how to get stains out, and your dad taught you how to be a gentleman? Donuts and offering up your car so I don't have to ride the bus? Our dad taught us how to evade the poli–"

"Zoe!" Her name squeezes out between my clenched teeth.

She stops talking immediately, her eyes widening as if she forgot that it wasn't just her and me in the room.

She mouths the word *sorry* to me, and I look away.

"No…" Malaki drags the word out. "I didn't have a dad growing up," he admits. "My mom taught me how to get stains out of pants *and* how to be a gentleman. I also know how to sew, and I'm not ashamed to admit that." He pauses and looks at me over his shoulder with a half-smile. "Probably not as good as you, though."

Surprise flickers throughout like a camera shuttering to take a photo.

He was raised by a single mom?

Is that why he was so willing to stay in this fake engagement with me?

Zoe places Charleigh on the ground and leaves the kitchen

to head to her room. She hates showing her emotions, but I know her like the back of my hand. She's embarrassed she just blew up like that about our parents.

I walk over and scoop Charleigh into my arms. She grabs the end of my braid and plays with the hair tie with a look of concentration.

Malaki spins around after wiping his hands on a nearby towel and stares at me.

I move Charleigh to my other hip and nervously blurt, "Is that why you're doing this? Because you know what it's like to be raised by a single mother?" I pause. "Is it because you feel sorry for me?"

There is a sliver of hurt that comes with the thought, but I have no idea why.

It doesn't matter why he's doing it, because at the end of the day, he's providing me with a safety I likely couldn't get anywhere else.

Malaki's forehead furrows as he studies me. His head tilts to the side, his hands gripping the back of the counter tightly. "What makes you think I feel sorry for you?"

I scoff, but it sounds more like a pitiful laugh. "I think you've been around me enough to know that I'm a mess, Malaki. My house is"—I shake my head—"*was* a shithole. I have basically nothing to my name, and I'm hardly making ends meet. The only true romantic relationship I've had is with a man who no longer wanted me after I got pregnant, yet now he refuses to let me go. I mean...just look at me!" I stare down at his shirt draped over my body. "You walk into your house, and I'm literally standing in the kitchen without a shirt, my hair a disaster, with a naked baby on my hip...not to mention, my ex on the phone, threatening me unless I video-chat with him."

I'm out of breath by the time I finish my rant. I'm so

embarrassed I shut my eyes so I don't have to see his pity, but then I feel Charleigh being taken out of my arms.

My first thought is that my sister was eavesdropping, and she's taking Charleigh because I just had a mental breakdown, but instead of Zoe holding her, it's Malaki.

She stares up at him with her wide eyes, full of curiosity.

"Do you think Mommy is a mess?" he asks her.

Charleigh smiles widely and snorts with a giggle.

"I totally agree with you," Malaki says matter-of-factly. "She is the prettiest mess we've ever seen, huh?"

Charleigh kicks her legs excitedly, and I try my hardest not to smile when Malaki leans closer to her, pretending she's telling him secrets.

He leans back and dramatically gasps. "You spit up on her on purpose? Just so she'd have to put my shirt on?"

I cover my mouth with my hand to hide my laugh.

"Then I guess I should thank you, huh?" he says to her.

He glances up at me with one lip lifted in a smile before turning back toward her.

"Why thank you, Charleigh-girl. I do, in fact, like seeing your mama in my shirt."

My stomach flips. *He does?*

Charleigh takes her hands and touches Malaki's face, rubbing her little palms against his scruffy jaw. He playfully pretends to bite her fingers, and I freeze. I step forward, thinking she's going to cry, but instead, she laughs so hard her cheeks turn pink.

I blink through my confusion.

"She likes you," I say quietly, in complete awe.

"Of course she does," he says with a wink.

I won't admit it aloud, but I think I like him too.

Twenty-One

MALAKI

TONIGHT ISN'T JUST any ordinary game.

Tonight, my fiancée is watching.

Fiancée, fake fiancée—tomato, tomahto.

The majority of the team is completely unaware of my sudden engagement, but after tonight, I'll make sure they know.

Will they be surprised? Maybe.

But I think they know me well enough now to know that I like to be spontaneous. I'm predictably unpredictable, a wild card if you must—but in the best way.

The stands are filling up, both teams on the ice for warm-ups.

I take full advantage of Coach being preoccupied with a reporter and search the stands for Reese. She said she's been to a game before, but never like this—with my ring on her finger.

I find her off to the side, talking to Daisy, and drop my attention to her left hand.

There it is. The ring that Benedict thinks is nonexistent.

After his last phone call, where he obviously doubted our engagement, he's been quiet.

I don't have high hopes that his absence will last, but I do have a feeling that his threat of gaining custody of Charleigh is just a strategy he's attempting to use to keep Reese in his left pocket.

For now, we keep up this charade and have a little fun.

I skate up to Reese just as Daisy takes the ice. "Hey, fiancée."

Reese, to my surprise, smiles. "Are you ever going to stop calling me that?"

I grin. "Yes. When we get married, I'll just start calling you *wife*."

Her deadpan look makes me grin.

She leans close and whispers through clenched teeth, "We aren't getting married!"

I put my gloved hand on my chest. "You just stabbed a knife in my heart."

She laughs, and those cute dimples dig the knife in even farther.

I quickly pull my glove off and pull on her Blue Devils shirt. "You need to wear my jersey."

Reese glances at her shirt. It's a blue t-shirt with our logo on the front and a long-sleeve shirt underneath it. "Why? Do I look bad?" Her words zoom out of her mouth nervously. "I borrowed this from Daisy. I don't have any Blue Devils merch, but–"

An unexplained energy flies to the tips of my fingers, and I find myself leaning over the edge of the glass to grab a hold of her chin. I squeeze her warm face, and she immediately stops talking to give me her full attention. She peers at me with the same brown eyes that Charleigh has, and my mouth opens before my brain even catches up.

"You look perfect," I admit. "I just meant you need to wear my jersey because you're mine."

She blinks once, and I do the same.

That came out...possessive.

I quickly attempt to remedy the situation with a shake of my head. "I just mean...because..." I stumble over my words.

What the hell is happening?

I look away, hopeful that the break in our eye contact will be enough to loosen me back up.

I clear my throat and make sure no one is too close to get an earful of my explanation. "I mean, most of the girlfriends and wives wear their significant other's jersey. Since you're my fiancée, you should probably wear mine...right?" I glance out at the ice, knowing I need to get back out there to stretch—and apparently, to focus. "I think we should act under the assumption that Benedict is always watching."

"Oh, yes. Right!" she agrees sternly.

Before I skate off, I give her one more glimpse. Her white teeth work into her bottom lip as she stares at the sparkly ring on her finger. She chews on the soft skin nervously, and a pang of worry eats away at me.

"Hey." I wait until her brown eyes find mine. "I've got you."

Relax, babe.

Reese's lip pops out from being trapped behind her teeth, and she plasters a fake smile onto her face. Daisy, in her Blue Devils costume, takes my place. I quickly skate off to join my teammates and put my focus on the game instead of the strange pull I keep feeling from Reese.

I'm all for a pretty girl catching my eye, which she has done from the very beginning, but to stutter over my words? That's unusual for me.

A tall presence skates up beside me, and I know it's Lars without looking up.

"Who is that chick you were talking to?"

I slide a puck off from the side and move it back and forth against the ice. "Why?"

Lars taps me with his stick, taking advantage of my slower pace. "Because she's smokin' hot."

"Didn't you see the ring on her finger?" I ask. "She's taken."

"She is?"

I follow his line of sight, and a feeling I haven't felt since my hot seventh-grade teacher informed the class that she was married settles into the pit of my stomach. Raging, hot jealousy sends my reflexes haywire as I stare at Reese bent over at the waist with her perfect peach up in the air, fixing something on Daisy's costume.

I lift my stick and jam it into Lars's stomach. *Relax, I sent it into his pads.*

"Yeah, she's taken." A hot flush spreads against my skin. "By me."

Lars shoves my stick away. "You're engaged?"

A few of my teammates come to a skidding halt against the ice. "What did you just say?"

I spin and skate backward to face my teammates, who all similarly share a look of shock. "Yeah." I'm nonchalant. "That's my fiancée."

"Bullshit," Hayes mumbles through a laugh.

Emory skates out from the net and angrily pulls his mask up. "It's true. Now quit gossiping and chuck some pucks at me."

"I didn't even know he was dating anyone," someone mutters on their way past.

I make eye contact with Emory, and he shakes his head with disappointment before he fixes his mask.

He has no room to judge, though. He married a stripper he barely knew, for fuck's sake.

Twenty-Two

REESE

I FEEL LIKE A FRAUD.

I'm sitting in the first row, right next to the bench, cheering on my pretend fiancé with a ring on my finger that doesn't belong.

The only thing that isn't fake about this entire evening is that I'm surprisingly absorbed in what's happening on the other side of the ice.

I won't admit that I'm actually impressed, but *wow*. Daisy wasn't kidding when she said the games are fast and exhilarating.

Kind of like this whole engagement with Malaki.

With Daisy being too busy to sit with me, I'm just waiting for the gleam of my ring to catch her eye before I fill her in—or maybe I'll get lucky, and she'll never notice, and I won't have to explain myself. She thinks I've finally just decided to take her advice and come to one of the games, which couldn't be further from the truth.

The whistle blows, and I'm back to cheering the Blue Devils on.

They're aggressive, and fast.

Especially Malaki.

It's hard not to gravitate toward him, and that has nothing to do with our growing *friendship*?

Are we friends?

Fake lovers?

I freeze at the thought. We are *not* fake lovers.

We're friends.

Friends who act engaged. Totally normal, right?

Emory, the goalie, blocks a shot, and the team takes a quick break. The majority of them skate over to the bench, Malaki included.

He finds me staring, but his grin is fleeting. He gulps down some water, then he's off again. Back and forth, skates cut against the ice, players shout random words, and at one point, a broken stick flies through the air.

It's thrilling. The game. The strength and endurance that these men possess.

I cheer for Malaki–a guy I hardly knew a week ago–like I've known him for ages.

A squeaky yelp rushes from my lungs with the loud thump against the glass. I jerk backward, and my hand presses to my heart. Two players fight over a puck in front of me, and my jaw drops. Everyone around me jumps to their feet, some of them banging on the glass.

Another blur of blue appears, and my breath catches.

Malaki uses his elbow and forcefully breaks apart the collision then turns toward me for the quickest second of my life. He smirks, and suddenly, I'm sweating.

It takes me a second to snap out of it, but I swear my cheeks still remain warm by the end of the game.

The men celebrate with each other until they skate off the

ice, only for Daisy, in her devil costume, to bring a few back onto it for Play of the Game.

I stay seated while other fans take off up the stairs, several of them likely calling Ubers.

I can't say I'm sad not to be on the clock anymore.

Malaki's name is called, and I'm suddenly on my feet, clapping. I'm not sure who I am when I cup my hands around my mouth and yell out like a crazed fan.

With a smile still on my face, I lower myself to sit but quickly stand straight up when I see who has taken the empty seat next to mine.

"So you're a hockey fan now?"

I'm instantly on edge. A blistering heat sweeps over my skin. "What are you doing here?"

Benedict chuckles with malice. His hand lands on my arm, and he tugs me to sit next to him. He looks back through the glass and relaxes in his seat.

"Just wanted to watch a hockey game," he answers cooly, running his hands down his slacks.

I'd bet my life that he came directly from work and bought a ticket from some random person on the street just to see if I was here.

Goosebumps fly to my skin at the thought of him watching me this entire time. He's probably been waiting for the game to be over just so he could corner me.

"Since when do you watch hockey?" I ask, a bite to my tone.

"Since when are you engaged?" he retorts.

My teeth grind.

Benedict is intimidating.

He comes from wealth and is used to getting everything he wants. He likes to be in control, and thrives on it. It's obvious he knows his control is slipping when it comes to me, considering he's beginning to act even more irrational than before. I want to smack him or take my sister's baseball bat to his prized possession, but I can't. There is too much at stake, and he knows it.

Benedict looks at me with his eyebrows raised. He's waiting for my answer, but I keep my mouth shut. As more seconds pass, his expression quickly shifts to something I can't name. His smooth chuckle is like fingernails on a chalkboard to my ears. "Does your little best friend over there in the hot devil costume know the answer? Maybe I should ask her how long you've been in a relationship with one of the players."

I pray he can't see the panic on my face.

Shit. He's been keeping tabs on me far longer than I thought if he knows that I'm friends with Daisy.

I grip the armrests of my seat. "Stop following me around."

I push up from my seat, climb the concrete steps two at a time, and disappear through the arena in hopes that he won't follow me.

He does, though. His voice hits the back of my head. "Well, when you avoid my calls, you leave me no choice."

I spin around so quickly my hair falls into my face. "If by avoiding your calls you mean I promptly hang up when you bring up something other than seeing your daughter, then sure, I avoid your calls."

I roll my eyes, pent up with irritation, and turn away.

Only, he grabs me by the arm to stop me.

I stiffen. "Let go of me."

His fingers uncurl around my bicep at the sound of my demand.

I'm confused as I take a step away.

"Hey, baby." Malaki's arm curves around my waist, and he tucks me next to him.

Ah, so that's why it was easy.

I tilt my chin and try my best to thank him silently. His

mouth tilts on one side, and his hand around my waist squeezes. It's the quickest warning of my life. He places his lips on mine, and I go from tense to relieved in the same breath. It's like all the tension in the air breaks apart, and I'm safe.

I reach up on my tiptoes to deepen our kiss. Malaki's tongue slips inside for a brief second, and it makes me forget all about Benedict standing a few feet away.

Malaki eventually breaks our kiss, and his eyes bouncing back and forth between mine.

He's so good at playing the part of my fiancé in front of Benedict that I'm almost fooled.

"Did you enjoy the game?" he asks, ignoring Benedict completely.

I gulp and lick his kiss from my lips. "Mm-hmm," I squeak.

"Hello?" Benedict snaps. "We were in a conversation."

Malaki cranes his neck toward Benedict. "It sounded one-sided. I thought you may be talking to yourself."

I slap a hand over my mouth when a laugh accidentally slips out.

Benedict blinks. He's clearly baffled.

"Well, I need to talk to the mother of my child *alone,*" Benedict growls.

Malaki shakes his head. "Not happening."

"This doesn't concern you," he argues.

Malaki clicks his tongue. "The second you put your hand on my fiancée, it concerned me." His airy attitude switches like a blink. "Don't do it again."

When Benedict doesn't say anything, likely too appalled that someone had the nerve to speak down to him, Malaki goes back to ignoring him.

"Are you ready to go home, babe?"

I nod. My lips sealed.

He takes my hand in his. "Excuse us."

Benedict makes no move to scoot over. His jaw flickers, his chest puffing with a sharp inhale.

Malaki's hand tightens in mine, his body heat climbing the longer we stand here.

The last thing I need is for my fake fiancé to assault Charleigh's dad, whether he deserves it or not. In fact, that's probably what he wants–a reason to get the police involved.

"Benedict," I say his name with conviction. "If you want to speak to me about Charleigh, then I am all ears. But other than that, we have no reason to talk. I would really appreciate it if you didn't show up at my fiancé's place of employment again."

His eyes narrow, and I know I've struck a chord.

It's very similar to what he said to me when I showed up at his office to inform him that I was pregnant with his child. He denied it, threatened to call security, and told me to never come to his place of employment again.

I haven't been back since.

Eventually, he moves out of our way. He gives us such a small passageway that Malaki's pads brush against his shirt. He towers over Benedict, and I hope it makes Benedict feel even a fraction of intimidation.

As soon as Malaki and I are let through a door by security, I release his hand and bend at the knees.

Malaki gently pulls on my arms so I'm looking at him. "Oh now, come on." His thumbs rub soft circles against my shirt. "I thought that went well." His gaze drops to my mouth, and I tingle in spots I shouldn't be.

"I thought you were going to hit him," I admit.

His lips flatten. "You don't give me enough credit, Dimples. If anything, I was going to kiss you in front of him again."

"You were?"

His lip hitches into a sly grin. "I'll take any excuse I can to kiss you."

My thoughts fizzle. *Do not smile.*

A second passes, and then another, and *damnnit!*

I smile because, after all, I *am* just a girl.

He shakes his sweaty hair out and chuckles. "Those dimples kill me."

I roll my eyes playfully but still move to cross my arms, because even though Malaki is putting me at ease, I'm still cagey over Benedict.

"Here." Malaki digs into the pocket of his uniform, and something crinkles. "Open your mouth."

I hesitate, but he sends me a look that has my lips parting. He grips my chin lightly, and the tangy taste of an orange Skittle plops onto my tongue.

"Better?" he asks, helping push my jaw closed with his thumb.

Oh my god.

He's completely ruining every man for me after this fake engagement is over.

Which is simply unacceptable.

I shrug and lick my lips. "Would've been better if it were a red Skittle."

Malaki laughs. "My bad." He tugs me down the hall toward the locker room. "I ate them all during my game."

Twenty-Three

MALAKI

I SHOULD BE SLEEPING.

Typically, the night after a game, I fall asleep right away, my body and mind both exhausted. But tonight, I'm unsettled. I can blame Benedict for that. Or can I *thank* Benedict for that? After all, if I didn't spot him harassing my fiancée from across the ice, I may not have kissed her like I did.

It felt so damn good to kiss her. When my tongue slipped past her soft, surprised lips, my knees grew weak. Now I lie in bed alone, full of dirty thoughts and guilt. Reese has been put in a position that she shouldn't be in, all because her ex is this controlling, obsessive asshole. I can't act on that. I can't swindle her into my bed because I can't move past my attraction. It would be taking advantage of her. She's too good. Selfless, a good sister, an even better mom, a damn good kisser with a body that my hands crave—*fuck*.

I fling the covers off my legs and clench my jaw.

Is it wrong to jack off to my fake fiancée, knowing that she's sleeping in the next room?

What would she think if she knew?

I know she is firm on the whole boundaries thing, and it's completely understandable. However, *the kiss.* It can't just be me whose skin prickles with energy the second we touch. Her flushed face gives her away—and the way her pupils dilate when I move close.

Damn.

I take the heel of my hand and push down on my cock.

I shouldn't picture her naked.

I shouldn't think about that night in her car, where she came all over my hand.

It was so fucking hot it was all I thought about for a week.

A noise catches my attention, and I hold my breath.

Excitement sends me upright in bed. Is that Reese?

I angle my head toward the door and strain to hear the noise again.

My shoulders slump.

Charleigh is crying.

Either that or a wild animal broke into the house.

I continue to stare at my door as Charleigh's cries grow louder. Since Reese has moved in, I haven't heard Charleigh cry once. She squeals with excitement sometimes, her giggle contagious, but she hasn't cried.

Not while I'm around, at least.

I glance at the time. It's well after two in the morning. Another minute passes, and she's still crying.

Worry gnaws at me.

Is she okay?

I don't have much experience with babies, but a cry is a cry, right?

I tug on a pair of low-hanging sweats and creep across the floor. I quietly open my door and peek my head out into the hallway. There's a single stream of moonlight from the window at the end of the hall and nothing else.

Charleigh's room is two down from mine—not that I've gone around snooping or anything. But the fact that her cries are louder the farther I walk down the hall, I can only assume. I stop at the room before hers, the one that shares a wall with mine, and listen. The door is cracked, just barely, so I rap my knuckles against the wood and wait for Reese to stir.

My heart beats faster as I listen to Charleigh cry. I want to text Rhodes and ask him if he thinks it's okay to go in there and pick her up, but he's likely sleeping, and if he isn't, he'll probably call me an idiot again.

"Reese?" I say her name through the crack.

Again, nothing.

Against my better judgment, I push on her door and poke my head inside.

With the blinds pulled, I can't see anything.

I walk farther into the room but stop when my foot nudges something.

Her breath catches from below.

"Malaki?" My name is a whisper in the dark edged with her sleepiness.

I'm confused, my eyes straining to find her bed in the dark. "Charleigh is crying," I say.

Her shadow moves quickly. She scrambles in front of me to stand on wobbly legs.

"Oh my god, I'm so sorry she woke you." She darts past me, her sweet, sugary scent stunning me long enough for Charleigh's cries to stop.

I snap out of it and flip on the light.

Shock keeps my feet planted as I gape at the floor.

A heaping pile of blankets and one measly little pillow stare back at me. Her suitcase is off to the side, next to Stella, the headless mannequin, and that's it. I shift my attention to the door, and then back to her makeshift bed.

Why is she sleeping on the floor? Where is her bed? Did the moving company forget it, and she didn't want to tell me?

I reach up and squeeze the back of my neck before exhaling deeply. I calmly flip the light switch off, shut the door, and walk into the hallway.

I rest my back against the wall, cross my arms, and wait.

With Charleigh's bedroom door cracked, I have the perfect view of Reese. It doesn't take her long to soothe Charleigh back to sleep. She stands in the middle of the mostly empty room in nothing but an oversized t-shirt that hits mid-thigh, her long dark hair in soft fallen waves behind her shoulders. She sways back and forth for a couple of minutes before padding over to a tiny crib-like bed for Charleigh with see-through mesh sides. Reese practically has to bend in half to lay her down, and the only thing that does is pull my eyes to her backside.

Her t-shirt rides up, revealing a round curve. Heat pools in my veins, but just as quickly as her ass appears, it disappears. She tiptoes backward out of the room, keeping her sights on her daughter before gently pulling the door shut and exhaling.

She turns, and her eyes grow wide. A hand flies to her mouth, muffling her yelp.

"Oh my god!" she whisper-yells. "You scared me half to death!"

I raise an eyebrow and keep my arms crossed. "What the hell, Reese?"

She glances to the ceiling as her shoulders slump. "I know. I'm so sorry she woke you up. I usually hear her. I think I was just so tired because of the game. I promise I won't let that happen again."

I pop up from slouching against the wall. "No. That's not–" I pinch the bridge of my nose. She thinks I'm upset because of her daughter crying?

"You're angry, right?" she asks quietly.

I drop my hand. "No! Wait, yes!"

Reese's eyes crinkle on the sides.

"I'm not angry about Charleigh crying. Why would I ever be upset with you over that?"

What kind of man does she think I am? And why am I so bothered over her thinking that I'm the type of man who'd scold her for something like that?

"I'm confused," she admits, nibbling on her lip.

"Me too." I reach out and grab onto her wrist. I gently tug her behind me into her room before shutting the door. This conversation calls for more than whispers in a dark hallway.

"I'm angry because you're sleeping on the floor." I gesture to the bundled blankets. "Where the hell is your bed?"

That pretty shade of pink spreads over her cheeks.

"Oh..." The word floats in between us like a feather.

When she doesn't answer my question, I decide to start guessing.

"Did the moving company forget your bed?"

Those big, round, brown eyes skip to mine, and she shakes her head.

"Did they break it?"

Again, she shakes her head.

"Was there something wrong with it? Was it uncomfortable, so you just left it?"

She looks down at her bare feet. "No."

I bring my eyebrows together. "Then what?"

"I don't have one," she admits.

Silence settles over us. My thoughts circle. What does she mean she doesn't have one? Where did she sleep before?

Finally, I break the quiet. "What?"

Reese hurriedly goes over to her 'bed' and bends to fluff the blankets. Her movements are jerky, her eyes never finding mine. "I don't have a bed," she explains. "When I moved into the apartment, I used all my money for the deposit and first month's rent. I told myself I'd get one eventually, but..." She shrugs. "I had other things to pay for. Sleeping on the floor isn't that big of a deal. I have plenty of blankets."

It takes effort to keep my jaw tight so it doesn't fall with shock. Reese gestures to her blankets with a half-smile, like she's trying to convince me that her rigged bed is a California king.

I walk closer to her spot on the floor and stare at the mismatched blankets. Is this woman out of her mind?

I'm almost afraid to ask but, "Does Zoe have a bed?"

"Yes..."

I raise an eyebrow at her skeptical tone and point to the floor. "This doesn't count."

She huffs and crosses her arms. "She is using an air mattress."

I sigh and aggressively put my hands through my hair. "I'm buying you both a bed."

Reese jumps up from kneeling. "No!"

My jaw aches. "Yes," I say through clenched teeth.

"I don't want you to buy us anything," she pleads.

Zoe will gladly accept a new bed. I don't have to worry about that one.

Reese, though. She's different. The more I'm around her, the more I notice how independent she is. It's part of why I was so intrigued by her to begin with. Hell, she even threw a fit when I tipped her for the Uber ride.

"Okay," I finally say.

Reese's shoulders sag. A breath of relief leaves her, and I can't help but smile. Her eyebrows fold inward when I advance. I scoop her up, her legs dangling over my arm.

"What are you doing?!" she exclaims.

Her arms find my neck, and the way her soft skin feels against my bare chest is just enough to get me toying with those dirty thoughts again. I walk us over to the door and open it before flipping the light off.

"If you won't let me buy you a bed, then you can sleep in mine."

Reese tenses in my arms. "I cannot sleep in your bed."

I quietly walk over to Charleigh's room and crack the door. That way, she can hear her better if she stirs.

"Malaki!" she hisses my name on the way to *our* room.

I glance at her. "What?"

"I can't sleep in your bed!" she argues.

I shrug with her in my arms. "Then let me buy you one."

A quiet growl echoes as she pouts. That plump bottom lip plops outward, and I force myself to look away.

I leave the door open to my bedroom and walk us over to the bed. The covers are messy from my restless half-sleep, but there's plenty of room for the two of us.

Unless she doesn't trust me…

I hold her steady. "I'll sleep on the couch."

Within the shadows of my room, I watch shock blanket her face. "Absolutely not."

"One way or another, you're sleeping in a bed. You either let me buy you one, or you sleep in this one."

There is no other choice.

She thinks for a moment, and I narrow my gaze.

"You know how persistent I am. So what'll it be?"

Her warm breath fans against my chest. "I don't want you to buy me anything."

"My bed it is." I drop her onto the soft mattress.

Dark waves frame her face before she pops up onto her elbows to gape at me. I get a glimpse of her soft thighs when her t-shirt rides up.

Yeah, I better sleep elsewhere.

"I'll be on the couch," I announce, backing away.

Those big, brown eyes turn doe-like as she watches me go. She looks so damn good on my bed—sweet but enticing.

I force my back to her.

I'm almost all the way through the door when she pipes up.

"Wait!"

One tiny word is all it takes.

I wait.

Twenty-Four

REESE

I SWALLOW my humility and stare at Malaki from across the room. As soon as the word *wait* blurted from my mouth, he stilled, and now there's nothing but silence separating us.

My stomach flutters as he slowly spins around. His hands grip the top of his doorjamb, and the only thing I can do to stop staring at his tight stomach is scramble to the opposite side of the bed.

"I won't be able to sleep knowing you gave up your bed for me," I ramble on, lurching to the very edge. My feet tangle in the blankets from my rushing, and next thing I know, my back is on the floor.

Malaki appears just in time for my embarrassment to settle.

He towers over me with a furrowed brow. "I know I'm a lot bigger than you, but I don't need *that* much room on the bed, Reese."

I snort out a laugh, and he chuckles. He pulls me to my feet and gently grabs my hips, guiding me to sit on the bed. I sink onto the mattress, and my body automatically lets out a sigh of relief.

It's cozy. The mattress, the blankets, the scent. All of it.

"Lie back," Malaki orders.

He takes the blanket out from underneath my legs and drapes it over me when my head hits the pillow. Then, he makes his way to the other side of the bed, hooks his thumbs into the waistband of his sweats, and pauses.

Warmth pools in between my legs, and I pinch my thigh to stop myself from going there.

Crossing the line with Malaki is the very last thing I need. It'd bring nothing but more drama into my—our—life, and this is something I can't afford to screw up.

Out of the corner of my eye, Malaki stands with his thumbs hidden beneath his pants. He shakes his head briefly before seemingly deciding not to shed them.

The bed dips, right along with my heart.

When was the last time I was in bed with a man?

Benedict's face flashes inside my head, and I hate the fear that follows it. I hate that I'm afraid of him. I hate that I don't see a future without him in it, one way or another.

Malaki's smooth voice drifts into the quiet room. "I'll still buy you a bed if you want your own."

I'm quick to refuse. "I don't."

"You don't?"

Is he flirting with me?

"Not because I want to sleep with you!"

He shifts beside me. "Who said you need a bed to sleep with me? We could do that anywhere. The shower, the kitchen, a car…"

I turn my head against the pillow and brush my hair away from my face to see him better. His hands are propped behind his head, the blanket pooled around his waist. He stares at the ceiling with a grin on his face.

"I did *not* mean it like that," I huff and turn away.

He chuckles. "I know, but it's fun to tease you."

I kick him under the covers. "I changed my mind. You can go sleep on the couch."

As soon as I move to drag my leg back, his hand lands on my thigh. "No take-backs, Dimples."

My heart races.

Heat sweeps against my skin like a flame.

When he eventually lets go, I quickly turn onto my side with my back to him.

Get it together, Reese.

I try my best to think of anything besides him.

Even when I attempt to think of Benedict and his threats, I end up circling back to the moment at the arena, when Malaki swooped in and kissed me.

We lie in the quiet of his room for so long I lose track of time.

My heart slows, the comfort of his bed reminding me of how exhausted I am.

When I think he's asleep, I allow myself to be humble. "Thank you for what you did at the arena." I wait for him to respond, but he doesn't, so I keep going. "Thanks for keeping the bedroom door open too."

I'm not sure if he left it open to make me more comfortable, or if he did it because Charleigh is two rooms down. Either way, I noticed.

Right before I drift off to sleep, I swear I hear him say, "Anything for my fiancée," in that cocky tone of his.

What time is it?

My groggy state tells me I didn't sleep enough, but when my eyelashes flutter open, I'm greeted with a stream of sunlight right across my face. I immediately shut my eyes again and groan.

Since having Charleigh, I've learned how precious sleep is. I take full advantage that she isn't crying and curl back into myself, desperate for more rest. I snuggle onto the pillow.

I'm warm, and my back doesn't ache from the hard floor.

I open my eyes fully, and my chest tightens.

I'm in Malaki's bed.

Last night replays inside my head like a jumbotron for all to see—and by all, I mean me, myself, and I.

As slowly as I can, fearful I'll wake him, I turn toward the other side of the bed, only to find it empty.

I quickly sit up and fling the blankets off my legs. I'm in the middle of trying to sort out my mixed feelings when the slightly ajar door opens farther.

I do my very best to focus on Charleigh instead of Malaki, but he stands there with his hair in a perfect, wavy mess, shirtless, holding my sleepy-faced daughter in his arms.

She smiles widely when she sees me, and to my complete and utter surprise, she buries her face in the crook of Malaki's neck to hide her excitement.

What the–

My lips part.

Has Malaki Young somehow wormed his way into Charleigh's heart?

"Sorry..." He shrugs while walking closer to the bed. "I heard her, and you just looked so peaceful sleeping, I didn't want to wake you up."

I blink past my confusion. "It's okay... but you know you don't have–"

Malaki's cocked eyebrow cuts me off mid-sentence. I close my mouth and manage a small smile. "Thank you."

"You're welcome."

Charleigh puts her hand on Malaki's scruffy chin and rubs it with curiosity. "Want to see Mama?" he asks her.

"*No*, she wants to see me," Zoe says from behind.

Malaki turns around with Charleigh in her arms, and Zoe stands at the bedroom door, fully dressed for class. She leans around Malaki and grins at me. "Well, well, well... What do we have here? You in your fake fiancé's bed? *Interesting*."

I sit up even taller. "It's not like that!"

Malaki peers at me over his shoulder, and Zoe takes full advantage of his attention being elsewhere. She winks dramatically, and I scowl at her.

"Sure it's not," she teases.

"He found out that I don't have a bed," I say. "He said he was just going to buy me one if I didn't use his, so..."

She laughs. "Yeah, yeah. Whatever you say."

I take the pillow behind my head and chuck it at her. She swats it away with another laugh.

Malaki steps in between us. "I heard you don't have a bed either."

"Are you inviting me into your bed too? Because that's where I draw the line."

Malaki coughs or chokes. I can't decide which.

"What? No! God."

"Why not?" Zoe retorts. "It's not like you two are doing anything other than sleeping... right?"

"Zoe!" I snap.

She takes Charleigh from Malaki and glances at me on his bed. "I'm kidding! Relax."

Charleigh pulls on Zoe's hair, and she winces.

Malaki walks over to his dresser and pulls out a shirt. His back muscles move languidly as he tugs it on. He turns toward Zoe. "Your bed will be here today."

He already bought one?

Zoe catches my attention with surprise, and I give her my best *say thank you* look.

Her shock lasts half a second. She looks at Malaki, says thank you, and begins to back out of his bedroom with Charleigh in tow.

"I'll feed her breakfast before I leave for class," she says.

"Thank you." *And thank you for showing gratitude.*

A shit-eating grin curves on my sister's face, and I prepare myself for whatever is about to come out of her mouth.

"I'm leaving in fifteen"—she gestures to Malaki and me— "so make it a quickie."

My face warms. "Zoe!"

Malaki's shoulders shake with laughter, so I climb to my knees, reach for his pillow, and chuck it across the room at him just like I did to her.

Of course he catches it. Natural-born athlete and all.

I blow a piece of my hair out of my face. "You two are going to be the bane of my existence, aren't you?"

He grins slyly. "Oh, come on, that's what siblings are for."

"And fake fiancés?" I retort, crossing my arms.

Malaki's eyes slip from my face, move to my chest, and then down even farther. I follow his line of sight. My old college t-shirt has ridden up with my arms crossed, showing off my very bare thighs.

I swallow.

Malaki shifts, but his eyes never leave the gap between my thighs.

Do I move? Do I try to cover up? Do I pretend like my nipples aren't poking through my shirt?

He clears his throat and repeats my question. "What are fake fiancés for?"

"Yeah," I choke out.

Finally, Malaki drags his gaze past my hips and lands at my

face again. His high cheek bones are a little flushed, and I can't stop staring at his mouth.

"You tell me, Reese."

Our eyes snag, the eye contact feverish.

My pulse flutters in places I didn't know it could.

Why do I want him to close the gap between us, sweep me beneath him on this very bed, and do dirty things to me?

The longer we keep a hold of each other's gazes, the more twisted my thoughts get. I lick my bottom lip, and he mirrors me.

Finally, he breaks the moment.

"I need a shower," he blurts.

I jump up from the bed and tug on my shirt to cover my legs.

"A cold one," he mumbles, heading right to the bathroom.

I barely make it out of his room before one last dirty thought about him in the shower enters my head.

Twenty-Five

MALAKI

"WHERE'S YOUR *FIANCÉE* TONIGHT?"

I'm lacing up for the game when Lars's smug grin comes into view. I'm someone who is hard to rile up, but his tone makes my blood run hot. "She's at home...in my bed." *Hopefully.* "Where's your mom tonight?"

Someone sniggers from a few lockers down, and I don't have to look to know it's Kane.

"A mama joke? Grow up," Lars sneers.

I wink. "Can't take the heat, stay out of the kitchen."

Rhodes busies himself with lacing his skates and asks, "How long have you and Reese been together? I'm surprised we haven't heard you spouting at the mouth about her if you're serious enough to get engaged."

I glance away as guilt hits me. I hate lying. "A while, but she wanted to keep things under wraps since I'm in the media."

"What's a while?" Lars asks in that annoying accent of his.

There's a twitch in his eye, which tells me he's skeptical. When I don't immediately answer, he squints.

If I'm not careful, he'll catch me in a lie.

When I don't answer, he questions me again. "A while, as in...she had your bub?"

"What the fuck is a bub?" someone asks from a few lockers over.

Lars answers, "Ah, sorry. The term bub is used for baby in Australia."

I grip my jersey tightly before pulling it over my head.

Through my rising blood pressure, I hear someone say, "A baby? His fiancée has a baby?"

"Well?" Lars's face comes back into view.

I ignore my unusual possessiveness. Charleigh isn't something I can lie about, so I tell the truth. "She's not mine."

There's a collective *ooooh* that moves through the locker room like a tidal wave, followed by the term, "Stepdaddy Malaki". I have to act like it doesn't irritate me, because any other day, it wouldn't.

"Hey, baby or not. She's fine as hell. I'd become a stepdaddy too."

I jerk upright and search to see who said that.

"Hey." Rhodes steps forward, his shoulders bundling with anger. "Show some fucking respect."

"Yeah." I try to brush off my anger with a joke, per usual. "Rhodes is the real dad of the bunch. Listen to him."

The chatter is broken up right away but not without a few chuckles here and there. Emory catches my eye across the locker room and flicks his chin to Rhodes. I nod, silently giving him the go-ahead to make Rhodes privy to my situation.

That's where I draw the line, though. I don't want anyone else to know about Reese's and my fake engagement.

I may be flippant and only appear serious when I'm racing

my opponent on the ice, but I understand the gravity of the situation I'm in. Being fake engaged is all fun and games until I remind myself that Reese is in a shitty situation with a man who has a vengeance for control.

Kane elbows me on the way out of the locker room, and I slow my pace to walk with him. He waits for some rookies to pass before leaning in, "I assume you're taking Reese to the charity function, right?"

My steps falter.

He rolls his eyes before pulling on his helmet. "If you want people to believe your engagement, you should probably take your fiancée as your date."

My fingers tighten as I grip my own helmet, but I make no move to put it on. *How the hell does he know the truth?*

He answers my silent question. "We lived together. I'm not a fucking idiot. You've either swept her off her feet in a couple of weeks—which is unlikely—or it's a fabricated engagement." He shrugs. "Plus, Daisy mentioned something being off too. She's just waiting for Reese to fill her in."

Great.

He calls over his shoulder as he continues toward the ice. "Text Reese and tell her to pick one of the dresses that I had her get for Daisy. She's on her way over there now to inform Daisy that she's going as my date."

I rush toward my locker. Placing my helmet on the bench, I dig for my phone.

Reese's name is already on the screen with a text message.

REESE

I found a bag of Blue Devils merch on the bed. I assume this is from you, considering there's a jersey inside that says, Future Mrs. Young on the back...

I grin.

ME

You're welcome 😊 Also, I need you to pick one of those dresses for the charity function you got for Daisy for yourself. You're coming with me.

My heart beats fast, and I haven't even climbed on the ice. I could blame it on game-day jitters, but I haven't been nervous for a game in years. Hockey is my calm, and apparently, Reese is my chaos.

When Reese doesn't text me back right away, I send another, because I have a feeling she's trying to come up with some excuse.

ME

It's time I showed you off...

REESE

Showed me off? Like I'm cattle? 😕

No, Dimples. Not like cattle.

ME

It's time I showed you off as mine. So pick a dress, and I'll see you tomorrow.

Oh, by the way, Kane and Daisy are onto us, so you might want to tell her something.

Night, Mrs. Young

I toss my phone into my locker and head for the ice, and what do you know? I'm no longer nervous.

———

The house is spotless when I get home. The scent of something sweet fills the air, and I have to admit, I'm not necessarily upset that Reese is taking this whole "work for me" thing seriously. Coming home after an away game to someone other than Kane *and* the house is clean? Who would argue with that?

The simple contract she made–not me–listed the tasks she'd take care of while we continued our fake engagement, and an entire monthly menu with lasagna on it twice. I decided to let her have her way. She's persistent when it comes to supporting herself and Charleigh financially, and I can't blame her for that.

I wonder if she'll notice me paying her more than agreed upon?

After placing my bag near the door, I walk down the hall in search of Reese. I stop in place when her conversation with Zoe carries throughout the house.

"Just act like you're not here. I'll tell him that I have no one to watch Charleigh," Reese rambles to Zoe, both completely unaware that I'm mere feet away, listening to their conversation.

"You are insane," Zoe states. "I'm not going to go hide in my room from your pretend fiancé because you're afraid to go on a date."

"It isn't a date, and I'm not afraid!" Reese argues. "And keep your voice down. I don't want you to wake Charleigh."

Zoe's sigh is still loud enough for me to hear around the corner. "Then why are you trying to get out of going? Do you really think Benedict is going to believe you two are engaged if Malaki is showing up to events without you? Especially if they require a plus-one?"

"Benedict just texted me this morning and apologized."

He did?

"He said he's going to respect my relationship–"

Zoe cuts off her sister. "Please tell me you didn't believe

that bullshit. He can't even respect you when you say no, let alone your relationship with another man!"

I cock an eyebrow. What exactly does that mean?

Reese begins to stammer. "I...I..."

"Remember when he refused to believe that Charleigh was his and belittled you for being a whore? He said that you were trying to trap him because he was wealthy! Oh, and do you remember the first time he actually met her?"

"Zoe," Reese warns.

"He came over and tried to get you to sleep with him even though you weren't cleared from the doctor yet! Then yelled at you when you refused? Or how about all the times he came to the apartment and didn't respect the fact that we didn't want him there?"

My heart pounds, and a thin line of sweat forms along my hairline.

"Don't even get me started on the time I found him shoving you around. If I didn't show up and threaten him with that bat..."

Zoe's voice trails, and I realize it's because I've stepped into their line of sight unintentionally. My sights are set directly on Reese. When she sees me, her lips snap together, and her gaze runs in the opposite direction.

I know a shamed face when I see one, and for some reason, it bothers me that she feels the need to hide. Now, more than ever, I want to have her by my side every chance I get, just to show Benedict that he can't have her.

It's a possessive thing to say, even inside my head, but I can't deny it.

Zoe takes Charleigh, who's fast asleep, from her mother's arms and scoots past me. She gives me a look that I can only assume means *help her* in reference to her sister.

I lean my shoulder against the wall and scan the kitchen. It's spotless, not a dish in sight. The only thing I see is a baby bottle that's drying on some weird-looking grass thing. It was one of the only things Reese had brought with her, besides baby bottles and clothes.

"There are some meals in the fridge for you, if you're hungry," she says.

"I'm not," I say.

Awkward silence fills the gap between us, and she eventually breaks. "How much of that did you hear?"

Enough to make me want to bury Benedict.

Instead of showing her all my cards, I play it off. "Not much," I say, lying right through my teeth.

Her laugh is abrupt, and I can't help but grin. She places her elbows on the counter and buries her face into her hands. "I'm choosing to believe that over the alternative," she mumbles.

"What if I told you I heard it all?" I ask.

Reese peeks at me through her fingers. Her brown eyes, soft and pretty, sober. "Did you?"

I push off from the wall and make my way toward the fridge. I open it up, grab the apple juice, and walk over to her. Instead of touching her, I lean my back against the counter and open the cap. "I heard enough," I admit.

As much as I want to know everything that's happened when it comes to her ex, I won't push. I think she's had enough of that over the last year.

I decide to change the subject instead. "So what dress did you pick?"

Reese pulls her hands away from her face to peer up at me from leaning against the counter. "You're asking me what dress I chose?" She drops her gaze to the jug of apple juice in my hand.

I hand it to her. "You look like you need a drink."

One of her dimples catches my eye, but instead of letting me see her smile, she looks at her feet. Her hair comes forward, hiding most of her face from me, and I involuntarily reach forward to push the long waves over her shoulder.

I inch the jug of juice closer.

She laughs, and my mouth curves.

Eventually, she takes it from me and tips her head back to take a drink.

When she's finished, she runs her tongue along the seam of her lips.

There's a pull in my groin, like I'm a fucking puppet.

I'm a grown-ass man with a career, investments, a mortgage, and yet…I'm turned on by a pretty woman drinking apple juice?

Jesus.

I take the juice from her, twist the cap on, and shove it back into the fridge. I hold my hand out to her, and she looks at it like it's a trap.

"Come on, let's go." I inch my chin toward the hall leading to the stairs.

She's about to protest, but I don't give her the option.

"You know I can't show up to this event without you," I say. "I'd be the world's worst fiancé if I didn't have you by my side."

She's hesitant, eyeing my hand like I'm taking her to the pits of Hell instead of a fancy event.

"Don't make me do it," I threaten playfully.

Reese narrows her eyes. "Do what?"

"I'll throw you over my shoulder and carry you upstairs right now if I have to."

The energy shifts around us. Reese pops a hip, crosses her arms, and narrows those pretty eyes. "And then what?" she questions. "Are you going to strip me out of these clothes and force me into a dress?"

I step forward. "Wanna test me?"

Twenty-Six

REESE

MALAKI'S GRIN challenges every excuse I've come up with to put space between us.

I know I shouldn't, but I do exactly what he says and test him.

"You wouldn't do that," I say teasingly.

God, what am I doing?

The more time I spend with him, the more I slip up. I need to stick by the book or, at the very least, reflect on that list of boundaries I'd given him.

Sleeping in his bed is nothing more than sleeping.

Kissing him in public is for the watchful eyes and that's all.

"Are you challenging me, Dimples?" Malaki stalks forward slowly, and my heart beats faster as I anticipate his next move.

I look past his hot grin and wide shoulders. If I run, he'll chase me, and the thought of that does nothing but send flutters in between my thighs.

"I'm fast," he admits out of nowhere, like he can read my mind. "The fastest in the league."

"Arrogant much?" I tease.

He shakes his head. "Just stating facts, baby."

My cheeks burn, and I'm so swept up in him calling me baby that I don't even realize he's swooping low and wrapping his arms behind my legs.

"Malaki!" I hiss.

His arms tighten around me even more as he heads for the stairs. We're face to face, our breaths mingling as he smirks. "I warned you."

I can't help but laugh, and God, it feels good.

I don't laugh anymore—not like I used to.

Our engagement may be fake, but the laughter that comes with being around Malaki is as real as it gets.

I wiggle my legs back and forth when he makes it to the landing. He opens the bedroom door, and he walks us into his–*our*—room. The dress I'm supposed to wear is hanging on the bathroom door, and I wiggle again, hoping he'll put me down.

Malaki's arms tighten, and our eyes lock. "You better stop doing that," he rasps.

His heart hammers behind his chest against me.

"Then put me down," I say quietly.

Malaki tips his chin, and I get a better view of his mouth. "Maybe I don't want to."

He shifts me in his arms when I start to slip. I graze something hard beneath his waist, and my stomach flips.

A slow swallow moves down his throat as he stares at me.

I force myself to say, "We're going to be late."

Malaki exhales, and then I'm slowly sliding down the front of his body. I brush against every one of his taut muscles before my feet land on the floor.

To hide the flush creeping along my skin, I race over to the bathroom and grab the dress from the hanger.

"I guess this means you're going, then?" he asks.

I turn around, and my breath catches.

It takes me a second to regain consciousness again.

"Malaki!" I chide.

God, stop looking!

Malaki is in his tight boxer briefs, still sporting that hard bulge I apparently didn't imagine a few moments ago. "What?"

"You're practically naked!" I exclaim.

Does he not understand that I'm highly attracted to him? Is he doing this on purpose?

"You're my fiancée...surely you've seen me in less clothing."

My lips flatten at his joke.

"You're only my fiancé when people are around! In case you haven't noticed"—I gesture to his empty room—"we're alone."

Malaki hums before going back to his closet. He reaches for something, and I stare at the defined muscles along his shoulders like I'm trying to burn them into my memory. I turn around in haste, clutch my dress, and walk into the bathroom.

"Thought it'd be good to practice," he says from the bedroom. "The more comfortable you are around me in private, the more comfortable you'll be in public."

"It just took me by surprise," I explain, my voice slipping through the crack in the door. I strip off my clothes and leave them bundled on the tiled floor. "I am comfortable with you."

More comfortable with him than I ever was with Benedict.

"Good." His voice is closer than before. "Then you won't mind if we share the mirror?"

The door to the bathroom opens all the way, and I yelp. My hands fly to my chest to hold the loose fabric there.

"Oh, my apologies."

I can tell without looking in the mirror that Malaki is smiling.

"If you want to see me naked, just ask!" I snap half-heartedly. "Though, I've had a baby, so you might not like what you see," I mutter under my breath.

While holding up the strapless dress in the front, I reach behind me and attempt to zip it up. I use the mirror to get a better look at the back of my dress and immediately catch Malaki's glower in my direction.

"What did you just say?"

"Nothing." My fingers freeze on the zipper.

Malaki stops buttoning his dress shirt to grip the edge of the vanity. The veins on top of his hands strain, and I tear my gaze away. I pull on the zipper but stop altogether when he appears behind me. One hand lands on top of mine, the zipper in my grip, while the other wraps around the front of my waist.

His warm whisper brushes the side of my neck. "Did you just say that I wouldn't like what I see because you've had a baby?"

Words are nonexistent.

He grips my wrist, removes my hand from the zipper, and places it on the wall in front of my face. I press my palm against it, still holding the front of my dress steady with my other hand. He tugs on my dress, zipping it halfway before stopping.

"Did he say that to you?" he asks in a low tone.

My heart beats so hard I feel it everywhere.

Benedict's opinion isn't the problem; it's the insult itself. I don't care if he thinks I'm more appealing in a size two with a toned stomach. It's the fact that my body is different, and my jeans don't fit the way they used to. When you've been told something about your appearance on more than one occasion, it's hard not to believe it.

"Reese." The strain in Malaki's tone pulls my attention to his face. Our eyes meet in the mirror, and for the first time, there is no amusement lingering.

"Yeah," I say. "He did."

Malaki's expression remains steady as he removes his hand from the zipper. A chill races down my spine from the touch of his knuckle skimming my skin. Then, he tugs me backward by my waist. I hit his hard chest, and a breath slips from my lungs.

"Well, I'm nothing like Benedict, Reese." Malaki's jaw is set in a firm line as he drags his knuckle back down my spine, landing at the zipper. "I can assure you that I'd love every single part of your body."

My breathing quickens, my lungs tight with trapped air.

Once Malaki finishes zipping my dress, he spins me around and grips my waist with both of his hands. I press against him, and he takes me in. "If you want me to prove it to you, just say the word."

I open my mouth, and nothing comes out. I'm flushed, and the room spins. I can't catch my breath, and I think he notices, because he finally backs away and puts space between us.

I inhale a gush of air and move my hair to the side to expose my warm neck.

"There's no rush, though." He goes back to the mirror to continue buttoning his shirt.

Wow.

He may not be affected by our little moment, but I most definitely am.

I spend the next twenty minutes pinning my hair back and applying makeup, all while refusing to give my attention to Malaki in his high-end, black suit. Benedict wears dress attire daily, yet I can whole-heartedly admit that I have never been this distracted by a man in a suit before.

Malaki is hot in his hockey uniform, especially on the ice, but it should be illegal for him to wear a suit.

It tangles everything inside my head.

"You ready, Future Mrs. Young?" he asks.

I can barely manage a glimpse at him leaning against the bathroom door. "Mm-hmm," I squeak. "Just let me check on Charleigh real quick and tell Zoe bye."

"I'll be downstairs."

After eyeing Charleigh sleeping in her room, I head to Zoe's bedroom and peek through the crack of the door. She's lying on her bed but pops up when she sees me creeping.

"Don't you dare try to sneak out without showing me your dress."

I slowly push on the door, and her jaw drops. "Now this is what I expected you to look like on prom night."

My shoulders fall. "I had better things to do than go to my senior prom."

"Better things?" She rolls her eyes. "I'm not sure I'd consider making sure Dad didn't choke on his vomit from drinking too much a better alternative."

I scoff. "Fine, I mean...I had more...important things to do."

My dress is pretty.

It's light blue, and the glossy satin looks good against my olive-colored skin.

It feels wrong, though.

"What's wrong?" Zoe asks.

She always knows when something is up with me.

I pull on the slit in my dress. "It feels wrong to get all dressed up and go to some fancy event with a man like Malaki. I should be staying in with Charleigh, but instead, I'm having my younger sister watch my baby and–"

"Reese." My sister scrambles from her new bed, which just so happens to be bigger and nicer than any bed she's ever had before. She places her hands on my bare shoulders and gives them a gentle squeeze. "You do know that you're allowed to be more than just a mom, right? You're allowed to have fun and get all dressed up to spend the evening on a date."

"It's not a date," I argue.

She shakes her head. "Whatever. Just..." She squeezes my shoulders again. "Promise you'll have a good time tonight. Charleigh is fine with me."

"I know she is. I wouldn't trust anyone else to watch her," I say.

Except Daisy.

And maybe Malaki.

Wait, I would trust Malaki?

"It's just..." I let my words fade because the real reason I'm being hesitant is simply a reaction to how I grew up, and we both know it.

"Just because you're going out for the evening doesn't mean you're turning into Mom."

I wince because I hate when she brings her up.

"I know that," I say, nodding.

Deep down, it's the truth. My mother left us alone with our alcoholic father more times than I can count just so she could escape a life she hated. Never once were my sister and I a priority or even a thought in her head.

The last thing I would ever want for Charleigh is for her to think that there is anything more important to me than she is.

"Then go have fun." My sister twists me around and shoves me out her bedroom door. "Hook up with your fiancé while you're at it. Maybe getting laid would help ease all that stress you're carrying around."

"Zoe!" I hiss.

Her laughter follows me all the way down the hallway.

Twenty-Seven

MALAKI

IT'S strange to have a woman hanging off my arm for an event like this. Showing up at award ceremonies, charity functions, or galas without a date is usually frowned upon, but I'm not necessarily huge on following social norms.

I'm not going to just go out and find some random woman and use her like arm candy for the media. I'm an athlete, not Hugh Hefner.

Most of the women I've come in contact with over the last couple of years are as shallow as a kiddie pool. There's no real depth to them, and we typically have nothing in common. Most of them don't even laugh at my jokes, either too incompetent to understand them or too afraid they'll get a laugh line or two.

Reese, though? She's not afraid of getting a laugh line or anything of that nature. In fact, she just admitted that she's afraid of making *me* look bad. What an absurd thought.

"What if I trip? Or say the wrong thing?" She tugs on the sexy opening of her dress in the front seat of my car. "What if they ask me a question about you, and I don't know how to answer?"

I try to hide my amusement. It's sort of adorable that she's so worked up over being my date. "Will you relax?"

"Relax?" There's fire in her voice. "How do I relax? I'm supposed to be your fiancée, and I don't even know your hockey stats!"

"My hockey stats?" I laugh loudly while I drive toward the valet.

I get a quick glimpse of Reese, and her angry glare only eggs me on further. I reach over and place my hand on her thigh that's been calling my name since the moment she sat in my car. Her dress fell open, and I haven't been able to concentrate on anything but that.

"Listen, I will handle it if someone asks you about how talented your future husband is." I give her leg a squeeze.

Reese exhales loudly, unbothered that we're skin on skin. "I want a detailed report on all things Malaki Young by tomorrow evening. I don't like to be unprepared."

"You know what I think you need?" I ask.

"A lawyer?" she exclaims. "I know! I've already thought about that. The moment Benedict threw the word custody around, it was my first thought."

I trace the outside of her thigh with the pad of my thumb. "No..."

I bought a pack of Skittles at the gas station earlier simply because she was on my mind, but now that I'm looking at her like this, I'm wondering if she'd be better off with an orgasm.

That's sure to relax her a little, take her mind off things.

But what do I know? I'm just her fake fiancé.

I put the car in park. "Look in the backseat."

"Did you get me Skittles?!"

I grin, and her eyes brighten. She smiles fleetingly at me and reaches in the back for the candy.

The valet comes around to my side of the car, and I hop out to hand him the keys. I walk around and open Reese's door, only to see her sitting there staring up at me.

She's wearing more makeup than I've ever seen her wear before, the dark mascara outlining the almond shape of her eyes. The shiny, pinkish color on her lips is a sucker punch to the gut, and I really have to focus on not staring at them.

"Reese?" I say her name, and her eyelashes finally flutter with a blink.

"You got a car seat?"

I grip the top of my car and stare down at her, attempting to read her reaction. "Yeah."

Those plump lips open and then close again. People are starting to stare, the valet being one of them.

"It's not a big deal," I say, holding my hand out for her to take.

Without hesitation, she places her palm in mine, and I pull her to stand. She peers at me, and one of her dimples appears. "Yes, it is."

Someone calls my name, but I can't be bothered to look. I hook Reese's arm in mine and pull her to the sidewalk. I lean in close, my mouth brushing against her ear, thanks to the way she did her hair. "You ready?"

She blows out a breath. "I'm nervous..."

"Nervous? Why?"

From the moment I met her, Reese never seemed impressed by me—or any other hockey player, for that matter. She is the furthest thing from a fan girl, money and talent having no interest to her. For her to be nervous is conflicting.

Is she nervous to act like we're a couple?

Is she nervous because of my teammates?

"I grew up in a trailer park, Malaki. Our yearly income was probably a week's worth for some of the people in there." She flicks her delicate chin to the doors we're about to walk through. "Including you. They're all going to know the second we walk in there that I'm trailer trash."

Before walking any farther, I pull her off to the side and spin her to look at me. I keep my arm around her waist, but the other goes to her chin. I tip her head so she's forced to meet my eye.

"One, it doesn't matter where you came from or how you grew up. And two, nothing about the way you look says you're trailer trash." Just to get my next point across, I tug her flush to my body. Her breasts press into my chest, and my entire body lights up. "Three...I never want to hear you insult my fiancée ever again."

Reese's mouth turns up on the side, her eyes rolling playfully. I pull her in tighter, just to feel her brush against me again.

"I'm serious," I press on. "Just because you grew up in a trailer doesn't mean you're trailer trash."

"I know," she admits quietly. "It's just a habit."

I take her arm in mine and start for the doors again. "What is?"

"To refer to myself as trailer trash. When you've been called that most of your life, it catches on."

The idea of someone referring to her as trailer trash puts my blood pressure at an alarming level.

The door opens in front of us, and with a tight-lipped smile, I nod at the man standing there. Once we're inside, the same man gestures at the door leading to the event. There are a few flashes of a camera, but we make our way without stopping for too long.

I place my hand on the small of Reese's back. I lean in and put my mouth against her cheek. "You ready?"

Our eyes lock. "Just...don't leave me, okay?"

As if I'd leave her in a tank full of thirsty sharks.

"I wouldn't be a very good fiancé if I ditched you at an event I begged you to come to," I note.

She laughs softly, and after seeing her all worked up with nerves a few minutes ago, my pride swells.

"Oh, and Reese?"

Her brown eyes twinkle under the glowing lights.

"You look beautiful," I say.

Warmth spreads onto her cheeks, and I walk into the event with satisfaction. For the first time in my career, I don't have to make light of the evening with humor to cure my boredom, because I've got my own personal little escape right beside me.

Twenty-Eight

REESE

I AM SO out of my element, and I fear everyone can tell. I wave to Daisy and send her a *help me* look, but the only thing she does is wiggle her eyebrows at my left ring finger. My ring gleams underneath the lights, catching everyone's attention. The engagement may be fake, but the diamond is not.

I'm learning that Malaki Young doesn't do anything halfway.

He gives his all to his career and skates with fierce determination during every single game. He suddenly becomes engaged to a poor, single mom, and he goes above and beyond to play the part—buys a real diamond, moves us into a picture-perfect house in a safe neighborhood, purchases a car seat for Charleigh, and he hasn't left me once since arriving at this charity function.

"This is my fiancée, Reese."

My stomach dips as I reach my hand out toward an older man standing with his wife. She's dripping in beautiful emerald and ruby jewelry and smells like expensive perfume.

"It is so nice to meet you," she says through a smile while her husband presses his mouth to the top of my hand.

I smile back. "Likewise."

After some small talk, Malaki excuses us. His hand moves to my lower back, like he's been doing all night, and I shiver from the touch.

"Are you cold?" He stares at my goosebump-covered arms with a frown.

Quite the opposite.

"Do you mind if I step away and check my phone? Just to make sure Charleigh is okay?" I ask.

I need some air.

The number of times Malaki introduced me as his fiancée is going to my head. My smile is a little less fake, and the butterflies are a lot more noticeable.

And he bought a car seat for his car.

It's such a small thing to him, but it's so big to me.

"Of course not." Malaki presses his hand against my back again.

His touch is so faint, yet I feel like his palm is burning me through this dress.

Once he pushes on the door, someone shouts his name from behind. We both look back, and it's his coach.

He grumbles before meeting my eye.

I laugh softly. "I know I asked you not to leave me, but I promise I'll be okay out here for a minute or two."

"Maybe I don't want to leave you..." he says. "But *fine.*"

I roll my eyes at the way he pouts and turn to walk farther into the hallway, only to stop abruptly when his arm winds around my waist. He pulls me backward, and I only manage one breath before he seals his mouth over mine.

I'm lost in the surprise.

His lips are so soft, but the way he works his mouth over mine is branding.

I can hardly stand when it's done.

He backs away, taking my breath with him.

"Hurry," he says quietly. "It's boring without my fiancée next to me."

I quickly glance around to see if anyone is watching us, but besides a few random glimpses, no one is paying us much attention.

Which proves my earlier notion: Malaki Young doesn't do anything halfway, even faking an engagement.

We go in opposite directions. He strides toward his coach, as if our quick parting kiss didn't affect him at all, while I nearly stumble over my dress to get away.

Instead of taking a right and heading toward the front doors where random people loiter about, I go the other way and turn toward the banquet hallway. I press my back against a door that reads, *Banquet Room Stage* and pull out my phone from the clutch I borrowed from Daisy.

My stomach bottoms out almost as quickly as it would if the text were from Zoe telling me something was wrong with Charleigh.

BENEDICT

You think an expensive ring and fancy dress is going to cover up the fact that you come from the south side of Chicago, Reese?

I jerk upright and stare into the empty hall.

Did he follow me to the event?

Is he here?

What if he's one of the donors? Benedict and his family absolutely have the funds to be invited to an event like this.

He's been surprisingly quiet after showing up to the Blue Devils game. There have been a few texts with an apology, but that's it. I never let my guard down when it comes to Benedict, but after Malaki swooped in and kissed me in front of him, I thought that maybe he'd back off.

I was stupid to think that.

The jealousy continues to eat him up.

He wanted nothing to do with me...until I wanted nothing to do with him.

After triple-checking that I'm alone, I rest my head against the door and clench my eyes shut. Deep breaths in through my nose and out through my mouth. I try to visualize the faces sprinkled throughout the sea of people attending the event, straining my memory for anyone I recognize.

"Need a Skittle?"

A yelp tears from my chest, and my phone flies through the air.

Malaki catches it with his fast reflexes before it clatters to the marble floor beneath our feet.

He chuckles at the device in the palm of his hand. "I'll take that as a yes," he jokes.

Just as he's about to hand me my phone, it vibrates. We both drop our attention to it.

Benedict's name flashes on the screen, and Malaki glances up at me with his finger hovering over the word *decline*. I nod, and he follows my silent command.

As soon as Benedict's name disappears, the last text he sent sits on the screen for Malaki to see. I quickly snatch it out of his hand and shove it into my clutch. Guilt hits me, but I have no idea why.

My heart pounds.

Malaki shoves his hands in his pockets and eyes me suspiciously. Those blue eyes, always dancing with mirth, narrow. "What's going on?"

I swallow my thick spit. "Nothing."

His jaw clenches, but he still manages to lift his lip into a knowing grin. "I can tell when you're hiding something, Reese."

My eyes flick in a different direction. "No, you can't."

His deep chuckle snags my attention, and I find myself meeting his eye again. "Your voice gets all high-pitched," he notes, taking a step closer. "And you always look away."

"I do not," I argue.

It takes everything in me not to do just that.

"Your pulse races too."

I scoff. "It does not."

He lifts an eyebrow, and before I can figure out what he's doing, he grips my wrist and presses his fingers to the skin below my palm. "Let's check it, shall we?"

I tug my hand backward, but he doesn't let go.

Malaki's brow furrows beneath the few strands of his hair that have fallen out of place throughout the night. He's silently counting under his breath, and the longer I stare at his mouth moving, the faster my pulse gets.

Those blue eyes flick to mine, and I freeze. "Are you going to tell me what's going on and why you snatched your phone out of my hand faster than I can send a puck flying into the net?"

The thought of going back into the event, with the pretense that Benedict or someone he knows is watching my every move, makes me nauseated, and whether I want to or not, I can't only rely on myself at the moment.

The second I lied and said that Malaki was my fiancé was the second I involved him.

I pull on my arm, and Malaki lets me go.

My hands hang by my sides. "I think Benedict is here." I wince with my admittance. "Or someone he knows. It wouldn't surprise me. He has money. His entire family does."

Malaki's swallow is loud enough for me to hear. His temples move back and forth with the grinding of his jaw, and

I don't know if it's the dark lighting of the hallway that's making him appear dangerous or if it's something else.

"Why do you think that?" he asks.

I reach inside my clutch and show him the message.

It was sent an hour ago, shortly after we arrived.

Malaki scans the text, the phone screen illuminating his stern brow. He quickly clicks my phone off, shoves it into his pocket instead of my clutch, and grabs a hold of my hand.

"I hope he is here," he says, tugging me back toward the event.

"What?" My steps come to a halt. "Why?"

Malaki angles toward me. The flirty glint in his eye switches to a blue flame full of determination and passion. "So I can show him that the ring on your finger isn't just for decoration."

There's a dip in my stomach, and this time, when Malaki tugs on my hand, I make no move to stop him.

Twenty-Nine

MALAKI

"IF YOU SEE HIM, you tell me, yeah?"

Reese peers at me from her shorter frame, that glossy lip tucked in beneath her teeth. She nods before scanning the crowd.

When I came to find her, after talking to Coach Jacobs about the potential to sit me out for the next game to lower the risk of injuries for the playoffs, I was ready to ask her if she wanted to leave, but now here I am, letting my protectiveness take charge.

Don't you mean possessiveness?

I give my subconscious the middle finger and wrap my arm around Reese's waist for all to see.

At least this gives me an excuse to touch her more—something I've been trying to reel in since seeing her in this dress. The slit in the fabric plays with my emotions, and the only thing I want to do is take her back to that hallway we were just in and have my way with her.

I reach up and loosen my tie.

Most of my teammates have made the rounds and left, though there are plenty of donors still lingering with full glasses of liquor.

"I don't see him," Reese says quietly.

I turn my head and brush my nose against her delicate cheek. She tenses at first but turns and gives me more access to her neck. My lips hover over her ear. "Of course you don't."

"Why do you say that?" she asks.

A man as vindictive as Benedict isn't stupid. He isn't going to put himself in a position that could come across as stalking.

"Because he's smart," I admit. "He won't show his face."

Reese's pulse picks up pace the longer we stand at a cock-tail table and scan the crowd. I stare at the little flicker against her neck for several minutes, and I can't stand it any longer. I pull her in front of me, grip her hips, and press her back against my chest. "You've gotta calm down, Dimples."

She inhales, her lungs tight with trapped air. "I know. I just can't."

"Take a deep breath with me." I inhale and hold my breath until she follows suit. Her chest expands, and I get an eyeful of her perfect cleavage.

I blow the air out slowly and watch her chest deflate the same as mine.

"There you go." I swallow. "Let's do it again."

I inhale, she does the same, and then we both exhale at the same time. My warm breath falls to the crook of her neck, and I stare with fascination at the goosebumps that appear on her flesh.

We inhale and exhale again, and this time, I make sure my lips graze the side of her ear. "Good girl."

Reese trembles in my grip, and my dick immediately hardens at the thought of her liking my praise.

Fuck me.

I have to be sensible.

I can't drag her out of this event with hopes of doing something filthy to her in one of the closets. It's not like that between us, as much as my body craves it.

A hot swallow forces itself down my throat when I exhale again, only to be knocked on my ass by Reese's sweet scent.

Quick, think of something that'll douse this fucking fire.

She shifts in front of me, and I grip her hips again. Her ass grazes my dick, and I can't stop myself from grunting.

She glances over her shoulder. "Are you okay? Did I step on your foot?"

I clench my eyes shut. "No."

"No?"

I make a mistake by opening my eyes, my gaze immediately dropping to her lips.

My mouth waters.

We should probably leave so I can put myself in the fucking corner.

"Are you less nervous?" I ask.

She glances at my mouth and then turns away. "Yes."

People are starting to head out, the event closer to ending. I give a tight-lipped smile to a few people I recognize before giving Reese all my attention again.

"You lyin' to me, Dimples?"

I hear her mouth open and then close again. It takes her a few seconds to answer me.

"I'm...distracted," she admits.

Heat rushes my veins, and a raspy hum vibrates my throat. "Are you calling me a distraction?"

She scoffs. "You know you are."

I shrug from behind her, doing my best to keep a little bit of space between her ass and my dick. "That wasn't my plan. But I have to admit it's a good one."

Reese shifts, and we're flush again.

"We should go." The three words slip out from in between my teeth on their own.

I don't want to go, but I'm antsy. My fingers beg to graze more of her body, and all I want to do is grind against her so she can feel how hard I am.

The thought of driving her ex mad gets me off too.

Before she has a chance to move away, I do something impulsive. As if my hand has a mind of its own, it sweeps against the satin fabric of her dress, brushes against the curve of her breast and ends at her chin. With my index finger, I angle her face toward her shoulder where my mouth is waiting.

A surprised noise slips from her, but instead of pulling away, she sweeps her tongue against mine to deepen the kiss.

My knees nearly give out.

Fuck.

I dig my fingers into her hip, and she quickly snaps out of it.

Our kiss ends, and her cheeks burst with heat.

My nostrils flare. "You ready?"

One sharp nod and we're heading outside.

The fresh air sweeps against my heated skin, and I quickly shrug my jacket off to roll my sleeves. I'm hot and bothered, and she knows it.

"Sorry." She nervously pulls on a stray hair that fell into her face. "I got a little carried away with the storyline."

The valet pulls up with my car, but instead of acknowledging him, I reach out and grab onto Reese's wrist. She stops mid-step toward the passenger door.

"Never apologize for kissing me," I say.

Her attention moves below my waist where she felt an obvious bulge a second ago.

Instead of being ashamed and acting guilt-stricken, I chuckle. I erase the space between us and wrap my arm around her waist while opening the passenger door with my other hand. "Don't worry about me," I whisper into her ear. "I know how to take care of myself."

She shifts, and we make eye contact.

The remorse in her eye is gone, and in its place is something so enticing I'm half-tempted to spin her around, press her against the side of my car, and grab that delicious thigh of hers that's been playing peek-a-boo all night and wrap it around my waist.

Jesus.

I am acting insane.

"Do me a favor and stop looking at me like that." I press on her waist and guide her into the car.

When she's tucked inside, I pull the seatbelt and drape it across her body just to get close to her again. For once, she doesn't put up a fight about me doing something for her. She lets me buckle her in without so much as a huff.

Before I shut the door, she stops it with her hand. I drape my forearm on top of the car and raise a brow.

"How am I looking at you?" she asks, fluttering those long eyelashes at me.

I don't sugarcoat it. "Like the idea of me stroking myself gets you hot."

Reese snaps forward and stares out the windshield.

But she doesn't deny it.

Which does nothing but feed my suspicion–my fake fiancée might just want me as much as I want her.

Thirty

REESE

IT'S as if fate knew I needed to be pulled away from Malaki the second we were in the house, because otherwise, I would've made a complete fool out of myself.

Charleigh snuggles into my chest, pressing her cheek against my bare skin with a wistful smile. I rock back and forth while still in my heels, my feet throbbing from all the standing. I wait until she's good and asleep before placing her back into her Pack 'n Play, but before I leave, I shut my eyes and pray that fate is still on my side by the time I get to my room.

Or Malaki's room—our room.

I quietly latch her door and stand with my back against the cool wall before attempting to get my bearings.

Malaki is the last thing I should be thinking about after getting that text from Benedict, yet here I am, full of eager anticipation.

My nerves are fried, and every brief touch from him left a lasting mark. I'm attracted to Malaki—who wouldn't be?—but crossing the boundaries that I vehemently laid out on the table would make me a hypocrite.

Or a woman with needs.

I roll my eyes.

Eventually, I push off from the wall and hobble down the hall. My body reacts as soon as I reach for the handle, as if it knows what's on the other side. I turn the doorknob, and my stomach flutters.

I find him right away, and although my nipples perk at the sight of him sitting up in bed without a shirt on, I silently curse him. If he were asleep, then maybe I could keep my composure. Instead, he's watching some race on the tv with intense concentration.

The lamp on my side of the bed is on, while the one on his side is off. Yet, as soon as he sees me, he turns off the tv, and shakes out his damp hair. "Everything good?" he asks.

My nod is sharp.

I'm clearly on edge, full of nervous jitters. I'm acting like a virgin at the sight of him on the bed, as if he's waiting to claim me.

God. I'm insane.

"I'm going to go get ready for bed," I say.

So I can escape your hot stare.

I take one step toward the bathroom and wince. This is what happens when you're not used to wearing heels. Your feet reject them.

Malaki pops up from the bed. "Are you okay? What's wrong?"

"Nothing. I'm fine–"

I pull my attention from his *very* toned pecs and scan the disapproval on his face.

"It's just my feet," I admit. "I'm not used to wearing heels." I laugh quietly.

I take another step toward the bathroom, and suddenly,

I'm forced to stop in place. Malaki's arm wraps around my waist, and he tugs me backward until he's able to sweep me off my feet.

Physically and metaphorically.

"Malaki! What are you doing?" I hiss.

A deep chuckle vibrates Malaki's chest as he carries me into the bathroom. He flicks the light on and gently places me on top of the vanity. I open my mouth to scold him for picking me up like I'm a toddler, but then he disappears beneath me and grabs my foot.

The pad of his thumb gently brushes against my skin, and I'm rendered speechless. He undoes the clasp around my ankle with his deft fingers, and it's instant relief. A breathy noise flows out of my mouth, and Malaki snaps his eyes to mine. His jaw tightens as he slowly pulls the heel off. He wraps his hand around my foot and gives it a gentle squeeze before massaging the sore skin.

"Better?" His voice is raspy.

I nod once and try to pretend like my heart isn't racing out of my chest.

I can't breathe, my lungs tight with need.

Malaki moves to the other foot with purpose, his fingers making their way to the clasp around my ankle where they brush against my skin. Goosebumps appear on every surface of my body. I inhale shakily, and I know he notices. His cheek twitches, the blue color of his eyes deepening and playing tricks on my mind.

When our gazes snag, his pupils dilate, and that talented tongue of his slips out from behind his lips to wet them.

"There," he says, dropping the other heel onto the floor.

I press my hands into the top of the vanity as hard as I can.

"Thank—" I can't even speak. "Thank you."

Malaki stays crouched below me on one knee with my

ankle still in the palm of his hand. "Need help with anything else?"

Heat prickles my scalp.

Malaki's thumb stops stroking the inside of my ankle, and our eyes catch. That tongue of his darts out again, and I'm suffocating on need.

"Reese?" The way he says my name has me wondering if the string tugging on my desire is tugging on his too.

I'm a ticking time bomb. One more hot touch and I'm bound to show him how desperate I am. All I hear is my heart beating inside my ears. The room narrows in on Malaki, and his hand travels little by little past my ankle and up to my calf.

He massages the muscle there, but I'm irrevocably focused on him.

A slow swallow moves down his throat, making his neck strain. His abs flicker as his fingers glide up to my knee. His hand leaving behind a trail of heat.

"You're trembling," he notes.

I exhale a shaky breath.

"Are you trembling for me, Dimples?" His voice comes out strained, and that's exactly how I feel with the teasing touches against my leg.

He moves up even higher, his hand no longer visible. My dress hides the way his fingers ghost against my inner thigh, and I can't take it anymore. I let my head fall backward and sigh wistfully.

How can a brief touch to my leg feel this good?

"You want me to stop?" he drags the words out slowly.

I make a noise that sounds an awful lot like *no*.

"Thank God," he chokes out.

Without hesitation, he grips my ankle and props it on top of his shoulder before quickly shoving my dress up to my hips. I grab the fabric, bundling the satin in between my fingers to give him more access.

He mutters from in between my legs, "I've been thinking about doing this all night."

Cool air sweeps against me as he pulls my panties to the side.

"We shouldn't be doing this." I say the words, but at the same time, I push myself closer to his warm breath, hoping it'll soften the ache.

"It doesn't have to mean anything, Dimples." He places a soft kiss to the inside of my thigh, and a breathy noise leaves me.

"Promise me it won't change anything," I whisper. "Tell me you won't throw me away after this and kick me out of your house."

Malaki nips the inside of my thigh with his teeth, leaving behind a bite of pain. "That's for even suggesting that I'd do something like that to you and Charleigh."

I swore I'd never trust a man again after Benedict, yet here I am, trusting Malaki with a lot more than just my body.

Malaki's tongue glides over the spot he bit, and the faintest moan slips from my mouth.

"Plus..." his whisper brushes against my skin. "This is just as much for me as it is for you, Reese. I've been craving to find out what you taste like since the second we met."

His candor takes me by surprise but not as much as his tongue does.

Thirty-One

MALAKI

I'VE NEVER BEEN SO passionate about something.

Not even hockey.

The thought of giving up my last breath to taste her was right there on the tip of my tongue, but then she gave me the go-ahead, and I fear I'll never be the same after.

Reese's breathy whimper echoes around the bathroom, and I push her legs farther apart for better access.

She tastes so good I want to spend my entire night with my face buried between her thighs. I flick my tongue against her clit, and her hips move closer. I let up on her for a split second to say, "Show me that you're just as needy as I am."

Our eyes lock and *fucking hell*.

Dazed and lust-driven, she peers at me. I lick her taste off my lips, and pleasure explodes in my blood. "God, you taste so fucking good."

I drop back in between her legs.

Her hips jerk, and I smile against her pussy. *She likes the compliment.*

She moves up and down, faster and faster, and I can't get enough.

I graze my teeth against her clit and groan when she grows wetter.

"I can't get enough." I die a slow death watching my finger disappear inside her. I use my fingers and mouth to bring us both to insanity.

She moans, and I know she's close. I push another finger inside of her, watch in awe at the way she takes them, and then move back to sucking on her clit.

"Oh my *god...*" Her sentence trails, her cunt tightening around my fingers.

I quickly look at her from below and feel like the luckiest man in the entire world.

Her mouth falls open, and a breathy whimper floats into the bathroom.

She is beyond beautiful, especially like this.

"There you go," I coax.

She coats my tongue, and my cock is aching to be inside of her.

"So perfect." I can't stop touching her. "Every single inch of you."

Her bottom lip is tucked in between her teeth, and she looks away.

I'm beginning to know her so well that I can read her mind. If she ends this night thinking that I'm lying about her being perfect, then I've failed.

I remove my fingers from her pulsing pussy and drag my wet fingertips down the inside of her thigh. "Are you trying to argue with me?" I ask.

She says nothing, and I'm quickly reminded of the man who had her before. I've never wanted to prove something to someone so badly before, but with Reese, I'm having all kinds of firsts.

I don't like the thought of his voice inside her head, telling her things that aren't even remotely true.

Nah, *fuck* that.

I stand with purpose and grab her by the hips, sliding her to the very edge of the counter. It forces her to gaze up at me, and it almost brings me to my knees. She's so damn pretty, especially with a fresh glow on her face.

"I can't let this night end without you understanding what you do to me, Dimples."

Reese's eyelashes flutter as I reach behind to unzip her dress. I watch as her back becomes exposed in the mirror and force a tight breath from my lungs. Her dress loosens, and I get a quick glimpse of her soft, full breasts.

She pulls on my strings by just existing.

"There's a reason why Benedict keeps coming back." My teeth graze her earlobe before I tug on it. "It's because you're the whole package."

Her wistful breath is music to my ears.

Blood pumps through my veins, my fingers itching to touch her elsewhere.

This wasn't how I thought the night was going to end.

I told myself to be a decent man and leave her be, but being so close to her all the time is a tease. I know right from wrong, but is it really wrong to indulge in something if it feels this right?

"His insults are a deflection," I say.

With one arm, I pick her up and pull on her dress until it falls to my feet in a heaping pile. "He thinks he can get into your head and make you believe that no one else will want you so you'll end up back with him."

I want to shove every insult he's ever said to Reese down his throat.

The nerve he has to treat a woman like that—especially her, the mother of his child.

He deserves every bit of jealousy he feels knowing she's in my bed each night.

Fake engagement or not, it's my hands that are on her body. Not his.

Instead of placing her back onto the vanity, I wrap her legs around me and walk us over to the wall near the shower. I press her against it, and she arches her back, pressing those soft, full breasts against my chest.

My thighs ache, and I kiss her without thought.

It's a deep kiss, one of carnal need. Her sweet whimper echoes inside my mouth as I plunge my tongue inside, desperate for more.

I break our kiss just long enough to say, "I want him out of your head." There's an edge in my tone, and for once, I hope she detects it.

She wets her lip. "Me too."

My fingers dig into the soft skin of her ass.

"Let me erase him."

It's not really posed as a question, but I wait anyway.

When she answers with a nod, I'm unstoppable.

I hold her steady with one hand and drop my pants. My dick is rock solid. Reese looks down, her eyes widening for a second, and then peers back at me.

"It's unfathomable that you think you're anything less than perfect." I grip myself and squeeze.

Reese exhales, her breasts pressing against me again. She reaches in between us to grip me, and I lose my grasp on reality.

I press her back against the wall and let my head tip backward. She strokes me a couple of times, my dick straining in her small palm, and then she guides me in between her legs.

Heaven.

I press into her, slow and steady.

She's tight, and hot pleasure shoots through my veins.

I grip her ass to slow my thrust so I don't hurt her.

"I'm on birth control," she blurts.

I don't think I care at this point if she's on birth control or not. There isn't much that could get me to stop this now that we're in it.

I keep her steady against the wall as I continue to push into her. I wait so she can get used to me. My entire body is rigid, even my voice. "When was the last time you had sex?"

She glances away, but I refuse to let her look anywhere but at me, so I follow her gaze as she looks in the mirror. She immediately finds me.

"The night I got pregnant."

Wait, what? Why does that make me excited?

"Can you tell?" she asks shyly.

I force a tight swallow down my throat. "You're tight," I admit.

"Sorry–"

My eyebrows cave instantly, and her mouth shuts. "You're sorry?" I shake my head. "You have no fucking idea how good you feel, Reese."

I pull out of her slowly, my heart beating a million miles a minute. She's so wet I swear her pussy is made of silk.

"Fuck," I mutter, pushing into her again.

I fuck her slow. I plan to take my time.

Sweet little whimpers begin to drift from her lips as I move. They do nothing but push me over the edge. I kiss her deeply, exploring her mouth like I need to learn everything there is about it, before moving to her breasts.

The smooth skin calls for my attention. I blow a hot breath against her nipples, and when they harden, I smirk.

"Your body is so responsive to my touch," I say, glancing up at her.

Her warm cheeks and dazed eyes send me to a new high.

If this is only a one-night thing, then so be it.

I'll keep this image of her for the rest of my life.

"Look." With my thumb, I grip the delicate side of her jaw and force her to look in the mirror at herself. "Look at how breathtaking you are."

Her hot noises have my fingers digging into her soft skin.

I clench my teeth. "If I hurt you, tell me."

I reach in between us and rub against her clit as I thrust my hips forward. No fiancée of mine is going to get anything less than multiple orgasms in a night.

"Malaki." My name on her lips is a mindfuck.

I want her to say it again and again.

Reese's hair has slipped out of her bun, tumbling down her back. I grab a hold of the strands and give them a gentle tug so I can press my mouth to her neck.

My heart stops for a second as she tightens around my dick.

Fuck me.

I suck on her skin to keep myself focused so I don't come before she does, but all it does is send her into a frenzy.

I pull back and stare at her in the mirror. She moves against my dick fast and hard with her mouth open and head tipped backward from the pleasure. Her pussy pulses around me from another orgasm, and I struggle to breathe.

Jesus. She's the hottest thing I have ever seen.

A guttural noise leaves me, and I quickly shoot my cum into her, not giving a fuck that I'm more of a *pull-out-just-in-case* type of guy.

I can't.

I can't break away from her.

It's too much.

I get the nerve to meet her eye, and my breath catches.

Her cheeks are as rosy as the flush working itself up my chest. I stare at her swollen, glossy lips and pray to God that this isn't a one-time thing.

Don't deprive me of a little slice of Heaven on Earth, please.

"You okay?" I ask, holding her tightly in my grip.

She places her hands on my shoulders before nodding. She looks exhausted...or sated. Maybe both.

Without letting go of her, I open the shower door and turn the water on. I wait until it's warm enough to create steam and walk us under the stream. I pull out of her, and she winces as I place her feet on the ground.

"You're sore," I say.

She lifts one shoulder, a small smile playing against her mouth.

"I'm sorry," I apologize, spinning her around to rest against me. Water rains on us from above, and she tips her head back to wet her hair.

I run my fingers through the long strands, and she sighs. Neither of us speak while I help her wash her body. I'm careful not to linger too much on her breasts or in between her legs, because it'll lead to places that will make her even more sore.

Eventually, I turn the water off and wrap her in a towel before wrapping one around myself. I stay in the bathroom and watch her get ready for bed.

I feel like a creep, watching her every move with fascination, but she doesn't seem to mind.

We make eye contact on more than one occasion, and each time, a cute blush spreads over her cheeks.

I'm obsessed with it.

Almost as obsessed with watching her eyes flutter closed as soon as she climbs into the bed.

The last thing I think about before falling asleep myself is how on earth can I get this girl to be my real fiancée, instead of my fake one?

Thirty-Two

REESE

WHEN I WAKE the next morning, the sun is already streaming through the window. I sit up and brush my hair out of my face. I immediately look to Malaki's side of the bed, my face heating from the instant memory of what we did last night, but it's empty.

Did that really happen?

I glance at the time on my phone.

Charleigh should be up by now.

My legs get tangled in the blankets, and I fall to the floor with a thud. I quickly climb to my feet and rush toward the door to throw it open. I'm instantly hit with the scent of... bacon?

If I hadn't just fallen like a bag of potatoes out of the bed and hurt myself, I would think I was still dreaming.

In fact, part of me wonders if last night was a dream too.

When I make it to Charleigh's room, it's empty.

Does Zoe have her?

I follow the scent of bacon down the stairs before coming to a complete stop at the sight.

My heart swells as soon as I lay eyes on Malaki, shirtless, holding my daughter. She's happily playing with a spatula, like she's the one cooking breakfast.

"Does your mama like eggs?" he asks her. "Or is she more of a pancake girl?"

Charleigh smiles, and I nearly faint at the sight of Malaki grinning back at her. "You could stop a war with that smile, Charleigh-girl."

And he can apparently stop my entire world by existing.

What have I gotten myself into?

I'm mid-panic when my sister's whisper reaches my ear. "Stop eye-fucking your fake fiancé and just do it already."

I yelp and slap my hand over my mouth to keep my response behind my trapped lips. The last thing I need to admit aloud is that I *did,* in fact, fuck my fake fiancé. I have no idea what he's thinking this morning. Was last night just a moment in time between us where our facade got the best of us? Is he going to pretend that it didn't happen? Was he being serious when he said all those things to me last night, or was he just caught up in the heat of things?

"Ma, ma, ma, ma!"

My hand falls, and I quickly banish the futile thoughts in my head for another time. I smile at Charleigh when Malaki turns to face me. Zoe brushes past with a quick snicker, and if I weren't too busy trying to act normal, I'd stick my foot out and trip her.

Brat.

"Good morning." Malaki's voice is smooth and steady.

Very unlike what I'm feeling at the moment.

"Hi," I squeak.

A loud laugh bursts out from my sister, and I send her a

scathing look. She stuffs a piece of bacon into her mouth to hide her amusement.

"How'd you sleep?" Malaki asks. The longer we stare at each other, the more curved his mouth gets.

I'm almost certain he's grinning at me because he knows I slept like a baby, thanks to the orgasms.

I shrug, playing it cool. "Fine. You?"

"Just fine?" he questions.

He looks at Charleigh with wide eyes. "Did you hear that? Just *fine?*"

"I feel like I'm missing something," Zoe mutters through a mouthful of bacon. "Did something happen last night, and also, I thought cooking was her job?"

"I gave her the day off," Malaki says. "We had a late night."

Malaki and I immediately make eye contact, and my cheeks burn. I walk farther into the kitchen and hold my arms out for Charleigh. Malaki's eyebrows furrow, and he spins away with her in his arms. "Stop stealing my girl," he chides.

His girl?

Why does that make my entire world tilt?

"Did something happen last night?" With a piece of bacon in between Zoe's fingers, she looks between Malaki and me.

"What happened was–"

I cut Malaki off. "Benedict texted me."

His jaw tightens, and the muscles in his temples flicker back and forth. He turns toward the counter, still holding Charleigh tight.

"What did he want?" Zoe asks.

"He wants Reese," Malaki mutters under his breath.

Zoe scoffs. "Well, he can't have her."

I pop a hip. "Obviou–"

"Agreed." Malaki throws his knuckles out for my sister to fist bump, which she does, replying with a stern nod. He then glances to Charleigh and holds his fist out for her too. She looks at it with confusion but smiles when Malaki forms her hand into a little fist and pretends to fist bump himself.

He cheers, praising her for the action, and just like that, I'm swept away into a fantasy land where Benedict doesn't exist and Malaki does.

"Shit. I gotta get to the arena." Malaki tenses before glances at Charleigh. "Don't repeat that word."

I laugh while Malaki whisks over to me. I hold my arms out for Charleigh, who happily climbs into them. "See you later, Charleigh-girl."

My heart warms as her little dimples appear, and I'm pretty sure mine are showing too. Malaki pauses in front of me, his eyes bouncing back and forth between mine. His hair is messy, a lock or two falling onto his forehead when he leans in closer. One of his hands wraps around my waist, and he lowers his voice. "Just fine, huh?"

My cheeks warm as I sink my teeth into my bottom lip. He pulls back slightly and stares directly at my mouth. I lift a shoulder, ready to play it off, but Malaki's cheeky smirk has my mouth twitching to hold back my own smile.

"That's what I thought," he says before bopping Charleigh on the nose.

He strides past us confidently and disappears down the hall to gather his things for their last away game of the season before the playoffs.

When I spin back around, my jaw half on the floor from Malaki's cool exit, my sister is resting against the counter with a sparkle in her eye.

"Don't," I warn, giving her a stern look.

"Do!" Malaki calls from down the hall.

A suck in a lungful of air, and swing around with Charleigh propped on my hip. Malaki winks at me, and this time, I make sure he is completely out of sight before turning toward Zoe.

"My, oh, my," she sing-songs. "You and your fiancé are very flirty this morning... I wonder why that is?"

I huff and grab my own piece of bacon. "Don't you have class or something?"

Zoe rolls her eyes. "Yeah, my friend is outside waiting for me."

I instantly go into mothering mode. "Your friend? Who?"

Zoe comes over and gives Charleigh a kiss on the top of her head before heading for the door. "You don't know him."

"Him?"

"God, not you too." Zoe sighs. "You and Malaki are two peas in a pod."

I take a bite of my bacon. "What does that mean?"

With her hand on the doorknob, she turns and sends me a deadpan look. "He saw Micha drop me off yesterday and quickly began questioning everything there is to know about him."

I slow my chewing. "He did?"

Zoe opens the door. "Yeah. I told him not to worry because I know how to use condoms...unlike my sister."

My mouth falls open, bacon still half-chewed inside.

Zoe laughs loudly. "Oh my god, I'm kidding."

"You better be!" I snap.

She's halfway out the kitchen door when she smiles deviously. "But seriously, there are condoms in my underwear drawer if you need any."

I shout after her, "I'm going to throw a fork at you!"

Unfortunately, she shuts the door before I can grab the utensil.

Charleigh looks up at me with curious eyes.

"Don't you start too," I say, wrinkling my nose at her.

She giggles. "Ma, Ma, Ma."

"Come on, Charleigh-girl," I whisper. "Let's get you ready. Daisy is waiting for us."

———

"Hold on, Char." I shush her whines as she fusses in my arms. "I gotta find my key."

Why is it that my bag turns into Mary Poppin's the second I'm flustered and desperately searching for something? Binky? Lost in no man's land. The house key? Who knows.

Sweat forms on my hairline. Charleigh's whine is three seconds from a full-blown cry. With my free hand, I push my hair out of my face and search again. My fingers brush against the crumbs at the bottom of my bag, and I silently curse.

"Charleigh-girl!" I freeze at the sound of Malaki's voice and frantically look around. I spin, look over my shoulder at our quiet street, and turn back toward the door. Charleigh is just as confused as I am. Her bottom lip stops trembling for a second, and she looks around too.

"Why are you crying?" Malaki asks.

I call out to the abyss. "Who? Me or her?"

"You're crying too?"

Still confused, I spin around once more before exclaiming, "Where are you?"

His chuckle is as smooth as ever. "I'm in Seattle, remember? But I had someone install an alarm with a camera. I kept getting an alert that someone was at the door, so I thought to check, only to find my adorable fiancée stressed to the max."

I follow the sound of Malaki's voice and find the culprit off to the side of the door. Charleigh fusses again, arching her back, seconds from a total meltdown. "Shh," I adjust her on my hip and rub a hand over my moist forehead. "I can't find my keys!"

"Relax. I've got you."

I hear the lock click, and I immediately turn the door-knob. "How did you do that?!"

"The alarm comes with a lock feature too. I can unlock it from my phone."

I glance at the camera with relief. "Thank you."

I'm halfway inside before I stop and lean out the door to look at the camera again. "Wait, when did you have this installed?"

"Today. While you were out." There's a pause. "I didn't like the feeling I had yesterday when I left for the airport."

Charleigh's head rests against my shoulder, seemingly to calm down.

"What feeling?" I ask.

"Uneasy," he says. "I don't like the thought of you and Charleigh being at home alone without me."

My eyes water, and I don't know why.

"Benedict's text bothered me," he adds.

There's a voice that echoes through the speaker, someone calling out his name.

"I gotta head out on the ice," he says.

Right.

He's in Seattle to play hockey.

"Okay..." I step inside the house but lean back once more to wish him luck. "Good luck!"

"I don't need luck. I've got you."

The speaker cuts off, and I dart inside the house to pretend his words had no effect on me.

When I glance at Charleigh, I realize she's fast asleep on my shoulder. Her plump, soft cheeks are no longer red with anger, contentment seemingly settling over her as soon as we made it inside.

Which, ironically, is exactly how I feel too.

Thirty-Three

MALAKI

IT ISN'T OFTEN that I'm completely wired after a game, but since the playoffs start soon, Coach only gave me a few minutes of skate time to eliminate the risk of injury before the most important games.

I easily pull off my dry pads, none of them wet with sweat, and toss them off to the side.

Lars takes a seat beside me on the bench. "You going out tonight?"

Typically, I'd go out for a little while just to keep an eye on Kane and his reckless behavior, but now that he's been tamed by Daisy, he no longer needs me as a babysitter.

I shake my head. "Nah, not tonight."

I've got energy to burn, but the thought of going out doesn't quite entice me like before.

"What? Why not? You always go out!" He stands up abruptly, clearly disappointed. "You hardly played tonight, so don't tell me you're tired. Plus, I saw you sleeping on the plane."

He's right. It's not often that I stay behind with all the married guys holed up in their hotel rooms, so why does the thought of going to the club, or at the very least a cool dinner spot, sound dull?

"Because..." Emory, already dressed with his bag slung over his shoulder, looks at Lars. "He's got a fiancée to spend his evening on the phone with. Maybe you should use that accent of yours and sweet talk yourself into getting a girlfriend."

"I would," Lars argues. "But every time I lay eyes on some gorgeous woman, she ends up being taken by one of you idiots."

A collective chuckle flows throughout the locker room. Everyone except Kane finds Lars's annoyance amusing.

He scowls at him. "Don't even think about Daisy."

"Easy, killer," I echo. "Everyone knows that Daisy is off-limits."

Reese too.

The locker room clears out as we all make our way to the bus. I finally grab my phone, eager to do exactly what Emory suggested.

And what do you know, I already have a text waiting for me from her.

REESE

Malaki.

That's all it says. Just my name. I grin because I know what's coming next. She's just waiting for me to respond.

ME

Dimples.

My phone vibrates as soon as I sit down, and I'm so excited to see her response my heart rate spikes.

REESE

Did you forget to mention that, in addition to an alarm system being installed, you had a crib delivered too?

ME

It was a two-in-one deal. Buy an alarm system, get a free crib. Since I know a baby, it would be crazy to turn it down.

I chuckle to myself.

REESE

That's the most ridiculous thing I've ever heard. Buy an alarm system, get a free crib?

ME

I don't make the rules.

We pull up to the hotel, and I shove my phone in my pocket to exit the bus. Coach Jones and Assistant Coach Crawford garner my attention, along with a few other defensive players, Rhodes included.

"You got plans? We're having dinner at the hotel restaurant and want to discuss some defensive strategies for the playoffs. The standings were just released. One more home game and then it's go time."

They immediately have my attention. "Who are we playing?"

Rhodes, in his gruff voice, answers, "Coyotes."

"Shit." *Talk about a hard opponent.*

Coach Jones raises his brows, waiting for my confirmation of attendance. The whole 'you got plans' wasn't really a question, though. It's implied that I sit my ass down and talk strategy.

"Let me go take my stuff up to the room, and I'll be down," I say.

I step on the elevator and wait until I'm away from my teammates to open my phone again.

REESE

I can't accept this crib.

I knew that was coming.

ME

Good thing it isn't for you.

REESE

Malaki.

ME

Dimples.

I can see her now, trying to hide her smile from me, which does nothing but deepen her dimples.

REESE

Take it back.

ME

Can't, sorry. They said no returns.

REESE

Malaki, please.

My fingers hover over my screen as I reread her text.
It's two words.
Yet, it delivers such a punch.
Reese is dependent on no one other than herself. That's the way she's been since the moment I met her–fighting me tooth and nail every step of the way if I do something that's out of the ordinary. I know she views it as charity, but even worse, she assumes I'll use it against her later down the road, which bothers me more than it should.

ME

> Do you want to know why I bought it?

I know I should put a pause on our texting as I head back out of my hotel room and into the elevator because minutes from now, I'll be in the midst of a game plan and defensive strategies against the Coyotes, except I don't want to end the conversation.

The thought of Reese thinking I'm going to take the crib back or somehow use it against her down the road, enrages me. The need to prove to her that not all men are like Benedict feels too important.

I watch as the floors on the elevator descend.

10, 9, 8, 7, 6...

I think about pushing the emergency stop button just so I can wait a little longer for her response, but I choose to send her another message before she can even type out hers.

ME

> You and Charleigh deserve the best of the best. You are my fiancée, fake or not. I won't let you have anything less.

I slip my phone into my pocket with a proud smile on my face and walk over to where my coaches are seated. Rhodes nods to the beer at the empty spot beside him, and I sit down.

Minutes pass, Coach Crawford speaking of the skill level of the Coyotes and a few players that I know will be difficult to keep up with–difficult, not impossible–and then the waitress comes to take our order.

I take the opportunity to check my phone beneath the table, eager to see if Reese has texted me back.

REESE

> You can't say things like that to me.

My brow furrows.

ME

> Why? Because you're not used to it? That's a tragedy, Dimples. You're just going to have to get used to it.

Rhodes elbows me, and I quickly check back into the conversation. I slide my phone into my pocket and take a sip of my beer. The vibration against my thigh pulls on my attention, but I do my best to stay checked in.

Coach Crawford looks to Coach Jacobs. "We need to change the lines."

Lines being the groups of players that head onto the ice together. Our lines and shifts are changed often, sometimes even during a game to better fit our opponents. Then there's the fatigue too. Sometimes I can barely make it to the bench after a long shift because of my speed.

Coach Jacobs nods sternly. "Tolliver and Page will be best matched up against you." He points to me. "They're just as fast, so you'll be able to keep up."

"Have you studied Berg?" Rhodes raps his knuckle against the table. "He's one of the best goalies in the league."

"Don't let Emory hear you say that," I mutter.

Rhodes chuckles, and the conversation shifts to offense.

My phone is burning a hole in my pocket, so I secretly check it again.

REESE

> You know you don't have to buy us things or treat me like I'm actually going to have your last name one day, right?

Oh, really?

ME

Who says you won't have my last name one day?

REESE

Malaki!

ME

Future Mrs. Young!

This time, I keep my phone in my hand instead of putting it in my pocket. A month ago, I'd be fully engaged in the conversation happening right in front of my face and thinking of nothing but hockey, but since Reese stepped into my life, I have a zest for something else.

There's a new objective that came out of nowhere, and even sitting at a table with two men who hold my future in their hands, I can't seem to dismiss it.

Thirty-Four

REESE

"FINALLY!" I pull the rest of the thread through the needle. My fingers aren't as stable as they normally are, and I'm blaming Malaki's last text for that.

I eye my phone laying beside me on the bed and reread it again.

Future Mrs. Young.

What do I say to that?

I most definitely can't respond in the way that my heart is telling me to, because it's obvious that I'm becoming delusional.

Malaki and his witticism aren't helping matters either. He's easygoing, and flirty, and completely unaware of how much his chivalry means to me. Which is why I have to remind myself that what's brewing between us isn't long-term—or even real.

My phone vibrates again.

I'm currently sitting on *his* bed, trying to convince myself that I'm not actually fantasizing about us being something real one day.

I pause my threading.

He already knows me too well.

I grab my phone and take a photo of my current project resting along my legs and type a follow-up text that says,

If it were anyone else I was texting, I probably would have lied and said I was doing something different, but Malaki has never once made me feel silly or like my hobby was obsolete, so I'll give him this one.

It takes him a little while to text back, but when he does, I slip into a state of insecurity.

I stare at the photo he sent–his large hand wrapped around a beer glass, the amber liquid almost gone. There are people in the background, though blurry, and I can't help but wonder if this fake engagement is holding him back.

What if there is a woman there he wants to pursue?

I know we crossed the line the other night, and Malaki sure does have a way with words, but it's not like we're in a relationship. If I know what's good for me, I won't let us slip up again.

I look at the half-stitched R and sigh.

I'm starting to get invested in us–the ache in my chest tells me so.

MALAKI

I'm supposed to be talking strategy with my
coaches for the playoffs…

ME

But you're at a bar instead?

I get through one stitch before my phone goes off again.

MALAKI

No. I'm at dinner, Dimples…with my
coaches. I'm just not really paying much
attention.

Relief settles in my stomach—something I'm ashamed of.

ME

Then you better put your phone away and
pay attention, Mr. Hockey Hotshot.

MALAKI

I can't.

ME

Why?

My head fills with all sorts of stupid things, like maybe he's too busy thinking about me to pay attention.

Ugh.

I'm acting like a teenager, not a scorned woman with a baby who has too much at stake to fool around with a guy like Malaki.

"Ouch!" I immediately put my finger in my mouth to sooth the prick from the needle. Malaki has me so out of sorts that I just stabbed myself.

MALAKI

Do you want the truth?

Do I?
I swallow and type:

Yes

MALAKI

I'm a little distracted because you sent me a photo of you in my bed where it looks like you're not wearing anything.

My body grows warm. I look at my embroidery hoop as it rests on top of my legs. Did I subconsciously send him a photo with me looking naked from the waist down?

God, I think I did.

Thankfully, I didn't pan the camera up even farther, because then he'd see that I'm wearing one of his shirts and get the idea that I miss him or something.

I'd have to explain that all of mine are in the laundry, which would sort of...kind of...be a fib.

They are in the laundry.

The clean laundry, but who's asking?

MALAKI

Are you?

I sink my teeth into my bottom lip. My fingers move faster than my brain, and before it catches up, I send off a text that I shouldn't.

ME

Guess you'll just have to wonder.

I quickly put my phone face down on the bed to try to focus on my stitch pattern.

It takes a few minutes for the vibrating to start again. The anticipation is so much that I practically throw the embroidery hoop off my lap to grab my phone.

He's video-calling!

Why is he video-calling me?!

I hit decline and toss it off to the side like it's a bomb.

MALAKI

Did you seriously just decline your fiancé's call?

My phone vibrates again, and if there's anything about Malaki I know, it's his unwavering persistence.

I answer at the last second.

"You declined my call," he says smoothly, his voice coaxing me into a state of delusion *again*.

His face comes into view, and his tight angular jaw paired with those blue eyes full of life do something wild to me.

"It...was an accident?" It comes out more of a question than anything.

Malaki chuckles, his lip lifting on one side. He glances away for a brief second before putting his attention back on me. His grin turns into a full-blown smile. "Are you wearing my shirt?"

My excuse is already locked and loaded.

I play it off by rolling my eyes. "Mine are in the laundry... that's okay, right?"

Malaki's neck bobs with a swallow, and the dark area he's tucked himself into while on the phone with me puts shadows on the defined curve of his jaw. "You can wear my shirt every night if you want to. In fact, I prefer it."

A breath catches in the back of my throat, and I hope he doesn't notice.

"Hey," someone says from nearby. "Food is ready."

Malaki nods. "Be right there."

"Did you need something?" I ask.

Malaki opens his mouth, closes it, shakes his head, and then opens it again. "Yeah," he says, voice lower than before.

"Okay..." I let the word linger for a second. "What do you need?"

He stares at me through the phone. "You."

My heart stops.

Every part of me knows I shouldn't engage in this because the more lines we cross, the more willing I am to erase them. I can't think of a time where I've ever craved someone's attention like this before. In fact, I've forbidden myself from needing anyone or anything for years. Yet, with Malaki involved...I can't seem to remember that.

"Don't stop texting me," he rushes out.

Then he hangs up.

My phone remains in my hand, and I stare at it with shock.

What just happened?

An incoming text buzzes against my hand.

MALAKI

I can't stop thinking about the other night.

For a split second, I swoon. But then I banish it away and remember what's at stake.

MALAKI

Do you regret it?

My fingers fly across the screen.

ME

No.

I stare at my response with wide eyes and type another message.

ME

I mean yes!

Ugh!

ME

I don't know.

I'm sweating. I pick up my needle and thread, as if needlepoint is going to distract me.

MALAKI

You do know. You're just trying to do what you think is right.

ME

How do you already know me so well?

I thought I was doing an okay job at keeping him at arm's length, but I was painfully wrong.

MALAKI

Because I pay attention.

Tell me something. Why does the other night have to be wrong?

ME

Because! There have to be boundaries.

It's to protect Charleigh—and myself. If Malaki and I start complicating things by adding whatever *this* is to the mix and then it turns sour...we'll be on the streets. Benedict will have an absolute heyday with that.

MALAKI

You should trust your fiancé, Reese. We're
going to be married after all. There's no
need for boundaries.

I can almost picture his grin.

He never misses an opportunity to mention that we're engaged.

MALAKI

Do you trust me?

My fingers still above my phone, afraid to send the message.

Deep down, though, I know the answer.

I think he does too.

ME

Trust is a fickle thing.

It takes him a few minutes to text back, and by the time he does, I'm pacing the bedroom.

MALAKI

That isn't an answer.

He's not going to give up until I answer him. I know it.

MALAKI

Don't let him make you untrusting, Dimples.
He's done enough.

My paces stop, my phone like a brick in my hand.

Malaki is playful and light-minded nine times out of ten, but then he says things that make me pause, and I realize he's so much more than he lets on.

I type something that sends a line of fear through me.

ME

I do trust you.

I shut my eyes and flop onto the bed with my phone pressed against my chest.

Malaki texts back quickly.

MALAKI

I won't betray it.

Please don't.

MALAKI

But now…I have another question.

Thirty-Five

MALAKI

I SLOWLY CHEW MY STEAK, only paying half-attention to my coaches. We've moved on from strategy building to trying to predict who will win what game and who we'll play after we sweep the Coyotes.

I'm floating after rereading Reese's text. She trusts me, and that means so much more to me than I expected.

I hope I don't fuck it up with this next text, but after the other night, I know she's gotta be feeling the remnants of my mouth on her just like I'm remembering how good her skin felt against mine.

ME

Have you ever sexted, Dimples?

I tip my beer back, the sweating glass moist against my hand. I wipe it on my pant leg, and it just so happens, my phone is laying there for the taking.

REESE

Do you consider someone sending me
unsolicited dick pics sexting?

Suddenly, I want to hunt down every man who's sent her an unsolicited photo of their dick and knock their teeth out.

ME

Not in the slightest.

I take another bite of my steak and nod along with Rhodes, who's much more involved in the conversation with our coaches than I am.

I don't even know what he just said.

My phone vibrates again, and I wait until the attention moves from me to glance down.

REESE

Then no. I haven't.

So I'll be her first?

I manage to keep myself from grinning slyly.

ME

Can I be your first?

The thought of taking all her firsts is tempting. It's such a possessive thing to want, but damn, I want it.

I bounce my attention back and forth from my lap to the conversation happening at the table. It's a task that I have to force myself into. Paying attention to Reese? I'm an expert. Listening to my coaches? At the moment, it's like pulling teeth.

REESE

I don't really know how to.

I know I have a baby and all, but I'm not as experienced as one would think.

That shouldn't be relieving to me, but it is.
I want her all to myself for as long as she'll let me.

ME

Want me to teach you?

REESE

Have a lot of experience sexting women, Malaki?

There's that streak of feistiness that only comes out every so often. I love it.

ME

I haven't sexted since I was a horny teenager… and I sure as hell have never sexted while at an important dinner with my coaches.

Not to mention, I've never sexted my fiancée before.

Every time I call her my fiancée, the more I love it.

REESE

*fake fiancée.

I snort and try to cover it up with a cough.

Rhodes glances at me sharply, and suddenly, my coaches are side-eyeing me. I clear my throat and make something up. "Sorry, I was just picturing Knight's face when he realizes that he's going up against me for the first game."

Knight's stats are constantly compared to mine. The media paints us out to be rivals, but the truth is, I don't even know the guy.

Thankfully, Coach Jones takes the bait. It sends the

conversation on a loop, circling back to the Coyotes' best players.

ME

> I was about to send you a dick pic, but never mind now.

REESE

> Are you using that as a punishment for correcting you?

ME

> For now, but just wait until I get home.

My dick gets hard at the mere thought of being with her instead of here.

REESE

> It's the truth, though. Our engagement isn't real, remember?

Stop reminding me.

I place my beer back to the table with a little more force than before.

ME

> Knock it off, or I'm going to have to make you pay when I get home.

All sorts of dirty things roam throughout my head.

REESE

> Pay how?

I can't decide if she's playing coy or not.

ME

Well, for starters… I'd wait until you were asleep, and then I'd pull you in extra close since I know how much you like to be the little spoon.

REESE

What? That isn't true!

I glance to the table, seeing that most of the plates are empty. *Thank God.*

ME

It is true. You like to cuddle in your sleep.

Each time her ass rubs against me, it's fucking torture. The first night she slept in my bed, I had to face the other direction to stop myself from sneaking off into the bathroom to rub one out like a perv.

REESE

That's so embarrassing.

MALAKI

It's not embarrassing to need me, Dimples.

"Are you finished with your meal, sir?"

I glance at the waiter. "Uh, yeah. I am."

He takes my plate, and Rhodes cocks an eyebrow. "You didn't eat much."

I shrug. "I'm tired."

"You barely played tonight. How are you tired?"

He tries to hide his knowing grin.

I turn away to ignore him and go back to my phone.

He chuckles and sits up a little taller, manhandling the conversation.

It may be my imagination that he's doing it so I can continue texting Reese, but I'll take it for what it is.

REESE

Just because I happen to accidentally bump you while sleeping does not mean I need you!

ME

Maybe…but you sure needed me the other night.

Quick visuals of Reese naked come to the forefront of my brain, and I'm forced to adjust myself.

Where the hell is the check?

ME

Not going to deny that? Good. Now let's get back to how I'd make you pay if I were there. After I pull you in close, I'd rest my hand against your hip, just like I've been doing every night when you press up against me.

REESE

You haven't been doing that…

Have you?

I place my Amex down before the waiter has a chance to dip away from the table again.

Coach Crawford laughs. "Eager to get to bed, Young?"

I shrug. "What can I say? Sitting on the bench is tiring."

Coach Jones digs for his wallet. "Gotta save your strength and energy for the playoffs."

I tip my beer at him before taking a gulp then immediately get back to my phone.

ME

> I have. You sleep better when I have my hand there.

It's the truth. Otherwise, she's restless. The first night I did it, I was cautious, afraid she'd wake up and accuse me of trying to touch her while she was asleep, but she sighed wistfully and didn't move an inch for the rest of the night.

REESE

> That's sort of…sweet.

> Unless you're being a creep and just wanting to cop a feel.

ME

> If I'm going to touch you like that, I want you fully awake so I can watch you come undone.

Rhodes elbows me from the side, and I snap my head up from looking at my phone under the table.

Goddamnit.

The waiter is in a fully engrossed conversation with Coach Jones about hockey—me in particular. They're both staring at me, dragging this night out even further. My credit card is in his hand with a pen and receipt.

"Need my autograph?" I ask.

The waiter's eyebrows shoot up. "Dude, yes."

My mouth twitches. "I was referring to the receipt, but I'll give you an autograph too."

Anything to get you over here faster so I can go up to my room and concentrate on these texts with my fiancée.

Mid-signature, I feel a vibration against my leg. I grip the pen tighter to keep myself from throwing it off to the side so I can grab my phone.

The waiter stares at my autograph. "Thanks, man."

"No problem."

He makes his way to Rhodes and the rest of the guys as I sit impatiently.

I sneakily read Reese's text.

REESE

So what you're saying is that you'd wake me up in order to pay me back?

ME

To start with.

Intrigued, Dimples?

REESE

Okay…then what?

I take that as a yes.

After glancing at the waiter, who's becoming a pain in my ass, I scoot my chair back to speed things up.

ME

I'd rub your hip until your shirt slipped to reveal your soft skin. Then I'd move my hand just a bit and start over on your skin.

My coaches stand to leave, and I quickly follow suit, pulling down on my pants to conceal my semi-hardon.

"Eager much?" Rhodes mutters.

"You would be, too, if you were in my shoes."

"You starting something with her?" he asks in a low voice, following everyone to the elevator.

According to her? No.

According to me? It started from the beginning.

I shrug and shove my phone farther into my pocket.

After saying bye and getting a verbal reminder of what time to be on the bus in the morning, everyone but Rhodes disappears in the other direction.

I stop in front of my door to let him pass. "Later," I say.

"Make sure to get some rest..." he calls over his shoulder.

I furrow my brow. Since when is he concerned about my rest?

He rounds the corner, and his voice echoes down the hall. "You know...in between beating your dick off to those texts."

"No promises," I call out jokingly.

But it's not really a joke at all, now that I think about it.

Thirty-Six

REESE

DAISY

A good friend would probably tell you to listen to your instincts, but I'm going to have to disagree with your instincts on this one. Keep texting him.

ME

My instincts are never wrong.

DAISY

Fine. Say you're right and this ends badly. You and Char can just live with me.

I roll my eyes. I'd never bombard a friend like that—not with all the baggage I have.

DAISY

Seriously, though. Might as well have some fun while you're playing make-believe, right? Knowing Malaki, he's probably trying to actually convince you to marry him.

I laugh.

She's right, even though I know he's kidding.

He has to be.

I'm a jobless, college-dropout, single mother with an obsessive ex.

Another text comes in right after Daisy's, and I already know it's Malaki without looking.

MALAKI

Either you're having second thoughts about sexting, or Charleigh woke up.

Since he loves to act like he knows me better than I think, I send him for a curve.

ME

Maybe the sexting is just that good that I was preoccupied. 😉

MALAKI

Mic drop

A laugh bursts out of my mouth.

ME

Kidding.

MALAKI

Good, because that'd be breaking the rules.

ME

There are rules?

MALAKI

Well, yeah, Dimples. So far, all I've said is that I'd be touching your hip. You have to do what I'd do if I were there. No other touching allowed.

My first instinct is to defy him, but then this whole texting exchange would be over. I'm sort of enjoying it. The anticipation of his message is exhilarating, so instead of putting a stop to it, I sink down onto the bed and get comfy.

ME

Okay, fine. So nothing more than minimal touching as of right now. Got it.

MALAKI

You got my t-shirt pulled up high so you can run your fingers along your hip and stomach?

I glance down and squirm, because of course I do.

ME

Yes.

MALAKI

Show me.

A shyness comes over me, but it only lasts a second. I think about the other night, and I'm suddenly filled with confidence. Remembering Malaki's rushed hands and his earth-shattering kiss had me thinking I was the most desirable thing he's ever seen.

I snap a photo, angling the phone to show my legs, panties, and bare stomach. His t-shirt lays just above my naval, and part of me wants to pull it up even more.

MALAKI

Look at you...already mastering sexting.

I blush from the half-compliment.

I've never craved to please someone so much before. I'll deny it day in and day out, but the slight ache in between my legs tells the truth.

My fingers brush back and forth against my warm skin,

getting closer and closer to the top of my panties. Another text comes through.

MALAKI

Tell me something…when was the last time you touched yourself?

My fingers pause. My heartrate spikes.
I type slowly and put my phone face down after I hit send.

ME

I…don't know. After having Charleigh, I went into survival mode. There isn't a lot of alone time when you have a baby, work all night, and share an air mattress with your younger sister.

MALAKI

Sounds like we have lots of orgasms to make up for, babe.

Why do I like that he called me babe?
Why do I like *him?*

MALAKI

Take your panties off.

I rush to pull them off, excitement flowing to my fingertips, but my phone goes off again.

MALAKI

Slowly.

My breathing is labored.
I do exactly as he says. I shimmy them off slowly and find myself picturing Malaki's fingers hooking beneath the cotton to pull them off himself instead of me.
I type **done** and hit send.
A minute passes and then another.

I watch little bubbles pop up, only for them to disappear.

The longer he takes to text me back, the more nerves fill my stomach. Where'd he go? I sit up on my elbows and glance at my naked bottom half before typing a message.

ME

Is this how you'd pay me back? Leave me half-naked on your bed?

I hit send, and no more than five seconds later, his name flashes on the screen with an incoming call.

I freeze, my fingers itching to answer.

I go back and forth over whether or not to answer, until I finally hit accept.

His smooth voice comes over the speaker, and goosebumps race against my skin. "She answers…"

"I know you'll just call back if I don't," I say.

"So you're learning." He chuckles. "Good."

I nibble on my lip. My panties rest right beside my foot. I'm tempted to put them back on, because what are we doing right now?

"Why'd you call?" I ask, my voice lower than before.

He makes a noise that resembles a hum. "I was arguing with myself…"

My brows dip with confusion. "About?"

"Whether or not I should continue texting you or video-call you."

I adjust the phone against my ear. "But you didn't video-call me."

"I know."

"Why?" I ask.

"Because if I see you in my bed, I might be tempted to book a red-eye back to Chicago."

A smile refuses to leave my face. "That would be crazy."

He scoffs through the phone, his voice echoing. "That's

sort of what you do to me, Reese. You make me want crazy things, and I find myself doing crazy things just to talk to you, or see you smile, or…"

His voice trails, and I swallow.

"Or what?" I whisper.

"Or touch you," he answers. "It wasn't my plan to cross the line last night after helping you with your shoes. I just couldn't seem to help it."

I bite the inside of my cheek while my head runs circles. I'm clinging to his every word like it's a cure to every one of my problems.

"I can't help it either," I admit. "Do you think I want to be lying here in your bed, desperate for your attention? It makes me feel weak…and needy." I laugh sarcastically. "I don't know what's wrong with me."

He's quick to respond. "There isn't a single thing wrong with you."

"I don't know about that–"

He cuts me off. "I like you like this."

Butterflies pull on every single string of my heart.

"I like you needy," he says. "I like you desperate for my attention too."

I think back to every time I've been called desperate or needy, and a sense of hurt comes with it. It was depicted as a negative thing from not only my parents but boyfriends too. Especially Benedict.

"I can't get you out of my head, especially knowing you're in my bed, desperate for my touch." He makes a noise that sounds a lot like a groan. "It's a turn-on, Reese."

A shaky breath leaves me, but I say nothing.

"That noise too," he whispers. "A total fucking tease."

"All I did was breathe," I argue.

"Exactly."

I laugh, but it's breathy. He makes another noise of satisfaction, and my skin heats.

"Tell me you're as desperate for me as I am for you."

My smile fades, and there's a pull in between my legs. I squirm against the covers. "I am," I admit quietly. "I'm desperate for a lot more than your touch, though."

"Tell me," he urges.

A tinge of embarrassment stings my skin. I reach over and turn the light off before admitting anything. At least now the walls aren't staring at me.

"I'm desperate for everything. Your attention, your touch, your kiss..." I can't believe I'm admitting this.

"Anything else?" His voice is edged with something tight.

When I say nothing, he sighs. "Don't get shy, Dimples."

"Your praise," I quickly blurt. "I like it, okay? I like... pleasing you."

He curses. "*Fuck me.* That might be the hottest thing I have ever heard in my life."

I put my phone on speaker but turn the volume down just in case Zoe happens to come home. My hands rest against my stomach, and my pulse beats everywhere.

"If you like pleasing me, then I want you to do exactly what I tell you to do."

I swallow.

"Can you do that for me?" he asks.

I shiver. "Yes."

"Spread your legs."

I spread my legs on top of the bed.

"Okay," I exhale. "I did it."

"Good," he murmurs. "Now slide your hand down your body until it's in between your legs."

My nipples harden as soon as I drag my palm past my belly button. Heat pools at my center, my body throbbing for my fingers in a way it never has before. I make a noise that sounds a lot like a whimper.

"That's it..." Malaki encourages. "Let me hear every sexy little noise."

My breaths are choppy, my chest moving quickly. "Now what?"

"Are you wet?"

I quickly skim my fingers against my warm flesh, not needing to slip a finger in between the folds to find out. "Yes."

"Good," he says. "Now give your clit the attention it deserves."

I waste no time.

My fingers find the spot my body needs, and I begin to unravel. I rub fast circles against my clit, my legs spreading even wider, desperate for a release. A slight moan leaves me in the midst of pleasure, and Malaki curses again.

"Fuck, I might get off just listening to you."

I whimper again, my fingers working faster than they ever have.

"Jesus Christ." His voice is strained, and it sends me into a frenzy. "Give yourself what you need, Reese. Put your fingers exactly where they need to go."

I take my other hand and slip a finger inside. When I realize it isn't enough, I push another one in and make a noise of satisfaction.

"How many fingers are inside?"

"Two," I breathe out.

"Your voice...*goddamn,*" Malaki groans.

I say nothing, too preoccupied in the pleasure.

"You're doing so good, Reese."

My entire body heats.

"Don't get shy. Your sweet moans are safe with me."

Oh my god.

I make one more noise, and suddenly, I'm falling into an altered state. My fingers work in overtime, my back arching for more.

"There it is." Malaki's voice is distant, but it's the final push I need to truly let go. "God, you're mesmerizing, even through the phone."

I'm still riding out my high when I hear Malaki groan on the other end of the phone. He curses under his breath, and the thought of me turning him on from across state lines is addicting.

My body finally relaxes, and I pull my fingers out from between my legs, letting my arms fall to my sides.

"That's my girl," Malaki whispers, his voice hardly hitting my ears. "I'm proud of you."

The smallest smile slips onto my lips.

"Sleep, Dimples. You deserve it."

It takes effort to speak, but I take full advantage of my high and say something I wouldn't have admitted prior. "I sleep better when you're here."

"I know you do," he says. "I'll stay on the line all night, babe."

I roll over, pull the covers up, and put the phone beside my ear. "Thanks."

"Sweet dreams, Dimples."

———

I smile with a coffee mug pressed against my lips, already done with cleaning the kitchen after prepping dinner for this evening. Charleigh is at my feet, playing with her new favorite toy—a spatula—while I daydream about a make-believe future with Malaki, who I'll see later on today.

My phone was dead as a doorknob this morning. I frantically sat up in bed, wearing nothing but Malaki's t-shirt, my panties thrown off to the side somewhere.

I quickly plugged it into the charger, and as soon as it came back to life, a text from Malaki was waiting for me.

MALAKI

Your phone must've died while you were sleeping. I'll be home later today. Can't wait to see you and Charleigh-girl.

I squealed like a teenage girl and flopped back onto his bed. While bouncing back and forth between rationality and a state of utter delusion where Malaki and I end up happily ever after together, raising Charleigh, without Benedict showing up like some sort of plague, Char woke up, and I slipped into mom mode.

That isn't to say I haven't been eagerly checking the time, waiting for him to walk through the door.

"What am I going to do, Char?" I ask, taking a sip of my coffee.

She looks up at me from the kitchen floor and smiles.

I bend and give her a kiss on top of the head. "I love you, pretty girl."

"Ma...ma!"

"What will we do when this is all over?" I ask. "Move into our own place? Stay friends with him?"

Charleigh smiles. "Ma...ma!"

"I'm not even sure when this will be over." I rub the pain in the center of my chest.

The thought of it being over should feel like a weight being lifted off my shoulders, because that means Benedict has finally moved on. Yet, there's dread that comes with it.

"Ma...ma!"

I smile. "Can you say... *Malaki*?"

Charleigh stares at my mouth.

"Right, that's way too complicated." I tap my chin. "What can you call him?"

"I know!" Zoe comes into view. "Dada!"

I stand abruptly. My coffee spills out from the top of my mug onto the counter. "That is not funny!"

"Daa."

I gape at Charleigh.

Her lips try to form the word again.

"Daaa."

Zoe bursts out laughing.

"Zoe!" I shout.

There's a knock at the door, and I'm pretty sure it's karma.

I point at my sister. "You better come up with other words that start with Da right now!"

My sister snorts out a laugh and gets on Charleigh's level. "Damnit?"

"Zoe, I swear!" I call out over my shoulder.

The fancy doorbell that Malaki had installed makes a chirping noise before being followed by another knock.

I open it, still preoccupied with Charleigh and the word dada to register who it is.

"Mrs. Moreno?"

I come face to face with a man who looks to be in his forties. There are dark bags on his face, his eyes tired looking. It sends me back to my childhood when my father tried selling vacuums for fast cash. He'd go door to door with hope gleaming in his eye, only to take out his frustrations on my sister and me when he made next to nothing on commission.

"Sorry," I apologize kindly. "We're not interested."

I move to shut the door but stop at the last second.

How does he know my name?

"Wait! Are you Mrs. Moreno?"

I pull the door open slightly, "It's Ms. Moreno."

He pushes an envelope into my chest. "You've been served."

The blood drains from my face as I watch him walk away.

Thirty-Seven

MALAKI

AS SOON AS the plane touches down, I turn my phone back on. My pulse thrums, eager to see a text from Reese. Surely she's awake by now.

Last night will live in my head for the rest of my life. Hearing her get off over the phone was better than anything I could've imagined, and I have a pretty wild imagination.

Once my phone is back in action, I frantically search the screen for an incoming text, but instead, I see a doorbell notification.

I get a notification every time someone leaves or enters the house. When I replay the video, I watch a man stand on the front porch with something in his hand. The only comforting thing is that it isn't Benedict, but I wouldn't put it past him to send someone else to torment Reese, because he's nothing but a coward in my eyes.

I wait until I'm in my car, away from my teammates, who are all just as eager to get home, to open the video again.

He says her name.

My spidey senses tingle.

"We're not interested," she says to him kindly.

He repeats her name, and I zoom in on whatever he's holding.

She corrects him with skepticism. "It's Ms. Moreno."

I think she means *It's Future Mrs. Young*, but I digress.

He shoves something into her chest, and my blood pressure rises. "You've been served."

I grip the steering wheel. "Fuck."

I quickly click my phone off and throw my car in drive.

My airy mood that carried on from our late-night phone call vanishes before I'm out of the parking lot. I have six days before we're on the road to play the Coyotes to help Reese figure out whatever it is that Benedict just pulled.

I hope it's enough time.

Better yet, I hope she's willing to let me in instead of trying to figure it out on her own.

I waste no time climbing the porch steps and walking into the house. I drop my bag and kick the door shut with my foot. "Reese?"

Zoe appears at the end of the hall from the kitchen. The closer I get, the more my shoulders tighten. Charleigh is on her hip and smiles at me immediately.

I grin. "Hey, Charleigh-girl."

Zoe tucks her lip beneath her teeth, just like her older sister does.

We make eye contact, but she says nothing.

"Where is she?" I ask.

Better yet, where is Benedict? I'd really enjoy finding him first.

"How do you–"

"Doorbell," I say.

She inches her chin toward the stairs.

Zoe's spunk is gone, which is unsettling to say the least. I follow her line of sight and see a manila folder on the bar top with a few scattered papers on top.

I quickly scan them, seeing the word *mediation* repeated several times.

"Mediation?" I repeat. "What does that mean?"

"It's where Benedict will probably spin the truth and paint Reese out to be a terrible mom in front of a third party, like a mediator, to try to force her hand into whatever he wants so they don't have to have a custody battle."

My eye twitches.

I know exactly what he wants, and it isn't Charleigh.

"And if she doesn't give in?" I ask.

Zoe sighs. "Then he'll probably drag her in front of a judge."

As if there's an invisible string tying me to Reese, I turn on my heel and head right for her. I begin climbing the stairs, only to stop when Zoe calls my name. I lean over the banister, my hand gripping the railing.

"She's freaking out."

I know she is.

"And she's going to shut you out."

I squeeze the banister tightly, my veins filling with hot blood. A desperation comes over me as I make my way up the stairs. I head for Charleigh's room. I don't know how I know she's in there, but as soon as I push on the door, opening the gap a little more, I see her.

She has her long hair piled in a high bun on top of her head, wearing a large sweater that swallows all of her curves and a pair of black leggings. Her bare feet slap against the hardwood floor as she paces back and forth, her thumb nail being gnawed off from her nerves.

I rest my shoulder against the doorjamb and cross my arms. My heart beats a million miles a minute as I try to come up with not only a plan to convince Reese that she doesn't have to face Benedict alone, but also a plan on how to give Benedict a taste of his own medicine so he'll stop harassing her.

Reese may be my fake fiancée and our engagement a ruse, but that doesn't mean I won't do everything in my power to protect her and Charleigh.

I'll marry her right now if that's what needs to be done.

I'll adopt Charleigh too.

I'd be an awesome stepdad.

Bro, chill.

"Reese."

Her gasp cuts through the empty room. She spins, and our eyes clash.

"Malaki." The hand she has up to her mouth drops. "I didn't realize you were home."

I narrow my gaze. I already know where this is going. "Everything okay?"

"Hmm?" Her voice is high-pitched. "Yes, everything is... great." She smiles, and although it takes my breath away, I can see right through it. "How was the flight?"

I push off from the doorjamb and shove my hands into my pockets. "It was okay. How was your morning?"

Don't do it.

Don't hide from me.

Reese brushes a tendril away from her face and glances at Charleigh's crib–the same one I bought on a whim because I was unsatisfied with what she was in before. Her neck moves with a slow swallow, her lower lip slipping beneath her teeth.

"Dimples."

I take a step toward her, but she doesn't look at me.

I've never felt a pull as strong as this. That invisible string tugs me closer, and as if the room is closing in on us, I end up right in front of her.

"You should really let me do my job," I say.

She turns, her eyes glassy. "Play hockey?"

I shake my head. "It's my job as your fiancé to give you a shoulder to lean on…"

"You're my fake–"

I grab her mid-sentence and pull her into my chest. I gently grip the side of her face, cradling her close. She freezes for a second, her shoulders tense, and I press my mouth to the top of her head, placing a kiss there. A shaky exhale leaves her, and something wet rolls over my knuckles.

"I'll marry you right now if that's what it'll take for you to stop saying that," I murmur against her hair.

She sniffles and shakes her head against my chest. "You're crazy."

I am. For her. For Charleigh.

I don't know when it happened, but I'm done for.

Moving her away from my chest, I grip both sides of her face with my hands and peer down into her watery eyes.

It cuts me to see her like this.

Pink splotches dot her cheeks, the warm brown color of her eyes filled with fear.

It does far more than increase my need to win this little game that Benedict is playing with her.

"We're going to figure this out together, okay?"

She tries to shake her head but doesn't get very far with my hands gripping her cheeks.

A shaky breath leaves her. "I think I've involved you enough. You have the playoffs to worry about—you know… your actual job, not the one where you pretend to be my fiancé."

I don't care.

Wait, I don't?

Instead of cracking open my chest and letting the truth spill out to scare her, like it just did to me, I lift a shoulder. "I can multitask, Dimples."

Her mouth twitches.

"I have the day off," I say. "Let me make you, Char, and Zoe—if she's staying in—dinner, and then we'll learn all there is to know about mediations and how to prepare. Yeah?"

She sniffles. "I already prepped dinner for you. That's my job, remember?"

Of course she did.

"Save it," I say. "I'm making dinner tonight."

Reese stares at me incredulously, a tiny line forming in between her eyebrows. "You can cook?"

"I cook and clean. The only reason I have you doing both is because I know you won't let me pay you otherwise."

Her lips flatten, but I know there's no use in arguing about it.

"I have a lot of skills..." I add. "Hidden skills." I wiggle my eyebrows in an attempt to lighten the mood.

A blush spreads over her cheeks, replacing the pink splotches from her tears. I interlace our fingers and guide us toward the door. "I'll show you those skills too," I whisper into her ear. "But later."

She huffs out a laugh and smacks me on the arm with her other hand, except I catch it midair. I tug her in close and wind my arm around her lower back to keep her steady. "You think I'm kidding, Dimples?"

I drop my gaze to her mouth, her lips begging to smile.

"I hope not," she whispers.

Green light.

I press a quick kiss to her mouth, catching a lost breath on the edge of her lips. When we pull apart, I force a swallow down my throat and keep her hand in mine as we make our way back downstairs.

When we get closer to the kitchen, I hear Zoe talking to Charleigh.

"No...say damnit," she says.

My brows furrow, and I glance to Reese.

She shakes her head. "Don't ask."

Thirty-Eight

REESE

"RIGHT HERE! LOOK AT MOMMY!" I snap my fingers a few times to get Charleigh's attention. "Charleigh-girl! Let me see your cute bow!"

Daisy laughs from the couch.

Charleigh is clearly ignoring me on purpose. She takes her little fingers and rubs them over the rug in the living room like it's some sort of magic carpet.

"Oh fine," I huff. "I won't send your picture to Malaki, then."

No more than a second later, Charleigh perks up.

"Da?" she says.

Not again.

When I say nothing, she does it again, only this time louder. "DA?"

"Is she—"

I interrupt Daisy. "No! She isn't."

"I'm pretty sure she's calling Malaki–"

I hop up from being on the floor. "Nope!"

"Okay...whatever you say..." she muses.

I flop onto the couch, my camera still ready to snap a photo. "It's Zoe's fault! She made a joke, and it stuck."

"It wasn't a joke." Zoe walks into the living room with popcorn. She sits it down on the coffee table—the same one Charleigh is using to stand. I smile at the colorful Skittles mixed in–something Malaki started the other night while we all sat in the living room, learning all there is to know about mediations.

He's kept my feet on the ground, always knowing when to distract me and even forcing Charleigh and me to his last home game just so I wasn't stuck at home, researching more custody cases.

That, and I think he may have wanted to show Charleigh off. He took her for a spin on the ice, and the image will stay with me forever.

"Either way," I reach for a Skittle, going back to the conversation. "It isn't funny."

"Malaki thinks it is," she mumbles.

I sit taller. "Excuse me?"

"Isn't that right, Char?" Zoe straightens Charleigh's blue bow, gifted to her by Emory's wife. "Malaki's been teaching you to say Dada, huh?"

Charleigh smiles. "DA!"

My jaw hangs loose.

"Hurry! She's smiling!" Daisy snatches the phone from my hand and snaps a picture. "Oh my god, look at how cute she is."

She angles the phone toward me, and I immediately smile.

"She is pretty cute, huh?" I take the phone back and glance at the TV.

It's only a few minutes until the puck drops for their first playoff game, but I take my chances and fire the photo off to Malaki with a message that says **Char says good luck**.

I settle back onto the couch. My stomach fills with nerves, like I'm the one who's playing in the playoffs.

"You know, this is all Kane has ever wanted," Daisy says, leaning back beside me.

We're both wearing Blue Devils jerseys, courtesy of Kane and Malaki. When she showed up to watch the game with me, wearing Kane's, she forced me up the stairs to wear one of Malaki's. She says it's a game-day tradition, something about it being good luck.

"You mean, besides having you?" I say, laughing.

Daisy tucks a strand of her blonde hair out of her face, showing off her blush. "Shush."

My phone vibrates in my lap with Malaki's name flashing on the screen.

"Why is he calling?" I exclaim. "Shouldn't he be on the ice by now?"

I glance at the TV, but it's a commercial.

"Well, answer it!" Zoe urges.

I scramble to pick it up. "Hello?"

Malaki, helmet and all, smiles when I come into view. Even with his helmet on, I can see his clear blue eyes as if he's in front of me and not in a completely different state. "Let me see my girl," he says.

I turn the camera quickly to hide my smile.

Charleigh's eyes light up. She moves up and down with her hands smacking on the coffee table. "DA!"

"Charleigh-girl! Are you rooting me on?"

She bounces again, her gummy smile so wide my heart catches.

She loves him. How could she not?

I turn the phone back around with the chatter increasing in the background. Several Blue Devils players appear in the frame, most likely walking toward the rink. "You better go," I warn. "It's not like you're about to play one of the most important games of your career right now!"

Malaki's eyes narrow through the phone. He pauses, the phone no longer swaying. "Excuse me, future Mrs. Young...are you wearing *my* jersey as opposed to the one I got you?"

I pan the camera to Daisy. "She made me! Something about it being good luck."

Kane's face comes into the frame. "That's right! Thanks, baby!"

She smiles. "Get on the ice, Barlow!"

I bring the phone back toward me. "You too, Young!"

Malaki starts walking again. "Yes, ma'am. Happy wife, happy life."

"I'm not your wife!" I remind him.

He smirks. "Yet. You're not my wife *yet.*"

I roll my eyes and scoff. "Bye..."

"Wait!" he says.

"Malaki!" I scold through the phone. "Go get on the ice!"

"I am, I am. But...you didn't say I love you."

My fingers tighten around my phone. Malaki's narrowed gaze is set in a challenge. I quickly scan the area behind him, but there's no one near that I can see.

"I'm waiting, Dimples."

My heart pounds, my stomach on a wild ride of confusion and butterflies.

Just because I say it aloud doesn't mean it's true.

Oh, but it is.

I rush the three little words out without thought. "I love you."

His face fills with surprise.

"Now go get on the ice!"

I quickly hang up the phone and toss it far away.

The only noise is the TV and my pounding heart.

Zoe, now holding Charleigh on her hip, stands with her

jaw on the floor. Out of the corner of my eye, I see Daisy staring at me.

I'm certain her eyes are twinkling, but instead of confirming, I snatch the bowl of popcorn into my lap and search for a Skittle.

"What?" I finally ask.

Zoe, for once, says quiet, but I wish she'd say something, because with the stark silence in the living room, we all hear my phone vibrate with a text.

Zoe laughs. "Ten bucks it's Malaki."

"Twenty." Daisy sticks her hand out.

I huff. "You two are ridiculous."

But sure enough, they're right.

MALAKI

Hanging up the phone before I can say it back doesn't negate the fact that I love you too.

ME

Are people screening your messages now too?

He does *not* love me.

MALAKI

Nope. That message is just for you, Dimples.

I glance at the TV, and Malaki's name is announced. The camera suddenly pans to him taking the ice.

I click my phone screen off and suck on another Skittle to keep myself from floating.

It's at this moment that I finally understand the term *lovesick.*

The thought of Malaki loving me is terrifying and

wonderful all the same. I want to argue that he doesn't, but I'm desperate to believe he does.

As if this strange, unexpected thing between us that started on a whim could turn into something more.

My phone goes off again.

I race to see what else he has to say, completely blindsided by my messy thoughts to remember he's on the ice.

BENEDICT

Since you don't check your email, I thought I'd give you a heads up that the mediation is moved to tomorrow at two. Wouldn't want you to miss it, and then we find ourselves in a courtroom.

And just like that, reality is back.

———

I haven't eaten all day.

I've done nothing but read between the lines of every message from Benedict over the last week since I was served with papers for this mediation.

BENEDICT

I didn't do this to be malicious, Reese.

There is no hidden agenda.

I came to terms with the fact that you are marrying another man, so there is no use in trying to get our family back together. Thus why I moved forward with a mediation.

Would you rather go to court and hash this out in front of a judge? We can do that, if you prefer.

> You'll need a lawyer for that. In case you're not up to speed on the process.

Of course I'm up to speed on the process.

Benedict has made it very clear in the past that he believes he's smarter than I am, given where I grew up and where I got my education from. I dropped out of college—something he likes to remind me of—whereas he graduated with honors and now owns a multimillion-dollar company.

It was handed down to him by his father, but he likes to leave that part out.

His reassuring texts hold the weight of a feather as I wait for the mediation to start.

"Ms. Moreno?"

My heels click to the shiny marble floor as I stand from the bench.

I smile at the woman, who I assume is the mediator. "Hi." I reach my hand out to shake hers and move toward the room. "I'm so sorry," I say, glancing down the empty hall of the courthouse. "I'm not sure where Benedict is–"

Shock fills me as I step into the room.

"Hello, sweetheart."

My limbs grow heavy, and my heels stop clicking against the floor.

Benedict, in a nicely pressed suit, sits across a large chestnut table with a tall stack of papers in front of him, clearly prepared for something I've been made unaware of.

"Benedict," his name ghosts out of my mouth.

A wicked smile curves against his mouth. "Sit, angel. We have a lot to discuss."

Thirty–Nine

MALAKI

I CHECK MY PHONE AGAIN, and I still haven't heard from Reese. She's busy with Charleigh, and half the time she loses her phone, but it's unusual not to hear from her at all by now.

Did I scare her off by saying I love you?

I'll admit it was an impulsive thing to do, but the thought of getting on the ice to play my first playoff game ever while holding in something that begged to be said just wasn't it for me.

I was probably more surprised than she was.

I'm the life of the party, the single-and-ready-to-mingle guy of all my friends.

Now here I am, secretly egging on my fake fiancée's daughter to call me dada and typing *I love you* multiple times a day only to erase them.

Who am I?

Kane breezes past me toward his car with his phone up to

his ear. I quickly catch up. "Hey, let me talk to Daisy real quick."

He pauses for a brief second. "No...and how do you know I'm on the phone with Daisy?"

I grab onto his arm. "Dude, please. It's important."

Of course he's on the phone with Daisy. She's the only person he talks to besides me, and that's at a minimum.

He rolls his eyes. "Make it quick."

"Daisy?"

"Yeah?"

"Have you heard from Reese?" I try to keep the concern from my voice.

"Not since last night..."

My stomach knots. "Was everything okay?"

She sighs. "Um...well..."

My hackles rise. "Was it because I said I love you?"

"No, definitely not." *Thank God.*

"Okay, well...then what's going on? I can tell something is off by your voice."

"Tick tock..." Kane groans.

"The date for the mediation was changed," she says.

My heart sinks. "What? For when?"

"It started just a little bit ago. I haven't heard from her yet."

I say nothing. My fingers wrap tighter around Kane's phone.

Why didn't she tell me?

It's like a punch to the gut.

"She didn't tell me."

Daisy sighs through the phone. "I know, and if I had to guess why, it's because she didn't want to worry you. You were in the middle of playing one of the most important games of your career when she got the email."

Yet, somehow the game doesn't feel all that important at the moment.

Before Daisy can say anything else, I hand Kane his phone. I jog toward my car. Kane shouts my name, but I keep going.

"Don't be late for practice!"

Right, practice.

We have to be back at the arena in a few hours to watch films and work out some kinks for game two. We didn't leave with the W last night, but I can't think about that right now.

Not as I climb into my car and head for the courthouse.

———

I'm horribly underdressed.

I pass by a few men in suits as I push through the court-house doors. They each glance at me awkwardly. Either they recognize me, or they're wondering why I look like I belong at a gym.

Black sweats, Blue Devils hoodie, and a backward baseball hat.

I flip my hat forward to block my face and scan the sign posted near the elevator.

Conference rooms.

Instead of waiting for the elevator, I round the corner and take the stairs.

I barely break a sweat when I reach the third floor. The door echoes behind me, and I drop my attention to the floor to be discreet. I pass by a couple of empty rooms and peek beneath the brim of my hat to see how many more there are to go.

I stop in place when I see her, all the way at the end of the hallway, sitting there on a wooden bench. Her hands are in her lap, her chin tucked as she stares at them.

I peer behind me and then at her once more.

We're alone.

I slow my strides, my heartbeat roaring in my ears.

"Reese."

As if she knew I'd show up eventually, she turns and looks at me without surprise. I lose my footing when our eyes meet. Her dimples are nowhere to be found, the warmth she usually radiates cold.

I take a seat beside her and remain quiet.

Part of me wants to demand she tell me the reason for keeping this to herself, fighting words resting on the tip of my tongue, ready to scold her for repeating the same patterns of relying on no one but herself. But after I sit beside her, all I want to do is pull her in close.

After a few minutes of the two of us sitting on the bench, I turn to stare at her. I trace the perfect curve of her button nose with my eyes, the same nose that Charleigh has, and silently beg for her dimples to show their face soon.

I break the tension, unable to take it anymore. "Reese, are you okay?"

The only response I get is a blink.

I'm not sure she even hears me, too swept up in whatever's going through her mind. A replay of whatever happened in the meeting?

My jaw flexes with frustration.

I stand up abruptly and walk over to the glass separating us from the conference room. I pray Benedict isn't in there, because if he is, I'll have to tap into any remaining energy I have not to end up behind bars.

An older woman perks up when she sees me.

I walk over to the door and open it without restraint.

"Can I help you?" she asks.

"Were you the mediator present with the woman out there?" I ask.

She looks me up and down once before locking onto my face. "Mr. Young."

Surprise lifts my eyebrow. "I'm guessing you don't know me from being a huge Blue Devils fan, and you know me because of Benedict Whitney."

That's right. Benedict Alexander Whitney.

While Reese has been filling her time researching custody cases, I've been filling mine with all things Benedict.

I know more about him than he thinks I do.

"I'm more of a football gal." She smiles cheekily.

Without asking, I take a seat across the table.

She eyes me incredulously. "If you're here to bribe me, it won't work."

Bribe her?

I turn on the charm, knowing it'll get me more information in the long run.

"Bribing isn't my style," I say, winking at her.

Her amused sigh floats across the table, ruffling the papers spread out in front of her. "I will tell you the same thing I told Mr. Whitney: I'm simply here to act as a neutral third party between two conflicting parties to help them reach a mutual agreement. I don't make the decisions. I only explore options to resolve disputes."

I want to be a smartass and thank her for the lesson on what mediators do, but again, that's no way to get information.

I force a casual smile onto my lips. "I completely understand. I'm only in this room because my fiancée is clearly upset, and I'd really like to know why." I inch my chin toward where Reese is sitting.

The woman follows my line of sight.

She glances away, not divulging anything, which is never a good sign.

"I'm not above begging," I add.

Her light laugh fills the room, but then she sobers. "The mediation was unsuccessful."

Great.

My teeth grind back and forth. "What did he ask for?"

She begins gathering the papers quickly. "I recommend a custody hearing," she adds, clearly unwilling to answer my question.

I glance over my shoulder at Reese, who remains in the same spot on the bench, unmoving. With quiet irritation, I head for the door. I glance at the woman before leaving, and she's staring at the back of Reese's head with her eyebrows drawn together, a frown pulling at her lips.

Apparently, the answer I'm looking for is right on her face. I don't have to look any further to know that Benedict is to blame.

The media may have me painted out as the golden retriever of the Blue Devils, but I don't think Benedict realizes that when he messes with my girls, he's messing with me.

Forty

REESE

CHARLEIGH RESTS her head against my chest, my heart still beating furiously behind my ribs. She squirms against me, fighting sleep. Either that, or she can sense my worries.

I haven't said a word to Malaki or Zoe.

Malaki didn't try to pry anything out of me after he talked to the mediator. I'm not entirely sure what she told him, but that's something I can deal with when I get my thoughts straight.

My head is too messy.

Benedict's lies tangle together, his opinions of me as a mother cutting so deep I ache.

The whole thirty-three minutes we spent in that cold room with lie after lie spilling from his mouth plays on repeat, my foolish, naive self unsuspecting that he'd go *this* far because of his jealousy.

Or whatever it is that is driving him to do this to me.

To us.

My eyes gloss over again.

I gently walk Charleigh over to her crib and place her inside of it, my heart tearing in half. The thought of Benedict taking me to court for full custody of Charleigh is unfathomable. If he continues to dig up things from my past to spin a narrative of how I'm an unfit mother like he did in the mediation, I don't see how the custody hearing could go any other way.

I hang my head and listen to Zoe and Malaki whispering in the hallway.

"She didn't say anything?"

"No. I figured it was best to just give her some space."

"Don't give her too much," Zoe says. *"She won't admit it, but she needs us."*

Malaki sighs. "I gotta go to practice...I'll be back around nine."

They part ways, and I see Zoe's bare feet stop outside of Charleigh's door. She walks the short distance to the opposite wall and slides down until her butt hits the floor.

My sister is almost as persistent as Malaki.

There is no use in avoiding her.

I wipe my eyes and walk into the hallway.

Zoe perks up, but she stays on the floor, knowing I'll find my way over to her.

Once I slide down beside her, she takes my hand in hers and squeezes.

It's just like when we were younger. Just her and me in a quiet house, with fear as our shadow, too scared to speak, too fearful to think of the future.

I know the minute I rehash what just happened with Benedict, my worries will become her worries, and that's not how it's supposed to be.

I'm the older sister.

I take care of her, not the other way around.

But the longer I sit with Zoe, the heavier things become, until I can't take it anymore.

"He's put me in an impossible position," my voice cracks.

"How so?" she whispers.

My bottom lip trembles, but my tears stay put. "He'll destroy me in court."

If he pulls a stunt like today in a courtroom, I'm done for.

"He'll gain custody of her, and my entire life will be in shambles." I sniff up a tear, refusing to let it fall. "I'm better off with him than without. At least I can be there to shield Charleigh."

Zoe's hand clamps onto mine tighter. "What? You can't be serious!"

"I don't have any other choice!" I exclaim. "If we go to court, he'll do exactly what he did today, and who is going to take my word over his?"

The lies.

So many lies.

Each with some type of corrupted proof. All the judge really has to do is look at his upbringing and then mine. There really is no question about who had better examples of parents.

"You may be able to shield Charleigh for a little while, but what about you, Reese?" Zoe snatches her hand out of mine and aggressively pulls her hair into a bun on top of her head, like she's about to enter the ring for a boxing match. "Eventually, Charleigh will catch on and realize that her mother settled for a man who doesn't deserve her. She'll grow up watching him treat you like shit. She'll hear how he talks down to you, and there will come a time where he'll put his hands on you. He's come close before, and you know it'll happen again." She shakes her head. "I won't have it."

I bury my face in my hands as a sob threatens to claw out of my chest. "I don't know what to do."

"You get fucking angry," Zoe seethes. "That's what you do."

I furiously wipe a tear away and drop my hands.

Zoe's lips are pursed, her eyebrows furrowed. "You get angry, and then you get even."

"How?" I cry. "I can't afford a lawyer!"

"Malaki."

I gape at her. "Malaki isn't paying me *that* much, Zoe. I do a few house chores and cook some meals. I made him promise to keep me at minimum wage, because otherwise, he'd go overboard–"

Zoe rolls her eyes. "I don't mean the stupid paycheck he's giving you. You and I both know that he'd pay for a lawyer if you asked him to."

My face pales.

"No."

"Yes," she argues. "You'll figure out a way to pay him back."

I shake my head, an argument threatening to come out of my mouth, but Zoe's fingers wrap around my wrist, pulling my eyes to her.

"Get angry, Reese. I know you have it in you. We share the same blood."

"You've always been the angrier one," I counter.

"That's not true." She shakes her head. "I'm just more impulsive than you."

Somehow, I manage a laugh, but there's next to no humor that comes with it.

"I'm not letting you do this alone," Zoe says. "And if you won't ask Malaki for the money, then I will."

I exhale deeply, our eyes locking.

"I'm going to be making him lasagna for the rest of his life in order to pay him back."

A loud laugh rips from her mouth, and I slap my hand over it to keep Charleigh from waking.

I shush her. "Shhh!"

We sit in silence, both listening to see if Charleigh wakes up. Zoe eventually slides her head against the wall to look at me.

"I'll watch Charleigh. Go find Malaki and talk."

An argument rests on the tip of my tongue, ready to go head to head with my sister.

But then my mouth closes.

Zoe's hand squeezes mine. "He showed up today...for you. Fake fiancé, real fiancé, boyfriend, friend...whatever he is, he's worth holding onto, Reese. Stop being so self-reliant."

I give her a look, and she shakes her head, dismissing me.

"Go," she urges.

I glance at Charleigh's door.

The thought of Benedict using her to get to me rears its ugly head, and I quickly climb to my feet with that anger Zoe told me to tap into.

She smiles cheekily. "There's that Moreno blood."

———

I shiver as I sit in one of the seats and watch the tail end of Malaki's practice. The Blue Devils skate with speed as they work on some type of new play. One coach is on the ice, sporting a beanie, sweatshirt, and sweatpants, with a whistle hanging out of his mouth that he blows every so often.

I hardly watched their game last night, thanks to Benedict's text. I'm a terrible fake fiancée for not even reaching out to Malaki afterward.

"Alright." The whistle blows again, Malaki and a few others coming to a halt on the ice. "That's it for tonight. Get some rest and be back at the arena tomorrow, three hours prior to game time. Losing on the road is never easy, but losing at home is even worse."

"Especially during the playoffs," someone says.

I nibble on my lower lip and watch everyone head for the locker room. Malaki ends up beside his goalie. They stop just before stepping off the ice, and suddenly, their attention is on me.

Emory smacks Malaki's chest once and then leaves him be.

The chatter of Malaki's teammates and coaches slowly fades, and my heart pounds.

We stare at each other for so long I shift in my seat awkwardly.

Malaki rests his helmet on the bench and vanishes out of sight.

I sit and wait with my lip still tucked beneath my teeth.

It only takes him a minute to appear in the aisle. He's in his hockey pants and a black long-sleeve shirt, sans pads, with sweaty hair. His face is flushed from the vigorous skating he was just doing a few minutes ago, and when our eyes lock, my breath catches.

"Hey, Dimples."

Forty-One

MALAKI

IT'S a breath of fresh air seeing her sitting up in the stands during my practice. Emory, having the best vantage point from the ice during drills, waited until we were done to tell me, knowing I'd be distracted.

It doesn't take a genius to know that something was up with me as soon as practice started.

I didn't make a single joke or even crack a smile.

Which, according to Lars, means the world has tilted on its axis.

More like just my world.

"Hey, Dimples," I say, meeting her eyes.

A swallow pushes down my throat when she turns and walks over to the stairs, climbing them one by one until she's standing right in front of me.

"Fiancé," she says in response, a barely there smile on her pink lips.

My eyebrows rise in surprise. "Fiancé, eh? Having a change of heart?"

She shrugs before crossing her arms over her thin shirt.

"Are you cold?" I ask, ready to shed my own. It's sweaty, but at least it'd be another layer.

"I'm sorry," she blurts.

She's sorry?

I try to think of a reason why she thinks she should be apologizing to me.

"I didn't even ask you about the game last night," she adds.

As if on cue, she begins nervously chewing on her lip, eyes anywhere but on me. Without thought, I grab a hold of her chin and pull on her lip so it plops out from behind her teeth. Those brown eyes send something warm into my chest, and I think I may be addicted to her.

"You have nothing to be sorry for. Me losing a game is nothing compared to your situation."

She huffs sarcastically. "It was selfish of me."

My eyebrows cave with anger, and my grip on her chin tightens. "Stop."

Her long eyelashes flutter as she peers at me. "Stop what?"

"Belittling yourself."

Her gaze skitters away with a long, drawn-out sigh. "I'm still sorry."

"Well, don't be."

We stand there in the quiet of the arena with my hand on her chin, her eyes staring at her feet.

I'm desperate for her to tell me exactly what happened in the mediation, but I know Reese better than before. She'll tell me when she's ready—*if* she's ready.

"Is that why you came to my practice?" I ask.

Surely it wasn't just to apologize about something she has nothing to be sorry about.

She finally swings her attention back to me. I beg to know

what's going through her mind. So many quiet truths and worries trapped behind her brown eyes.

"No," she breathes the word out. "I came because..."

With a shaky hand, she grabs onto my wrist, her fingernails digging into my skin to garner my attention.

"I came because I need you."

My world stops spinning.

She needs me?

I stare down into her eyes with my chest threatening to break open so I can hand her my heart.

"You need me?" I repeat. *Did I hear her right?*

Reese nods softly, her cheeks ripening with a flush. My mouth curves as my other hand snakes around her waist. I pull her into my chest, a quick breath leaving her mouth.

"I'm here," I utter. "What do you need?"

"At the moment? I think I just need you."

"You have me, Dimples," I say.

Without missing a beat, I pick her up, cradle her legs in my arms and take a seat. She sits on my lap and holds on tightly to my neck. I shoot her a crooked smile, and she laughs quietly.

The moment doesn't last long, though.

Reese's grin fades into a somber look. She relaxes on top of me, her hands landing in her lap. "Today didn't go well."

"I assumed as much," I say. "I already have a list of family lawyers who come highly recommended ready to go."

She jerks backward. "You already have a list?"

Of course I do.

Then she shakes her head. "They're going to be too expensive."

"I don't care how expensive they are." I start to get up, holding onto her tightly. "The list is on my phone. Let me go get changed and grab it–"

"No!" she blurts.

I sit us back down. "No?"

She shakes her head, strands of her long hair falling from her messy bun. "I mean, yes, I want to see the list, but I don't want you to think I only came here to ask you to help me with a lawyer." She stares out at the ice. "I don't know if a good lawyer will even help at this point."

"These lawyers are highly recommended–"

Reese peers at me, her thick eyelashes batting against her cheeks. "He lied up and down during that mediation...he was convincing too. I probably would have believed him if I didn't know firsthand that what he was saying was completely false."

I let her go when she scooches off my lap. She stands in front of me, her arms crossed defensively. "I mean, he lied so well that, at one point, I started to wonder if I did the things he said."

"He's manipulative. He knows how to get you riled up."

And I have to admit, I don't fucking like it.

Reese huffs and tilts her gaze to the ceiling of the rink. "He painted me out to be an unfit mother, showing the mediator text messages that weren't even from me."

I sit up tall, my hands gripping the edge of the chair arms with force. "What? That would never stand in court."

"He brought up my father, even though I haven't spoken to him in years. I mean, he doesn't even know I have a daughter! Which is exactly what I said, and you want to know what he did after that?"

I'm not sure that I do.

I nod anyway.

"He threatened to tell my father about Charleigh. His reasoning was that it's my father's right to get to know his granddaughter, just like it's his right to get to know his daughter. Never mind the fact that I've given Benedict multiple opportunities. I'm not keeping her from him on purpose."

My teeth clench together.

The more Reese rehashes everything from the mediation, the more riled up she becomes.

Once she starts to nibble on her thumb nail, I know it's time to put a stop to the frenzy. "Hey," I say, trying to soothe her.

She continues to chew on the end of her nail. "He only threatened that because he was trying to scare me. He knows I don't want my father anywhere near Charleigh."

Now, she's pacing.

"Reese."

When she doesn't stop, I wait until she's right in front of me, mid-stride, and grab onto her waist. I spin her, the long stands of her hair whizzing past her face.

"Take a breath, Dimples."

A line of worry or anger, maybe both, etches in between her eyebrows. She attempts to inhale deeply, and the only thing I want to do is give her air.

"I can't!" she exclaims. "Zoe told me to get angry, and now that I am, I can't seem to stop! I just sat there in that mediation and let him walk all over me. With every half-truth and snarky jab, I felt myself grow smaller and smaller until I couldn't take it any–"

Unwilling to let her keep going, I stand abruptly with my hands still on her hips. I pick her up effortlessly and bring her legs around my waist before sitting us back down.

"What are you–"

My lips seal against hers mid-sentence, stealing every last word off the end of her tongue. It takes her no time to catch up. She opens her mouth, and she lets me in with a sweet whimper. Lost in the kiss, I move my tongue against hers in slow strokes, begging her to relax.

I break the kiss when we're both gasping for air. Reese's hands press into my shoulders.

"What are you doing?" Her soft voice sends chills to my arms.

I adjust us on the chair, my already hard cock brushing against her jeans. My fingers slip beneath her long-sleeve shirt, her flesh hot to the touch. "Building you back up, Dimples."

Forty-Two

REESE

WHY AM I so turned on right now?

My body is in a state of chaos, yet the only thing I can focus on is the way Malaki's tongue just slipped out of his mouth to wet his lip.

"Take your anger out on me, Reese," he chokes out. "I beg you."

Just hearing his voice sends tingles to the quiet parts of my body. My breasts ache so much that I reach behind me and unclasp my bra without thought.

Malaki wastes no time gliding his palm against my skin until he slips beneath the cup to feel my hard nipple. Our eyes stay locked as he touches each breast, his breathing fast and swift. I arch my back and press myself closer to his hand. My head tips back with the faint skim of his fingers against my nipple.

"Don't hold back," he presses. "Take what you need."

Doing exactly as he says, I unbutton my jeans and take his

hand from beneath my shirt. I slowly guide it down the front of my body and push his fingers there.

With his other hand, he grips the back of my head with tender force and brings my face to his. I'm sent to a completely new high when he kisses me deeply, his tongue exploring every inch of my mouth like he wants to memorize it.

He breaks away. "I like you angry," he murmurs against my lips. "You're so wet and needy."

I gasp when he pushes a finger inside of me.

"*Yes,*" I moan. "Right there."

I'm out of control with need. The day melts away as each of my emotions comes together as one.

My hips rock back and forth as I chase the high. Malaki's fingers work their magic as his other hand roams my body. "Look at you letting go," he groans. "I fucking love it."

I drop my forehead to his shoulder and curve my hips to meet more of his hand. "Malaki." His name hardly makes it out of my mouth before I'm tumbling into an abyss. Heat covers me from head to toe, a line of fireworks shooting down to my toes.

"Just like that." His hot breath coats my neck. "You soaked my hand just like you needed to."

My body ignites into a full-on fire, and suddenly, I want *more.*

I quickly climb off Malaki's lap, and he immediately adjusts himself, pressing hard on his dick. He follows my every move with a hazy look, his gaze trailing my movements as I shimmy out of my jeans, kicking them off to the side.

"Goddamn," he murmurs. "You're perfect, Dimples. You know that?"

I glance away until his hands grip my hips again. He tugs me in between his legs. "Do we need a mirror again so I can show you all the parts of your body that are perfect? Cause I'll take you in the bathroom if you need me to."

Feeling bolder than ever, I shake my head. "I want you to take me right here."

His pupils dilate. "That's the hottest thing I've ever heard you say."

Malaki lifts up, pulls his pants down, and sits me on top of his lap within record time.

A rushed gasp floats from my lips when he pulls my panties to the side and angles himself. The tip of his dick nearly slides in on its own, but he stops for a quick second. I stare down at him, ready to sit, but he shakes his head and pulls on my thin cotton panties quickly, tearing them from my body.

My jaw drops, and he grins.

Then he pushes into me at once.

"Spread wide," he demands. "I'm not even close to being done with you."

He grunts when he pushes in deeper. A shattered breath escapes my lungs, and Malaki catches it with his mouth. His hand goes around my neck as his tongue flicks against mine. He kisses me until I'm seeing stars, and my skin prickles with heat.

"Fuck, Reese," he rasps. "This body. It was made for me."

I think he may be right.

I moan, and the bundle of pleasure starts to untie.

"You like that?" he mutters. "You like knowing you were made for me?"

"Malaki."

"My name falling from your lips..." he groans. "Say it again."

"*Malaki–*" I can't hold back any longer. An orgasm shatters through me, ripping me apart from the inside out. Malaki's hand covers my mouth to quiet my moans while pressing up into me with a long pause.

"F-fuck," he hisses. "Come here."

Suddenly, Malaki is on his back, and I'm lying on top of him. I tremble, my body still riding the high of what we just did.

"Shh," he whispers into my ear, rubbing his hand down my spine softly. "Coach Jones."

My body stills.

Malaki's mouth hovers over my ear. "Don't worry, Dimples. I'd rather die than let anyone see that pretty, orgasmic glow on your face. That's for me and only me."

My heart moves, like it's trying to make space for him.

"You're my fiancée." He pushes my hair away from my ear, giving him more access to whisper. "That means you're mine to protect. Always."

For the first time since we entered this facade, I don't correct him.

———

"Zoe!" I shout up the stairs. "Are you ready? I don't want to miss warm-ups."

Charleigh wiggles in my arms, her blue bow poking me in the eye. "Ow." I grab my eye and plop her onto the ground. She quickly crawls for the stairs, as if I'm not going to be right behind to redirect her elsewhere—apparently, with only one eye.

I squint through the burn and swoop Charleigh up to place her farther down the hall. "No way, missy! You're not old enough for stairs yet."

"Da!"

I put a hand on my hip. "Malaki isn't here to save you from mean ol' Mommy," I tease.

Charleigh sits on her butt and stares up at me. "DA!" she repeats, only this time louder.

"He's corrupted you," I mutter through a smile.

She smiles at me, her freshly cut tooth peeking through the swollen gum. I sigh. "Don't worry, baby...he's corrupted me too."

I call up the stairs again. "Zoe! I'm leaving without you."

Her voice echoes, "I'm coming! I'm coming! Jeez!"

My only response is the jingling of my keys.

Charleigh has made her way over to the banister to pull herself up. I quickly bend to snap a photo of her in the little Blue Devils jersey I found in her room this morning, courtesy of Malaki.

Young is printed on the back, the number 5 the size of her entire torso. It fits her like a dress, so I paired it with a cute pair of bloomers I found at Goodwill months ago. I sewed ruffles on the butt to give it some more life, along with her socks so she matched.

I fire the photo off to Malaki, letting him know we're running late, and as if Charleigh somehow knows, she yells, "Da!"

"He's at the rink, baby." I angle my chin up the stairs and raise my voice. "Which is where we should be!"

Zoe's head appears over the top of the banister, her voluminous dark waves hanging low. "I'm coming!"

"Wow," I say. "Look at you. Hair done and everything?"

She pretends to be bashful. "Oh, stop it, you." Then she disappears again.

I snort and glance back at Charleigh. My stomach drops when she isn't in the same spot she was in a second ago. I spin around in a circle until my sights lock onto her tiny jersey.

"Charleigh!" I shriek.

I'm halfway to her when a blur of blue whooshes forward, heading toward the hard floor from the third stair.

I dive, but her thud comes before mine.

My shoulder bangs against the wall, and Charleigh's head hits the last stair.

"What was that–" Zoe gasps.

"Charleigh!" Ignoring the pain in my shoulder, I scoop her up into my arms.

Her cry is delayed, which is how I know it's bad.

As if she ran out of air, she pauses and then *screams*.

"Oh shit, Reese." Zoe is behind me. "Do not panic."

I pull Charleigh from my chest and freeze.

Blood pours from her forehead, mixing in with her tears as she cries harder.

Zoe presses a towel to the gaping cut, and then we make eye contact.

"Hospital," I choke out.

"I'll get the car."

Forty–Three

MALAKI

"THAT WAS A FILTHY ASSIST, Young! Finally getting your head in the game." Kane slaps me on the back before the rest of my teammates do the same.

I gladly accept the praise from them.

Lars skates past, getting in position. "How did they cream us for game one but are skating like a bunch of bitches today?"

"Don't jinx it," Kane snaps.

I turn and glance at the stands.

Where are they?

"Focus." Volkova's voice is stern, like a father's. "Don't worry about it."

I mentally shake myself and focus. If I don't, he'll give me another pep talk.

When Reese and Charleigh didn't show up for warm-ups, I couldn't seem to get my shit together for the game, and thanks to Coach's last-minute defensive strategies after the first quarter, I didn't have time to check my phone to see what was going on.

Then quarter two rolled around, and I was just as sloppy.

Rhodes pulled me to the side, wrapped his bare hand around the back of my neck, and squeezed tight. *"What is your problem?"*

I quickly explained in between whistle blows, and he shook his head, reassuring me that if something were wrong, I'd know by now. Not to mention, kids are unpredictable–he knows that better than anyone.

And he was right.

I was able to check my phone after the second quarter, and I saw a picture of Charleigh in the jersey I had made for her with a text that said they'd be late.

However, the clock is dwindling, and I still have yet to spot them in the crowd.

Maybe Charleigh spit up everywhere, and they needed an outfit change.

Or maybe she fell asleep, and Reese didn't want to wake her by bringing her into a rowdy arena with screaming fans. Reese did say that Char's been trying to cut a tooth, which means she hasn't been sleeping well.

The whistle blows, and we lose the faceoff.

I skate fast, showing off what I'm known for.

I'm behind the backside of the goal in record time, my eyes tracking the little black puck like it's the only thing that matters.

"Left!" I shout.

Shavings fly from my hashmarks against the ice, and I block the shot before it can head for Olson.

I send it teetering down the ice where Rhodes is waiting.

The wingers take over, and before I know it, the game is over.

My breaths are labored, my legs ache, but we won.

I wait until the hurrah is finished and race past everyone to get to the locker room.

"Mittens?" someone shouts from behind me.

I pull them off and toss them toward the equipment manager without breaking stride.

"Jeez," Corbin, a veteran player who doesn't get as much action anymore, sits on the bench and watches me rush toward my locker. "You're never the first in here after a game."

I chuckle, half paying attention, and pull out my phone. *Nothing.*

There's no missed call. No text message.

Something isn't right.

I feel it in my gut.

My heart skips a beat on the first ring.

She answers on the second and sounds out of breath. "Malaki."

"What's going on? Is it Benedict?"

"No," she rushes out. "I was waiting for the game to end before I called you. I didn't want you to worry."

Too late.

The locker room starts to fill. I turn my back to block the chatter.

"It's Charleigh."

My shoulders tense. "What do you mean?"

Reese's shaky breath echoes through the phone. "She fell before we left for the game. I'm at the hospital."

My world stops.

Panic like I've never felt before slams into me.

I press a fist to my chest to stop the tightening. "I'm on my way."

———

I'm sweaty and short of breath by the time I walk through the ER doors. It's nearly empty, only a few seats taken, one by an elderly couple and the other by a mom and a coughing toddler.

"Reese Moreno," I say as soon as I walk up to the reception area.

The woman's eyebrows furrow. "Um?"

Anxiety claws at my chest. "I'm here to see my fiancée. Our daughter fell, and they're in a room somewhere."

Our daughter?

Did I really just say that?

Either way, it worked. The woman clicks a button, and two swinging doors open. "Go through there. Take a left down the hall. They're in room four."

My strides are hurried, my forehead tacky with sweat. I grip the curtain, peek behind it, and immediately spot Charleigh.

Relief and worry hit me like a tidal wave as I take in the scene.

Charleigh is lying on Reese's chest with a bandage wrapped around her entire head, the blue bow holding her tiny ponytail still intact. Dried blood is sprinkled all over her new jersey and her mom's too.

"I'm going to start calling you Rocky instead of Charleigh-girl," I utter, heading right for her.

Reese looks up and blinks the exhaustion from her eyes. "Malaki."

Charleigh's eyes grow wide with a smile. "Da!"

I sit on the edge of the bed and look her over quickly. Other than the bandage around her head, she seems okay. Fully intact. Still smiling and warming me from the inside out.

"Did you fall?" I ask her, bopping her on the nose.

"Da!"

I chuckle and hold my hands out to see if she'll give Reese a break.

She leans forward, and I take her in my arms before

swinging my legs over the bed and resting beside Reese. She scoots over to make room as Charleigh's little hand reaches for Reese's phone that's playing an episode of *Ms. Rachel*.

She settles onto my chest, fully content.

"I assume no concussion if she's watching *Ms. Rachel*?" I ask, peering at the top of Reese's head. She's so much smaller than I am that her head hardly reaches my shoulder.

Reese's chest expands with a heavy breath. "No. Just twelve stitches and years off my life."

My chest vibrates with a quiet chuckle.

I take my hand and interlace our fingers together before giving them a squeeze. "You okay?"

She glances down at herself. "Why? Do I not look okay?"

Dried blood is smeared all over her chest, her hair tangled at the ends. One of her dimples appears, followed by her cheeky smile.

Oh, she's got jokes tonight?

"You look stunning. Even with blood all over you."

"I think that makes you a psychopath."

I hum under my breath. "For you? I'd be anything."

She snorts out a laugh, her smile growing wider. "I don't know how you can make me laugh after the night I've had."

"It's a talent of mine."

"That and hockey," she says.

I rest against the back of the bed and haul Charleigh up to make her more comfortable.

"Well...if you managed to watch the game, one could argue that hockey is not my talent."

At least during the first two quarters. I was on fire during the third.

"What? Why? What happened?" Reese's voice brinks on the edge of panic, so I squeeze her hand to get her to relax.

"I was...distracted."

"Distracted?" she repeats.

I glance over to see her silent question on her face.

"I was worried," I admit. "When you two didn't show up for the game. I didn't have a chance to look at my phone, and all the stuff with Benedict...I was worried something happened."

Reese shuts her eyes and brings her hand up to squeeze the bridge of her nose. "I'm so sorry. I should've had Daisy pull you to the side. I didn't want to distract you from the game or worry you."

When is she going to realize that she's always a distraction to me? If she isn't in my line of vision, I wonder where she is. If she doesn't answer my calls, I think about sending a search party for her. I'm half-tempted to turn on her location services just to ease my mind.

Our eyes meet, but before I can say anything, the curtain slides open, and in walks Zoe holding two to-go cups of what I assume is shitty hospital coffee.

"The hoops I had to go through for these!" she announces.

Once she sees me, she stops abruptly and pulls the cups to her chest. "Don't you dare. If you want coffee, you're on your own."

I make a disgusted face. "I don't drink coffee."

Zoe stares at me. "So you were just born with energy?"

I shrug. "I've always been a little hyperactive."

"Or insane," she mutters.

She walks closer to the bed while mumbling under her breath, "*Doesn't drink coffee...what a psycho.*"

Teasingly, I reach for her cup. She sends me a glare that rivals a wolf but quickly wipes the look off her face when the doctor walks in.

"Aw." She smiles at Charleigh resting against my chest. "Looks like Daddy is all you needed."

Zoe's coffee sputters from her mouth.

The doctor leans backward and grabs onto her pager, like she's ready to let the trauma team know they have a choking patient in the ER.

"Are you okay?" she asks Zoe.

"She's *fine*," Reese seethes.

Zoe slaps her chest a few times, her face red. "Coffee went..." She pauses to cough. "Down..." Another cough. "The wrong tube."

I bite down on my tongue to keep myself from laughing.

The doctor walks over to Charleigh on my lap and gently lifts the bandage to inspect the stitches. "These look great. I think we're ready to discharge her."

I sit up a little taller. "Any precautions for the night? No concussion, correct? Allowing her to sleep is okay?" I rattle off questions one by one, not caring if Zoe is going to make fun of me for being overprotective later. I mean, the doctor did refer to me as her father, so I might as well act like it, right?

"Correct. There is no concussion. Just a bad tumble on the stairs that led to a nasty cut. I'll get your discharge papers."

As soon as the doctor leaves, I turn toward Reese. "She fell down the stairs?"

Damnit, I should have gotten one of those gate things.

She immediately looks elsewhere, hiding her face from me. "It was just the first two. I only looked away from her for a split second. I had just moved her away from the stairs, and by the time I looked over, she was on them again. I *swear* I was watching her, Malaki." Her explanation is rushed, the words flying out of her mouth at record speed.

"Hey, whoa." I pull on her hand to get her to look at me. "You don't think I'm mad, do you?"

Reese peeks at me with too many hidden emotions for me to even begin to decipher. "I...no? I don't know."

Zoe chimes in. "It's because Benedict would use this

against her if he knew. Blame her and make her feel awful for it."

I let go of Reese's hand and touch the side of her cheek to turn her to face me completely. "I am nothing like Benedict, Reese. My only thought was how I should've gotten a baby gate for the stairs."

She blinks several times, her eyelashes fluttering back and forth like the wings of a butterfly. "Oh."

"As a matter of fact..." I pull my phone out of my pocket, while making sure not to disrupt Charleigh watching *Ms. Rachel*, and type in the words *baby gate* into the search engine. "I'm buying one right now."

Reese's warm laugh brushes against my skin. "You don't have to do that. This is my responsibility–"

The words die on the end of her lips when I flick my eyes in her direction. She shuts her mouth instantly and turns away with her dimples showing.

Doesn't she understand that she and Charleigh are my responsibility now?

Or at least, I want them to be.

Forty-Four

REESE

I PEEL my eyes open slowly and blink through the blur. The gleam of the moon lies still on Malaki's bedroom ceiling, filtering in through the window.

What time is it?

I turn at the sound of shuffling and watch as a tall, shadowy figure strides toward the bedroom door with a pillow in tow. Malaki's side of the bed is empty, along with said pillow.

Without asking him what he's up to, I watch him quietly open the bedroom door and disappear down the hall.

My phone, somehow beneath the covers that I don't remember pulling up, is dead.

I must've fallen asleep when Malaki was showering.

How long ago was that?

Charleigh fell asleep on the car ride home and, surprisingly, went down easily after I got her bathed and in a fresh diaper.

By the looks of the dark bedroom and groggy state I'm in, I'd say it's past midnight.

After flipping the covers off my legs, I walk across the bedroom floor on my tiptoes and peek my head down the hall.

It's empty.

I walk farther and stop in front of Charleigh's room to check on her before attempting to find wherever Malaki just disappeared to.

Her bedroom door is cracked, as always, so I peek my head inside. What on earth–

I shake my head and blink, but it's the same scene as before.

Malaki, shirtless, in his low-hanging sweats, is lying in the middle of her bedroom floor, with nothing but his pillow.

"Malaki!" I whisper.

He crunches upward, his abs flexing beneath the shadows. His brow furrows when he sees me standing at the door.

"What are you doing?" I mouth to him.

He angles his head to Charleigh, who's sleeping on her back, arms and legs both sprawled out without a care in the world, as if she didn't scare me half to death hours prior.

Malaki climbs to his feet and strides over to the door. He grabs a hold of my hip and tugs me out into the hallway, away from Charleigh's door.

"What are you doing?" I ask again, still whispering.

Malaki's mouth opens, but nothing comes out. He squints, and I can tell he's trying to figure out what to say.

"Are you sleepwalking?" I snap my fingers in front of his face.

"I haven't done that in years," he says in a low voice.

"Then why are you lying in the middle of her floor?"

Malaki crosses his arms defensively. "You know...just..." He shrugs and looks past my head at the wall.

I cross my own arms, just like he is, and watch him squirm. He shifts on his feet, and I can't help but feel amused.

"Wow," I say, voice full of mirth.

He peers at me warily. "What?"

"I have never seen you this uncomfortable before."

His jaw flexes. "I'm not uncomfortable."

I poke his hard stomach. "You *so* are."

When he still doesn't budge with an explanation, I start guessing. "Was I snoring?"

His mouth twitches. "No."

"Was the bed uncomfortable? Thought you might be comfier on Charleigh's bedroom floor?"

His quick eyeroll makes me smile. "No..."

I open my mouth to list off another guess, but he stops me.

"I was..." Malaki snakes his hand up his chest and lands at the back of his neck to give it a tight squeeze.

For a split second, I let my eyes wander down his tight torso before he starts to explain.

"I was worried. Okay? What if she needed something? What if the doctor was wrong and she does have a concussion? What if the medication wears off and her head hurts? I figured if I slept on her floor, I'd be there if she needed me." Malaki's worried gaze flits between mine, and I suddenly have a knot in my throat.

After a few seconds pass, I uncross my arms and let them hang down by my sides. "You were going to sleep on my daughter's floor?" My voice is wobbly. "In case she needed you?"

Malaki exhales slowly. His jaw flexes, and he shrugs. "I know she's not *my* daughter, but–"

I erase the space between us without thought. My arms wind around his waist, and my head presses against his chest.

The speed of his heart pounding against my ear tells me all I need to know about him.

Malaki Young is one of a kind. He may be my fake fiancé, but I still can't help but feel lucky.

He says my name hesitantly while wrapping his arms around me, keeping me pressed against him. "Reese?"

I angle myself away from him slightly and look up at him with blurry eyes. "You are going to make an amazing father one day, Malaki." I force myself to smile, even though it hurts me to think he'll be this for someone else. "And husband."

Our eyes lock, and at that moment, something binds us together.

We move at the same time.

The sliver of space between us vanishes, and our mouths press together. I kiss him deeply, every concealed thought I've ever had about us showing itself in each stroke of my tongue.

"Kissing you messes with my head," he says in between kissing. "Makes me want to say things I'm afraid you don't want to hear."

I take my hands from around his neck and pull on his wrist to pull him back to the bedroom. The door latches behind us, nothing but the moon and stars lighting the way to the bed. Malaki's large hands reach up underneath my over-sized tee where he grips me by the waist. He edges me toward the bed until the backs of my thighs hit the side.

"Do you want to hear them?" he asks.

The rasp in his voice sends a shiver down my spine.

He slowly peels the shirt off my body, and I'm surprised to find him still gazing into my eyes instead of taking in my naked body.

"I won't say them if you don't want to hear them."

"You think you're afraid?" I whisper.

He squints, like he's trying to figure me out.

"I'm terrified, Malaki." I slip my fingers beneath the waist of my panties and push them past my hips until they fall in a pile at our feet.

"What are you terrified of, Dimples?" His voice is so low I hardly hear him.

With shaky fingers, I do the same to Malaki's pants and boxers, slipping my fingers beneath his waistband to shove them to the floor. He kicks them off to the side and wraps his arm around my lower back.

Our naked bodies are flush, and he stares down at me, waiting.

"I'm terrified I'll believe you," I finally say.

Malaki grips my thigh to haul it up around his waist. Heat builds between my legs. Malaki's warm breath fans against my skin as his nose skims my neck. I shake in his grip, and when his mouth hovers over my ear, I'm a goner.

"You never have to be afraid when it comes to me, Reese." He peppers faint kisses against my jawline until his mouth hovers right over mine. Butterflies fill my stomach, and my heart races so quickly I can't breathe. "So believe every single word I'm about to say to you...because I mean them."

Forty-Five

MALAKI

EVERY TIME she lets me have her like this, it's like holding a ticking time bomb in my hands. I don't want to come on too strong and fuck everything up. What started out as a minor infatuation fueled by attraction has turned into something so much bigger than I ever expected.

Half the time, I chalk my behavior up to playing the part of her fiancé, but the truth is, I'm not just fooling Benedict and everyone else around us. I'm fooling myself too.

"I want you," I say, the words burning my throat as they come out. "I want your body." The way she shivers beneath my palms as I graze her curves ignites a fire inside of me. "I want your mind, just like you have mine." I lay her back on my bed with my legs between hers. "You're all I think about, Reese."

I grab both of her wrists in my hand and push them up above her head. Her back arches, her breasts on full display for me.

Fuck.

Her nipple tightens in my mouth, and she spreads her legs wider. I'm right at the center, but I don't give in yet. I rub against her, her whimpers fucking music to my ears. After spending enough time on one breast, I move to the other.

They're full and perky. I could spend the rest of my life touching them and watching her eyes haze over with lust.

"Malaki."

My fingers clamp around her wrists as I haul myself up. I hover above her, my dick inching closer to the heat between her legs. I stare down at her, and the look of need on her face tethers me right to her.

"Do you wanna know what else I want?" I ask.

Her chest rises and falls swiftly. "What?"

I grip her chin and push inside of her. A hot gasp flies from her mouth, but we stay locked on each other's eyes, waiting for her to adjust. "I want you to want me just as badly as I want you."

Reese arches her body, seemingly pulling me closer to her. The space separating us is gone, our bodies pressed together as I move above her. With each thrust, I fall a little deeper. I touch every inch of her body, memorizing every single dip and valley. Her fingernails dig into the back of my neck as she pushes my face toward her to deepen our kiss, her cunt tightening as I move quickly.

"Tell me you believe me," I force between tight teeth. "Tell me you know that this thing between us isn't just because of that pretend ring I put on your finger."

She nods fast, her forehead moving against mine.

Thank fuck.

I kiss her again, this time so forcefully our teeth clank.

My thighs ache, pins and needles prickle all the way down to my toes, and we're suddenly both coming. Her cry of pleasure is muffled by my mouth, and I collapse with her in my arms. My legs give out, and she lies on top of me with her forehead resting on my shoulder.

It takes us so long to catch our breath that the sweat dries on our flushed skin.

She sighs wistfully as I pull out of her.

We lie there for a while until she pops up and makes eye contact with me. She smiles shyly, her dimples rooting me in my spot, and then she climbs off me.

I prop myself up on my forearms and watch her get dressed. She tosses my clothes at me and then steals her pillow off the bed.

"What are you doing?" I ask, pulling my boxers and pants on.

She shrugs sheepishly. "If you're sleeping in Charleigh's room, so am I."

My lip hitches.

"Plus…" She walks over to the door and glances at me over her shoulder. "I sleep better next to you anyway."

———

"Da!"

I peel one eye open and immediately lock onto Charleigh. With her wild hair, she grips the edge of her crib and smiles at me. I grin and sit up slowly.

"How are you feeling, Charleigh-girl?" My voice is hoarse from lack of sleep, but I don't regret last night's escapade at all.

The spot next to me on the floor is now empty, nothing but Reese's pillow there. I climb to my feet and pull Charleigh out of her crib. I gently brush her hair out of her face and survey her stitches.

She remains still and lets me look. After I'm convinced they look okay, I let her hair go. Her soft hand touches the side of my face, the rough stubble scratching her palm.

"Ma?" she asks, pulling her hand away.

"Should we go find her?" I ask.

She bucks in my arms, and I chuckle. "Looks like we both look forward to seeing your mommy in the morning, huh?"

After checking our bedroom and finding it empty, we head for the stairs.

I lecture Charleigh the entire way down, forbidding her to ever climb them again unless I'm there to catch her. I also inform her that I'm installing a baby gate.

"No ifs, ands, or buts," I say. "No more stairs for you."

The scent of something sweet fills the air the closer we get to the kitchen.

At first, I wonder if Reese has broken into another pack of Skittles, but instead, there's an entire buffet of breakfast food waiting on the island.

French toast sprinkled with powdered sugar, bacon, sausage, fruit, and of course, a jug of apple juice sits in the middle, next to a stack of plates.

Reese is bent over at the waist, wearing my shirt from the night before. It rides up, revealing her ass, and I have to forcefully pull my gaze away.

I clear my throat. "Good morning."

She jumps up and spins. Powdered sugar is sprinkled across her cheek, and it immediately makes me grin.

"Good morning." She smiles at me and then to Charleigh.

Her gaze moves to Charleigh's stitches.

"They look great," I say, moving her hair out of her face again to show Reese.

She comes over, a spatula in her hand that Charleigh steals right away.

God, I could really get used to this. Charleigh in my arms, her mom standing in the kitchen with my shirt on, making breakfast.

Reese angles her face up to Charleigh and nods. "You're right. They aren't even red."

I stare at the stripe of sugar on her cheek and reach up to swipe it away. My thumb rubs against her skin, and she blushes.

I show her the sugar on the pad of my finger. "Powdered sugar."

"Oh," she laughs, and then I do something I shouldn't.

I look at her mouth and push my thumb past her lips to lick the sugar off. Her eyes widen, but her pupils suddenly dilate. Surprise takes me under when her fingers wrap around my wrist. She sucks the sugar off, her tongue swirling around and around.

Holy shit, I shouldn't have done that. Charleigh is distracted by the spatula, but still.

"Do I smell bacon?"

I quickly pull my hand back at the sound of Zoe.

Zoe staggers down the hallway, hardly awake.

"Me first!" I blurt.

I move toward the island but not without winking at Reese.

A flush works over her face, and I fucking *love* it.

Forty–Six

REESE

THINGS ARE DIFFERENT.

The ring on my finger doesn't feel as heavy.

The house isn't so foreign.

The spot next to me in bed is no longer untouched.

With a smile on my face, I pour a cup of coffee. I sip on it leisurely while simultaneously watching Charleigh crawl around the living room.

Three of the five lawyers from Malaki's list have already gotten back to me, one of them ready to schedule an in-person consultation as early as Friday.

A week ago, I would've gone by myself.

But I find myself scheduling the appointment for when I know that Malaki is back in town, so he can come with me.

I type a quick text to him with the details and place my phone on the coffee table to keep an eye on Charleigh. Although Malaki installed the baby gate before leaving for the arena, I'm not sure I trust her not to climb the thing.

With each passing day, she becomes more daring.

I think she may get that from Zoe.

My phone pings with an incoming text, and I already know it's Malaki.

I smile.

MALAKI

> Are you sure you don't want to fly out here and watch the game?

Flying with a baby sounds like a nightmare, especially one as mobile as Char.

ME

> Sorry. Can't. Charleigh is still grounded.

> Could you imagine her on a flight? I'd have to let her roam the aisle.

MALAKI

> At least there are no stairs.

ME

> 😐

MALAKI

> Is the baby gate holding up okay? What did she think of it?

I glance at her, and as if she senses that I'm looking at her, she turns to glance over her shoulder while holding onto the gate.

"Charleigh..." I warn.

She grins, the mischievous glint in her eye loud and proud.

I shake my head and quickly type Malaki another message.

ME

> The baby gate is perfectly sturdy, but I think she's conjuring up a plan to climb it next.

Maybe we should look for a one-story
house?

My stomach tumbles.

What?

Is he serious?

I look at Charleigh and picture the three of us house hunting together. Butterflies take flight, and I'm suddenly sweating.

We can't just get a new house because of
Charleigh falling down a few steps.

Says who?

Says me! That's insane.

Plus, I could see Benedict using it against me that I'm moving again.

I also want you to have the house you want.

This is the house I want—including the people living in it.

I like this house.

I walk over to Charleigh and sit to get on her level. She flops into my lap, and I quickly pull her upright so she doesn't hit her head on my leg. "Do you like this house?" I ask her.

Her little eyebrows furrow, and her eyes drop to my mouth as she tries to figure out what I'm asking her.

My phone buzzes, and Charleigh reaches for it.

"This is Mommy's," I say.

"Da?" she asks questionably.

I stare at her, phone in my hand.

Surely she isn't asking if it's Malaki.

Right?

MALAKI

But do you love it?

Charleigh scurries off toward the living room, and I follow after her. With my eye on the time, I turn on the channel the game will be on so I don't miss a thing. I reread Malaki's text, my fingers hovering over the keyboard.

A house is a material object, and material things don't really matter in the grand scheme of things. I've lived in a house, a trailer, a dorm room, a shitty apartment, and now here.

Not many of those felt like a home to me, and I most definitely didn't love them.

What I did love, though, was all the nonmaterialistic things.

The feeling of independence.

The idea that I was the only one who had a key to the door.

Zoe being next to me.

And now...Malaki.

We could live in the middle of the forest somewhere, in a dilapidated cabin without electricity, and I think I'd be happy. It's not the walls that surround us or how sturdy each brick is that make me love this place.

It's who I share it with.

Whether or not it was unplanned, or started off as a ruse, somewhere along the way, Malaki became my home, and that's terrifying.

"Da!" Charleigh shouts excitedly.

She stands with her hands on the coffee table—the same one that Malaki taped pool noodles to so she wouldn't bump her chin on the edge. She's gawking at the TV, watching the Coyotes skate across the ice as they wait for the Blue Devils.

"Da!" she shouts.

I laugh. "That's not Malaki," I say. "But close."

Her pretty brown eyes turn to me with a quiet question, but then she turns toward the TV again.

"Da...da."

I pause.

My heart takes a tumble.

"What?" I whisper.

"Dada!" she shouts.

I blink though watery eyes.

Zoe comes flying into the living room, sliding across the hardwood floors in her socks. "Did she just–"

I nod.

Charleigh says it again, and it's the final push I need to type exactly what my heart is begging me to.

ME

> A house is just a house. I love the people in it, and that's enough for me.

A few Blue Devils players spill onto the ice. Charleigh bounces up and down. "Dada!"

Oh my god.

Suddenly, his name is flashing on my phone screen. My heart leaps as quickly as my finger moves to answer it.

"You better get on the ice," I say as soon as his face comes into view.

He's in the middle of getting all his gear on, the locker room quieter than normal. "Is that just one of your cross-stitch sayings, or do you mean that?"

He stops getting dressed, his eyes focused on my mouth.

"I mean it," I say.

His lip hitches, and I can't help the smile sliding onto my face.

"Dada!"

Malaki's eyebrows shoot upward, his smile frozen. "Did she just say what I think she did?"

"She did!" Zoe shouts from the other side of the couch.

"Let me see her," he pleads.

I turn the phone around, and it catches Charleigh's eye. The smile on her face could brighten an entire room. "Hey, Charleigh-girl," Malaki coos.

"Dada!" she repeats.

Her hands, still resting along the coffee table, give her enough stability to bounce up and down on her tiny legs with excitement.

"Reese."

I turn the phone back around. "Yeah?"

He exhales before looking directly into the camera. "I know it started out as a joke...but I sort of love that she's calling me dada...and I also love that you refer to me as your fiancé."

I smile and nod, too afraid to say anything.

His throat moves with a swallow. "And I love you...and Charleigh."

My eyes water.

Charleigh, now beside me, grabs for my phone. It falls to the floor, and the only thing in the frame is her chubby face. "Dada!"

Malaki chuckles, his smile matching hers.

"Say bye to Dada," he says. "I gotta go win a game so I can get back to my girls."

His girls?

We're his girls?

I smile to myself.
We are *his* girls.

Forty-Seven

MALAKI

WITH THE SCHEDULE of the game and different time zones, we won't be back in Chicago until tomorrow, which is unfortunate because all I want to do is celebrate the win with Reese and Charleigh. Zoe can tag along too, I guess.

She doesn't scare me anymore, but I most definitely won't cross her.

I may get her a new baseball bat for Christmas, though, just to be funny.

I spot Rhodes walking ahead of me and jog up next to him. I know he's one of the only ones who probably listened when Coach was talking so I ask, "When does the flight leave?"

"Supposed to take off at nine." He stares at his phone. "There's a storm coming, though, so it may be delayed."

Mother Nature, don't fuck with me.

I sigh annoyingly and sling my bag over my shoulder.

Rhodes chuckles.

"What?"

"Oh nothing."

I keep up my pace beside him. "No, tell me. What is so amusing to the grumpiest man on the team?"

He scoffs. "I'm not the grumpiest on the team—not anymore, at least."

"True. Not after a *Little Miss Sunshine* walked into your life," I say.

He rolls his eyes, but he doesn't argue. He, along with everyone from here to Chicago, knows it's true.

"It's just funny to see you so cagey after a game for once. Mr. Never Settling Down is itching to get back to his girl."

"Girls," I correct him. "I'm eager to get back to my girls."

Rhodes shakes his head, but he can't hide his smirk. He gets it, which is exactly why I nudge him with my elbow and say, "Guess what?"

"I'm not guessing."

Fair.

"Charleigh called me Dada."

Even hours later, I can't stop smiling.

I'll admit, when I first found out the woman I was lusting over was a mom, I was shocked. The thought of heading out the door was there, but I'm not one to back down from a challenge or help a gal out when she needs it, especially Reese.

So I willingly took charge and accepted my new position as her fake fiancée.

Now look at me.

I'm so high on life that I'm walking on clouds.

Rhodes stops beside me, and there's *almost* a smile on his face. "Did she?"

I nod. "Yeah, just before the game."

We continue walking, a few of our teammates squeezing past. "How does Reese feel about that? Has she been trying to get her to say that?"

I'm quick to defend her. "No, most definitely not. It

started out as a joke because of her sister..." I shrug. "But it kind of stuck, and now I don't ever want to unhear it."

"And her biological dad? What is he going to say when he hears his daughter call you Dad instead of him?"

Anger surfaces. "He'd have to be around for that to happen."

"So he's given up on Reese? The whole fake-engagement worked, then?" He looks surprised.

I wince. "Not exactly."

"Well, did you get a hold of Mel? Did he have any contacts for a private investigator?"

Mel, an old-time friend of Rhodes who I knew carried out the background checks on his nannies, did give me a contact for a freelance PI he'd met while working cybersecurity. He just hasn't found any dirt on Benedict.

I wait until Lars buries himself in his phone to answer Rhodes, because the less people that know, the better.

"He did, but so far, Mark hasn't found anything useful. Her ex has been eerily quiet since the mediation."

"Snakes are quiet," Rhodes mutters. "He's going to strike."

He doesn't have to remind me. It's been on my mind since the beginning.

Men like Benedict don't give up easily, and if they're so willing to point out all the bad in someone else, then that tells me they have their own skeletons.

I'm going to find every last one and put them in my back pocket to use at the right time.

———

Dread keeps me planted in the same spot. I stare at the screen hanging in the middle of the lobby. *Delayed due to inclement weather.*

"This is bullshit," Kane curses.

"Fuck Mother Nature," I mutter.

Lars pushes his head in between ours. "Will you two stop being babies? It's just a little rain. It'll pass."

"It delayed the flight," Kane snaps.

Lars wraps his arm around my shoulder but thinks twice before doing the same to Kane. "More reason for us to get a drink."

I shrug his arm off and pull out my phone to call Reese. It's early, but with Charleigh, I'm positive she's awake.

"Hello?" she sounds out of breath, like she's rushing around.

"Hey," I say. "You good? Charleigh got you chasing her or something?"

"Um, no..."

I walk around the corner for privacy.

Her voice is off.

"Is everything okay? I was calling to let you know that our flight got delayed because of the storms. Do you know where the flashlights are in case the power goes out?"

The other end of the line is quiet.

"Dimples? If you tell me that Charleigh is in the ER again..."

"No!" she exclaims. "She's fine. She's with Zoe."

I do the quick math again, just to make sure I have the time right. "It's seven-thirty in the morning. Where are you going this early?"

"I'm on my way to the courthouse, Malaki."

My bag slides off my shoulder and lands on the floor with a thud. "What?"

Her shaky breaths echo through the phone, and I swear I can feel them against my skin. "Benedict found out about Charleigh falling. He filed an emergency motion yesterday, and I was just told about it an hour ago."

Anger claws at my neck. "For what?"

"Neglect and abuse."

I clench my eyes shut and pinch the bridge of my nose so hard water pricks at the sides.

"I don't even have a lawyer yet," her voice breaks.

"How can they do this?" Panic rushes through my veins, but I keep it under wraps with her on the phone.

She sniffles. "I don't know, but I have to go. I can't get worked up any more than I already am."

"Don't worry, Reese." I'm already coming up with a plan to get home. "I'm on my way."

We both hang up without another word, and I jog over to Coach. He stares at me over the brim of his to-go coffee cup. "I can't control the weather, Young. I already told Barlow that."

"I have to get home."

He surveys my face and apparently comes to the realization that I'm not messing around, like usual. "No matter the airline, the flight will still be delayed."

"Then I'll fly into a different city and drive the rest of the fucking way," I argue.

Rhodes catches my eye and walks over. "What's going on?"

I say one word. "Benedict."

Rhodes turns to Coach. "It's an emergency. I'll go with him if that's the issue."

He sighs exasperatedly. "Fine. Let me see what I can do to get you home sooner."

He turns and pulls out his phone.

If he doesn't find a way, then I will.

One way or another, I'm getting back to Chicago.

Forty-Eight

REESE

I'M SHAKING, and I'm not sure if it's from anger or fear. I was told about this hearing without even enough time to shower, so I didn't exactly have time to call any of the lawyers I've been in contact with. How could I ask them to meet at the courthouse within thirty minutes when they haven't even agreed to work with me yet?

The security guard waves me forward through the metal detector, and it buzzes. He has me go through again and... same thing.

"Do you have anything on you?" he asks.

I blink several times, and I'm still just as confused. My mind is too messy, my blood pressure through the roof. "Like a weapon?!" I squeak.

His head jerks, and he reaches for his side.

Someone chuckles behind me. I glance over my shoulder, and the blood drains from my face.

Benedict walks through the detector as casual as ever,

snakes an arm around my waist, and looks at the security guard. "Don't worry. She's harmless," he muses.

His hand on my hip is like a cage.

I slap it away and step toward the security guard. "What the hell do you think you're doing?"

Benedict smirks and pushes his hands into his pockets.

He's someone who looks prepared for court.

Me? I'm wearing the heels I still haven't given back to Daisy from the fundraising gala, a thrifted dress, and hardly any makeup because I cried it off on the way here.

"Miss?" The security guard has his wand out, ready to wave it over me.

I spread my arms and legs, all while Benedict is watching.

"Are you waiting for something?" I snap at him as the security guard bends down with his wand.

"You're good to go," he says, stepping away to let me through.

I brush past Benedict, leaving his chuckle behind like I wish I could do with the memory of him.

"You know running away from me won't make me disappear, sweetheart. I'll see you inside those doors in just a few minutes."

I spin around in a haste, anger not even touching the feeling inside of me. "Why are you doing this?"

He stops his slow strides, and his smug smile stalls. His eye twitches as he scans me up and down. I cross my arms defensively because I can already hear the words that are about to come out of his mouth.

I beat him to the punch. "Is it because you still want me? Or are you just jealous of what I have with another man that you can't just let me be? You and I both know that this has nothing to do with Charleigh."

His glares at me. "She's my daughter. Of course it has something to do with her."

It's as if he's slapped me in the face.

"You called me a whore when I told you I was pregnant. Then you refused to believe that she was yours." I stare down at my heels and attempt to lower my voice. "I've given you multiple opportunities to have a relationship with her, and I still adhere to that, Benedict."

I look up at him, and his jaw is flexing with anger, per usual, but I've got news for him: I'm angry too.

I press my finger into his chest. "You just don't want her unless you can have me too."

His lip curls. "You think I'm doing this because I want you? Why on earth would I want a gold digger like you?"

I gape at him, my jaw falling open. "A gold digger? I've never asked you for money."

He hums and walks toward the two large oak doors leading into the courtroom. "First, you get pregnant on purpose..."

Shock ripples throughout my body. "What are you talking about?"

"And then when I decide to move on, you find another rich man and convince him to put a ring on your finger." Benedict's mouth curves into an all-knowing smile, and he heads back over to me.

I place my hand on my stomach to ease the roll of nausea.

"That is not true," I seethe. "And you know it."

He shrugs. "Maybe. But the judge doesn't."

His cologne burns my nose when he leans down to whisper in my ear, "But honestly, sweetheart, you jump into bed with a man you barely know, get engaged, and just expect I'll be okay with him being my daughter's stepfather? Do you even know him?"

Of course I do.

"What kind of mother are you to jump headfirst into a marriage this quickly?" His laugh is menacing, and I know he's using insults as a weapon to put me into a nervous tizzy.

But it's working.

I find myself hesitating...and doubting myself as a mother.

Is he right? Am I a terrible mother for jumping into things with Malaki so quickly? Of course, we're not really engaged, but there is some truth to Benedict's jab.

Am I being naive when it comes to Malaki?

Have I even thought of the consequences if this blows up in my face? Not only will I have to piece back together my crushed dreams, but I'll have to mend a broken heart.

I'll have to mend Charleigh's broken heart too.

It's not just me that I have to worry about.

"Are you rethinking things, sweetheart? Realizing that I have you by the throat?"

I know that if I give in to him, he really will have me by the throat, so I push past, my shoulder bumping into his, and say, "No."

Despite Benedict's false accusations, I walk into the courtroom with confidence.

I've always fended for myself, and today is no different.

———

I sit on the bench outside the courtroom with my hands underneath my thighs. What's the point in being here by eight if there are multiple hearings before ours? Is it to make me second-guess every little thing? Because if so, it's working.

My eyes burn from staring at my phone screen. I've learned all there is to know about custody cases and emergency motions from sitting here researching. My head is spinning by the end, and my nerves are no less fried than they were hours ago.

I close my eyes and press against the cool wall. Benedict

has been huddled next to his lawyer on the other side of the hallway, the pair of them muttering back and forth to themselves like they have some grand plan to take me down.

The only good thing about his lawyer showing up is that he hasn't said another word to me.

I hop to my feet on shaky legs when the door opens.

"Parties for Whitney vs. Moreno, Judge Ramirez is ready for you."

My stomach turns.

Benedict and his lawyer stand up, neither one looking in my direction as they stride past. I run my sweaty palms over my dress and exhale a breath.

The bailiff gives me space but eyes me closely. After another breath, he says, "Are you ready?"

Am I ready?

No, I'm not fucking ready.

I nod anyway.

"Reese!"

Mid-step, I pause.

Malaki rushes toward me while tightening his tie.

"Malaki! What are you doing here?" I glance back and forth between him and the bailiff. His hand is on the door, waiting for me.

My heart aches to reach for Malaki, my legs begging me to rush over to him so I can feel his arms around my waist. I want to bury my nose into his shirt and be engulfed in his familiar scent. But instead, I hesitate. I force him away.

"Malaki. You can't be here right now."

He comes to a sudden stop, his fingers clamped onto his tie. "What? Why?" He glances at the bailiff, who is becoming impatient. "Is it not open to the public?"

"Nothing good is going to come of you being here." It pains me to say it, but it's the truth.

With Benedict's words playing ping-pong inside my head,

I know that Malaki sitting in the courtroom will only provoke him further.

Malaki runs a hand through his hair, and from the looks of the messy ends, he's been doing it for hours. "Stop it," he says.

I furrow my forehead. "Stop what?"

"Stop pushing me away." His jaw tightens. "I'm not letting you do this alone."

"You're just going to make it worse." I force between tight teeth. "This is my thing to deal with and–"

Malaki steps forward, his hand gently grazing my forearm. "With all due respect, this isn't just your thing to deal with anymore."

"But–"

"You and Charleigh are a part of my life, Reese. No matter how it started or how it ends. So I'm staying."

"Ms. Moreno."

The bailiff reaches the end of his patience. He opens the door and gestures for me to head inside the courtroom. With a fleeting glance in Malaki's direction, I head through the doors, even more worried than before.

Forty-Nine

MALAKI

I MAY FIND myself in a similar courtroom if I get my hands on Benedict.

The number of times I've pictured myself choking him out is enough to forbid myself from ever being alone in an empty room with him anytime soon—or ever.

The judge slams his gavel, and Reese jumps.

I squeeze my fists, my fingers aching from how tight they are. I've never endured torture like this.

Skating suicides for hours before I threw up? Shitty. That time I took a puck to the nose and gushed blood on the ice? Hurt like a bitch. Hearing Reese tell me to leave the courthouse? Knife to the heart. But watching her struggle up there alone? I'd rather die.

"Mr. Whitney, since you filed the emergency motion, you may proceed."

Instead of Benedict standing up and speaking to the judge directly, it's his lawyer.

"Your honor, my client fears for his child's safety and well-being."

My teeth grind against one another. *This fucking asshole.*

"Ms. Moreno is erratic, indecisive, and impulsive. Just the other day, the child was in the emergency room getting stitches—"

"Do you have evidence of that?"

The judge is calm, but I'm shifting in my seat every few seconds. Reese's head is hanging low, but she remains quiet.

The bailiff takes a paper from Benedict's lawyer and hands it off to the judge. He scans it and then eyes the lawyer once more. "This is proof of the child being in the emergency room. This isn't enough evidence to say that the mother did something to cause the injury or that the safety of the child is jeopardized. Was Children Services called?"

"Well, no—"

Benedict interrupts his lawyer, all eyes flying to him. "Of course not. She knows how to spin a story, but my daughter sustained the injury while on her watch. Who knows what she and her fiancé were up to when this occurred."

The judge is irritated. He slams his gavel again. "Mr. Whitney, if you would like to speak, please take the stand. I do not tolerate speaking out of turn."

It only takes a minute for Benedict to be sworn in by the bailiff, then he's spouting at the mouth with all sorts of lies and exaggerations. A drop of sweat slips down my spine, my jaw aching from clenching.

"Mr. Whitney, did you personally witness any harm to your daughter?"

"Well, no, but—"

"And no report was made?" The judge flips through the documents again, and it's obvious that Benedict is angry he's not getting his way. I wouldn't be surprised if he threw a tantrum. He goes on and on, bringing up past incidents and even Reese's home life before moving in with me. At one point, he even says that Reese was charged with a misdemeanor as a minor because she assaulted her father's friend.

"So, just to be clear..." Judge Ramirez looks to Reese and then to Benedict. "You're asking me to remove custody from the child's mother based solely on your word and past allegations that aren't documented?"

Benedict pounds the table. "There's documentation!"

Benedict's lawyer whispers something to him, clearly attempting to calm him down.

Judge Ramirez raises his voice. "You are not helping your case by acting out in my courtroom. I suggest you listen to your lawyer."

Benedict shoves his lawyer's hand away and crosses his arms.

The judge turns toward Reese, and my heart pounds. "Ms. Moreno, I'm going to give you a chance to respond to the allegations."

Reese stands nervously. Her breaths are shaky, her back straight as a board. "Your honor, my fiancé wasn't even home at the time of the incident, and I wasn't distracted while caring for my daughter. She is nearly a year old. She's beginning to pull herself up and take risks. She's fast too." Reese laughs softly. "She climbed the first two stairs, and before I could run over to her, she fell and hit her head. There was no abuse or neglect. It was simply an accident."

"Was it an accident when you bashed someone's knees in with a baseball bat at the age of seventeen?" Benedict shouts. "Who's to say you won't do that again in the presence of my daughter? Or worse, *to* my daughter."

Reese winces.

Judge Ramirez bangs his gavel. "Mr. Whitney, this is your last warning."

I wipe the back of my hand over my damp forehead. *I'm*

going to take a baseball bat to Benedict's knees when this is all said and done.

Benedict sits with the help of his lawyer gripping him by the shoulder and forcefully pushing him into his chair.

The judge bounces his attention between Reese and Benedict, and it's obvious he wants to give into Reese, but he's hesitating.

"Listen. I am not dismissing the seriousness of the claims from Mr. Whitney. I take the safety of children very seriously, and without corroborating evidence from either side, this court is in a difficult position. As of right now, it's your word against his."

So what does that mean?

Benedict's lawyer stands. "May I speak, your honor?"

He nods.

"Considering Mr. Whitney has never had an incident like this happen or ever been accused of harm to their daughter, I feel that temporary custody with the father would be beneficial until the custody hearing."

Reese shoots up out of her seat but waits until the judge nods in her direction. "That's because he is never with his daughter." She glares at Benedict and his lawyer before looking back at the judge. "And that is not my doing. The offer is always there, and I've been willing to compromise, but–"

The judge puts his hand up to stop her. "This is becoming messy, and I don't like messy. You have both put me in an impossible situation. Your word against his."

Suddenly, I find myself standing. "Your honor, if I may..."

A hush travels through the courtroom.

All eyes are on me, and my heart pounds so hard my chest tightens.

I make no move to look at either Reese or Benedict. I put all my attention on Judge Ramirez.

"And you are?"

"Reese's fiancé. Malaki Young."

He nods.

Before I can think things through, I go with my gut instinct and continue. "I'm willing to take temporary custody of Charleigh until this is resolved."

I glance at Reese briefly. Shock ripples across her face. The light above her head shows just how glossy her eyes are.

I move my attention back to the judge. "I can provide a safe environment. A baby gate has been installed since Charleigh's fall, and she's grown comfortable with me since her mother and I have gotten engaged. Reese's sister, Zoe, is a college student but is around often enough that she'll be another familiar fa-"

Benedict stands abruptly. "This is ridiculous! He's known the mother of my child for no more than-"

"Sit down, Mr. Whitney!" The judge's voice booms throughout the courtroom.

Judge Ramirez eyes me closely, and I can tell he's considering this to be the best option.

Reese and I will figure out the rest after this case is closed, or at least while it's on hold, but there is no way in hell I'm allowing a man like Benedict to take Charleigh into his possession like she's a bargaining chip. And the mere thought of Charleigh being removed from Reese and thrust into the arms of a stranger kills me just as much.

I'd adopt Charleigh right now if that's what it took.

My heart races, and I open my mouth to say just that, but then the door flies open behind us.

"Your honor!"

I turn, and my vision tunnels onto the PI I hired weeks prior.

"I apologize for the abrupt interruption, but I have evidence relevant to this motion."

Mark eyes me with a tight-lipped smile, but I stay rigid in my spot.

Fifty

REESE

I'M ROOTED IN PLACE.

A man comes rushing into the courtroom, and I'm sick with fear.

He says he has evidence, and I'm terrified to see what Benedict has constructed against me by using this man.

The bailiff steps forward.

"Let him through," the judge orders.

I'm shaking. I can't even fathom looking at Malaki because I'll break.

Not only did he stay after I had a spiraling meltdown and told him to go, but he just offered to care for my daughter.

If I make eye contact with him now, I'll crumble to the floor.

"Here." The man hands the bailiff a folder, and I eye it the entire way until it lands in Judge Ramirez's hand.

Benedict and his lawyer are muttering to each other, and to my surprise, they don't seem to know who the man is.

"And who are you?" the judge asks.

Everyone turns toward him.

"My name is Mark Poole. I am a freelance private investigator hired by Mr. Young. Those documents show Mr. Whitney has intended to use this custody filing to punish Ms. Moreno for refusing a relationship with him."

What?

Benedict's lawyer grips onto his arm as he tries to stand. He glares at him and pulls Benedict to sit.

The judge says nothing as he flips through the papers, his eyes narrow as he scans each one. "How did you obtain these?"

"They were obtained through a cooperating witness, your honor. They are willing to testify to that if need be."

The judge blinks after staring long and hard at the PI.

He turns to Benedict's lawyer. "Care to explain why I'm holding copies of multiple emails from your client to various outside sources regarding his plan"—he flips to the first paper—"to destroy Ms. Moreno?"

I gasp.

The judge flips to another page. "And this email in particular is to you..." He flicks his glare onto the lawyer. "It reads, 'If she doesn't cave, then I'm taking that kid. It's only half hers anyway. Figure it out, and figure it out fast.'"

"It?" I press my hand to my mouth. "You called your daughter an 'it'?"

"This is fucking ridiculous!" Benedict shouts. "He probably constructed these emails himself!" He stands and turns toward the PI. "What cooperating witness do you even have? You're a lying piece of shit!"

"Your personal assistant," he says. "The one who filters all your emails."

Benedict looks as if someone slapped him. "Tell her I said she's fucking fired."

The judge slams his gavel three times. I jump with every

loud bang. He stares at Benedict. "This motion is a misuse of the court's time. The evidence clearly proves your bad faith, Mr. Whitney, as well as your behavior in my courtroom."

I almost sag with relief.

"This was not an emergency–it was retaliation. Therefore, this emergency request is denied and dismissed. I strongly advise you to think twice before filing further unfounded claims again."

Judge Ramirez looks to his bailiff. "Escort him out of my courtroom immediately. I want him off the premises."

The bailiff heads for Benedict as Judge Ramirez continues on.

"And if he acts disorderly in any manner, I will hold him in contempt of court."

I swear the bailiff's mouth twitches. "Yes, your honor."

Benedict's jaw is rock solid, the angular side of it sharper than ever. He brushes his lawyer's hand off his arm and walks out of the courtroom without looking in my direction.

My eyes fill with water, but I bite the inside of my cheek to keep my emotions in line.

"You are dismissed, Ms. Moreno."

I smile tightly at the judge.

"And for what it's worth...I think your daughter is just fine with you and Mr. Young."

Me too.

He stands and then exits the courtroom to his chambers.

I turn around and immediately search the room for Malaki, only to find him right in front of me.

Our eyes lock, his blue eyes filled with worry as he scans my face.

He takes a step toward me, and I can't take it.

I break in half, right there in front of him, in the middle of the courtroom.

A sob climbs from the deepest parts of my body, and before I collapse, he's there to catch me.

"Dimples," he whispers against my hair. "It's okay."

It is.

For now.

Hopefully forever.

"I'm so sorry," I choke out.

I furiously wipe my tears but stay pressed against Malaki. His heart beats as quickly as mine. Being wrapped in his strong arms has me hating myself for pushing him away.

"Please stop crying," he pleads. "I really can't take it. It's almost as bad as when Charleigh cries."

I sniffle and shake my head against him. "I am so sorry for what I said. I'm so sorry I pushed you away and told you that you were going to make things worse." I sniffle again. "It's not true. My life is so much better with you in it."

"Obviously," he jokes.

I finally pull back and stare into his eyes. A line of worry etches in between his eyebrows. He grips my face and uses his thumbs to wipe my tears.

"You hired a PI?"

He nods. "There was no way I was letting him take you or Char from me."

"And you were going to take custody of her if it came down to it..." Another tear slips from my eye. "You really do love her, huh?"

He wipes my face again. "I love both of you, Reese. Don't you understand that?"

My lip wobbles. "Why? I'm a–"

Malaki's hands weave through my hair as he brings me closer. His breath fans across my face, silencing me.

"You're you," he says. "That's why. I love everything about you. Your kind heart, the way you take care of everyone around you, your dimples, your laugh..." His mouth hovers over mine. "I think about you every single minute of the day. Coming home to you and Charleigh—hell, even Zoe—is the one thing I look forward to above everything else.

"Did it come as a surprise? Maybe a little. I didn't necessarily think our fake engagement would turn into forever, but goddamn do I want it."

I'm completely swept off my feet in love with him too, and this may be the first time I actually let myself feel all of it.

I wrap my fingers around his wrists. "I love you too."

His perfect smile is the last thing I see before he's pressing his mouth to mine. I close my eyes and let the warmth of stability and love fill me to the point that I forget where we are.

Someone clears their throat, and we break apart.

The bailiff stands there with an awkward smile on his face.

"Sorry." Malaki removes his hands and interlaces his fingers with mine. "We will see ourselves out."

The bailiff chuckles as we head for the doors.

Right before Malaki pushes through, he stops walking and peers down at me. I look up at him, my eyes puffy from crying. "Unless..."

"Unless what?"

His eyebrow crooks upward. "Wanna get married? We're already in the courthouse."

I pause for a moment.

Malaki snickers. "I'm kidding, Dimples. I think Zoe would take a bat to my knees if we got married without her to witness."

I laugh abruptly as Malaki pulls me down the hall. "You're right," I say. "And Charleigh would make a super-cute flower girl."

His fingers squeeze mine. "True."

We step outside, and fresh air fills my lungs.

"Malaki?"

He peers at me. "Yeah?"

I exhale. "I don't want this engagement to be fake anymore."

His steps falter, and he spins me to stand in front of him. A slow smile curves on his face as his hands fall to my hips. "It never was for me." His blue eyes move back and forth between mine, and he says, "Pick a date, Dimples."

Epilogue

MALAKI

Five months later

"How do I look?"

Charleigh is strapped into the best stroller on the market while I stand behind her, pushing it throughout the living room.

Reese stops working on her cross-stitch. "Hot."

I wiggle my eyebrows.

Zoe fake gags.

"Oh, knock it off," I say. "I saw you and that loser with the shitty car last night when I came home from the rink."

Reese sits forward and looks at her sister. "Wait, what?" She turns to me. "What did you see?"

Zoe gasps. "You said you wouldn't say anything!"

"Sorry." I push Charleigh around some more because she seems to be enjoying it. "But come on, Zoe. You can do better than him. Does he even have a job?"

"Yes!" she snaps. "And just because I'm hooking up with him doesn't mean we're a thing!"

"Hooking up with him?!" Reese jumps to her feet. "In the car? On the street? Zoe!"

"Yeah, who would *ever* do that?" I shake my head. "He must be a bad influence on you."

Reese snaps over to me, and the realization hits her. I flick my eyebrow, just barely.

Mm-hmm, remember when we did that?

"Who's the bad influence now?" Zoe asks, crossing her arms.

"Hey now!" I put my hands up. "We're engaged! That's different."

Zoe looks at me suspiciously. "Were you two even engaged at that point?"

Shit. No, we weren't.

"Ha!" Zoe points at me. "See! You're a bad influence too!"

Charleigh shouts, like she wants to be included in the conversation too. I bend my head forward and look at her. "I know, Charleigh-girl. Do you hear how she's talking to me?"

She kicks her legs excitedly. "Dada!"

"I agree," I say, acting like we're in a full conversation.

Zoe wants to laugh, but she turns her nose up instead. "I'm taking your wedding gift back!"

Reese pipes up. "You got us a gift?"

"Yes, but I'm about to take it back."

"There are no takebacks in this house," I remind her. "You know that."

She rolls her eyes, but I know her well enough to know she's just playing around.

Reese runs after her, her socks sliding across the floor. "What did you get us? I told you that you need to save your money!"

I already know that it didn't cost anything—she's going to watch Charleigh for us while we go on our honeymoon.

The wedding is going to be low-key; only our closest friends are invited. Zoe is the maid of honor, and Charleigh is the flower girl. I had the guys pick from sticks on who will be my best man because, to be honest, the only thing I really care about is marrying Reese.

Lars picked the shortest stick.

He was all for it, though, when he found out he'd be walking Zoe down the aisle.

I chucked a puck at him on the ice after that, but I'm not sure he got the hint. I don't think I have to worry, because apparently Zoe's into guys with crappy cars and no brain cells. I highly doubt she'll be impressed with Lars, considering she's still not into the whole sports thing—never mind the fact that her future-brother-in-law is a pro hockey player.

Either way, in a few short weeks, before the season starts, Reese will have my last name.

In years to come, I hope Charleigh will too. But that's not something we're willing to mess with just yet–not with Benedict still lurking around. With him dropping the custody issue altogether after the fiasco at the courthouse, we're unwilling to provoke him into pulling the same shit again.

What I do know is that Charleigh is a part of me whether she shares my last name or not.

I barely remember life before that night at the casino when I talked Reese into giving me a ride home. But after playing her fiancé and hearing Charleigh call me Dada, I know going back would mean losing something I never knew I needed.

"Zoe!" Reese's voice echoes throughout the house as she chases her sister around. "Tell me what you got us."

"Nope."

I chuckle and push the stroller in the direction of their voices so I can enjoy the show.

Charleigh cranes her head back and glances up at me.

"This is amusing, huh?"

She smiles wide, her two front teeth fully grown in, making her look so much older than before. She happily goes back to watching Reese chase Zoe around the house, laughing every time they pass us.

"She's almost as fast at me," I say to Charleigh.

"I am faster!" she says on her way past.

I dig into my pocket and pull out some Skittles. I pop an orange one in because, naturally, all the reds have been taken by Reese.

"Throw me one," she says, skidding to a stop in front of me. "I need some sugar."

I chuckle and throw one up into the air.

She moves underneath it and catches it on her tongue.

I raise my brow, impressed.

She winks at me, and my tongue slips out to lick my lip.

Yeah...there is really no going back after being Reese Moreno's fiancé.

S.J. Sylvis is an Amazon top 50 and USA Today bestselling author who is best known for her new adult sport romances. She currently resides in Arizona with her husband, two small children, dog and cat! She is obsessed with coffee, becomes easily attached to fictional characters, and spends most of her evenings buried in a book!

Stay up to date at: sjsylvis.com

Also by S. J. Sylvis

Bexley U Series

Weak Side

Ice Bet

Puck Block

Chicago Blue Devils

Play the Game

Skate the Line

Rush the Edge

Test the Ice

Shadow Valley Series

Sticks and Stones

Heart of Thorns

The Christmas Playbook (releasing 11/2025)

Cross the Line (releasing 12/2025)

English Prep Series

All the Little Lies

All the Little Secrets

All the Little Truths

St. Mary's Series

Good Girls Never Rise

Bad Boys Never Fall

Dead Girls Never Talk

Heartless Boys Never Kiss

Pretty Girls Never Lie

Standalones

Three Summers

Yours Truly, Cammie

Chasing Ivy

Falling for Fallon

Truth

Acknowledgments

THANK you to every reader for being patient with me to release the last book in the Chicago Blue Devils series. As most of you know, I'm a mom of two and a marine wife, which means my work schedule is typically messy and chaotic. Between extracurriculars and my husband working away from the home more often than not, it took me a little longer to publish Test the Ice, but I hope you enjoyed every second of it because I know I did.

I am so sad to end this era. The Blue Devils have been my home for over a year, and I love every single character I've created within this world. I hope you always find comfort in these stories, and I am so grateful for each and every one of you. <3

I'd also like to shout out all the people in my life who support me and help make these books come to life! My family, as always, for loving me and putting up with me when my head is somewhere else (like in Chicago with Reese and Malaki ;)). My besties for always encourage me. My right hand gal, Emma, for *literally* everything. My editor for never batting an eye when I'm late on my deadline. My PA who keeps me in line, and to every one of my readers!!

Thank you for being you.

I couldn't do this without you!

xo